Like Mother, Like Daughter

GEORGINA BROWN

07913581

Black Lace novels are sexual fantasies.
In real life, make sure you practise safe sex.

First published in 1999 by
Black Lace
Thames Wharf Studios
Rainville Road, London W6 9HT

Typeset by SetSystems Ltd, Saffron Walden, Essex
Printed and bound by Mackays of Chatham PLC

ISBN 0 352 33422 3

Chapter One

*H*e wouldn't have known she could see him standing there naked. But such was the angle of the mirror that the slightest gap in the door meant she had a good view.

This wasn't the first time she had watched him peeing. Not the most erotic of pastimes but somehow it had intrigued her. On that previous occasion, she hadn't seen any bare flesh. But his buttocks were tightly clenched against the confines of his jeans. The fact that she knew he would be holding his cock at a suitable angle was oddly arousing. In her mind, she could see his fingers positioned like a flute player, perhaps stroking it, coaxing the liquid to come out that much quicker.

She had admired his buttocks. They had the sort of shape and firmness that brings to mind a powerful thrust at the moment when it really counts. Hard and smooth to the touch, she'd bet.

On that occasion her pleasure had been interrupted. Her daughter, Rachel, had come out of her

1

bedroom and taken her by surprise. Liz had presumed she was still downstairs in the living room, explaining to her father why she didn't want the one-bedroom flat in Balham and why she did want the two-bedroomed one looking out over the river on Canary Wharf.

'Mum! You could have coughed, you know.' Rachel said it low as she softly closed the bathroom door.

Liz had shrugged, then reached out and adjusted the landing mirror. 'I couldn't see anything.' She'd smiled when she thought of what she had seen. 'That was the trouble. I was living in hope.'

Rachel had grimaced. 'Mum, you're incorrigible.'

Liz had smoothed her bobbed blonde hair and tucked it behind her ears. Sometimes her daughter made her feel as though she were the wild child and Rachel the responsible adult. Why didn't she give a little? 'And you, my dear, are a spoilsport.'

Rachel had shaken her head and clucked like someone three times her age. Her final words had cut deeply. 'You're too old to be looking.'

'Too old!' Liz had stopped dead in her tracks. As she'd watched her daughter trip off back down the stairs a terrible truth had taken hold of her. She was now fifty. Her daughter really was seeing her as someone beyond all that. Hadn't she heard that a woman at this age was incredibly sexually responsive?

Since puberty, Liz had taken her sex life for granted. Everybody did. A shiver ran through her. She rubbed at her arms. She didn't want her sex life to end. The thought of it doing so triggered a desperate urge, deep in her soul. There were too many things she hadn't done. Too many things curtailed by inhibitions imposed by the time and society she had grown up in.

Tonight, Ian, Rachel's latest boyfriend, was staying the night. It was late and he had obviously presumed both parents were asleep. He had needed to use the bathroom. This time, he was naked. The door was only half closed and Liz had been unable to sleep.

She had no need to go to the bathroom herself. Her bedroom was en suite. But she had heard movement, had guessed who it might be and had hoped – yes hoped – that this time he would not be dressed.

Black satin dressing gown tied loosely round her middle, she stood on the landing, her back to the bathroom and facing the mirror. The gleam of the bathroom light turned his body to gold. She caught her breath as she eyed the strong shoulders, the curve of his spine, round buttocks. Her attention lingered on the latter items. She imagined herself crawling across the floor, nipping at one firm orb and then the other. He stood with his legs slightly apart. His balls hung like ripe fruit. Peaches, she thought, covered in a light, furry down. Imagine the smell of them, the velvet softness of his skin against my mouth.

Lustful fantasies. Mentally she rebuked herself and argued the case for going back to bed and forgetting she'd ever seen his body or ever imagined herself biting his behind. But anticipation and dreaming of what might be were too powerful to be ignored. Old memories, old sensations came flooding back, as though the years in between had never passed.

Why, she wondered, did the sight of his naked

youth arouse her more than the sight of her naked husband, even her naked lover? Was it the onset of the twilight years, when the last remnants of a taken-for-granted sexuality were slipping slowly away? Fear of the middle fifties was a tangible thing. Some people considered it the beginning of the end. It might be so but, for her part, she didn't want that end to begin, not yet. She wasn't quite ready. Besides, she might not have the curiosity of youth, but she did have experience born of a relaxed familiarity.

At the sound of the flush, she made a snap decision. 'Ian!'

Did she sound surprised, even disgusted?

Ian certainly looked it. His cheeks reddened. He began to apologise. 'Mrs Carr! I'm sorry, I thought everyone . . .'

'Was in bed?' She smiled and raised an eyebrow.

Face pink with embarrassment, he cupped his genitals with his hands. They covered little. Black hair escaped and curled like small springs over and between his fingers.

'Yes. That's what I thought. I apologise,' he said.

He tried to squeeze past her. She stood in the doorway, daring to study his body, daring to look down to where his hands clutched at his cock.

Breathing deeply, she leant towards him, smelt the faint aroma of fresh underarm sweat and of recent sex. A tightening gripped her groin. A familiar tingling ran between her legs. It felt as though her pubic hairs were curling and unfurling with anticipation.

'You're a very naughty boy, roaming about my house naked.' She looked up at him. Some need, some hidden wickedness inside, urged her to do

4

more than that. 'I don't know what Rachel's father would say.'

Ian swallowed. 'Look, Mrs Carr . . .'

But Liz wasn't interested in excuses. The urge to touch, to take some pleasure from his youth, was too strong to ignore.

Slowly, as if afraid he wasn't real, she reached out for him. She ran her hand over the hard contours of his chest, down over his stomach. His muscles tensed beneath her fingers. The feel of his flesh was like fire beneath her touch.

Unblinking, she looked deep into his eyes. He stared back at her, mouth slightly open, as if he wanted to speak but could not find the words.

Her fingers burrowed behind those that he used to cover his embarrassment. She sighed then moaned approvingly as she felt the warmth and energy of his cock. A vein throbbed. The heat rose.

'Mmmm. A pleasure to meet you, too.'

'Please,' he said. His eyes were closed. Veins stood proud in his neck. 'Please. Don't!' His hands fell to his sides in supplication. He was hers.

She looked from his face to his cock. Her spirits soared. Warmly pulsating, it rose from its crown of dark, crinkled hair. Regardless of age or that she was Rachel's mother, he was becoming erect, proclaiming his own lust for her.

It would be so easy to gently tap the glistening tip, to stroke gently, pull on it once or twice, feel his fluid spurt into her palm. But now was not the time.

Seducing him was no longer of any great interest to her – at least, not for now. The fact that she could still elicit such a reaction had fired her imagination and heated her body. She stood aside and let him pass. Instinctively, she knew he would remember this night, knew he would think of her in his dreams and want more.

'Good night,' she called out.

'Good night, Mrs Carr.'

The moment of being just a man and a woman was gone. She was again Mrs Carr, Rachel's mother. He was her daughter's boyfriend.

Sleep was difficult. Each time she closed her eyes, she saw his body and his cock rising to meet her fingers. It brought back so many memories. Not so much the identities of boys and men she had known, but the sensations she had felt at the time. How sweet they had been and how difficult to confine entirely to the past.

A sense of urgency was born tonight, she thought. This is my awakening to things I thought I no longer needed and now find that I do. From now on, I am on a voyage of discovery. In my youth, handsome young men seduced me. The time has come for me to seduce them.

Rachel looked up as Ian came back into the bedroom. The curtains were open and there was a full moon, so the room was not entirely in darkness. Its light touched his body, the hard curves of his muscles outlined in silver.

'I thought you'd got lost. Are you all right?' she asked.

There was no reason why he shouldn't be. He'd stayed overnight in her parents' home before, so he knew where the bathroom was. She hadn't told him about her mother watching him on the last occasion.

But the sight of his cock had triggered the question. Rigid and standing at full length, it drew her attention. After all, he'd only just paid a visit to the bathroom. Didn't an erection take a while to come back?

'I'm fine.' His voice was slightly husky, his face a little pink.

Intrigued but disinclined to interrogate, she rolled over on to her side as he slid in beside her. Somehow it annoyed her to see him erect, especially when she had played no part in getting it hard. Nothing much could have happened between her bedroom and the bathroom. So what had he been thinking about? What outrageous fantasy had prompted such a virile reaction? Even now, it dug into the small of her back.

'You're hurting,' she said, and couldn't help sounding resentful.

'I'm sorry.' He moved. The digging ceased.

But she knew he was still hard. Imagine the feeling in his loins, she thought. Imagine having this pulsing creature growing into something that dragged at the body, pulled it forward. Imagine the tightening of the buttocks as exploratory thrusts drained the energy from the body, dragged it into itself until the penis was a projectile of pure physicality.

He began kissing her shoulders, small, gentle kisses that begged her forgiveness. The kisses were welcome and very persuasive.

'That's nice,' she said as he kissed the nape of her neck, his fingers gently brushing away stray strands of hair. It needs cutting, she thought in an absent-minded manner. Murmuring approvingly, she closed her eyes as his fingers traced delicate patterns over her shoulders and down her spine.

7

'And my bottom,' she added. She rolled on to her belly.

That's what I like. An obliging man, she thought.

His touch was light at first, fine feathery strokes that sent icy tingles of delight over her skin.

'More,' she said.

The pressure of his hands intensified. With the flat of his hands, he performed circular movements over each buttock.

This is queenly, she thought – in the ancient sense, of course. And Ian is nothing more than my slave – my sex slave, who responds to my every whim.

The thought pleased her. As long as she kept that idea in her head, she would enjoy having more sex tonight – just as long as Ian fulfilled her ideal role.

'Enough of that.' She rolled from under his hands and over on to her back.

Ian looked down at her but did not move. He looked wary of making the next move. She enjoyed the moment: looked at his face, then at the beautiful stiff prick rising like an iron rod from between his thighs.

Raising her eyes back to his face, she smiled at him, enough of a signal for him to kiss her.

His kiss was not so much demanding her body as asking for her approval, her permission to proceed.

When he tried to kiss her again, she turned her head to one side. Ian took the hint. His next kiss was for her breast, his tongue licking each nipple before taking it between his teeth, gently sucking on it, nibbling at it, then releasing it again.

Ian's eyes met hers. She saw the look in them, knew he understood.

Lowering his head, he ran his tongue down to her belly.

Soft, spine-tingling shivers spread over her body. She closed her eyes. Ian was still there with her. But behind her closed lids, he was merely an extension of her mind, a physical part of the sexual fantasy occurring in her mind.

Ian could not possibly know that he no longer existed. And what did it matter? He was enjoying licking her flesh, tickling her clitoris with the tip of his tongue. She was enjoying the ensuing sensations. But the thrill, the scenario created by her mind, provided the delicious embellishments.

Red walls, dark shadows thrown by lit torches from cold stone walls. Leather straps bit into her wrists and ankles. She was naked, just as she was in reality. But this nakedness was more vulnerable, more excitingly dangerous.

In reality, Ian was doing delicious things to her. If she wanted to stop him, she could. In her fantasy, she was at the mercy of a leather-clad man. Her cries of protest went unheeded. He told her he would do whatever he wanted. He licked away the juices that ran between her legs. He nibbled and sucked at her nipples and clutched her buttocks with dirty, uncut fingernails. When he had finished with one side, he turned her over. Her mouth was open, as if crying out in protest, yet no sound came. His nails scraped her backside and his thumbs delved between her buttocks. She felt shamed, she felt exhilarated. She felt helpless at the same time as feeling empowered. As she moaned in the ecstasy of reality and the imagined unease of fantasy, he entered her.

Chapter Two

'You look pleased with yourself,' Mark said as he grabbed his briefcase.

'I am,' Liz replied. They exchanged a knowing look. There were secrets in their marriage. Not secrets from each other, but shared secrets they hid from the outside world.

He gave her a quick peck on the cheek as she zipped up her own briefcase. His hand lingered on her behind before he moved away and she was left with only a hint of his aftershave.

'You've remembered I'm in Manchester for the rest of the week and weekend, have you?'

She didn't answer but glanced meaningfully at the navy-blue tapestry holdall that sat next to his feet and raised an eyebrow. He grinned and his eyes sparkled in the same wickedly exciting way that had first enticed her to his bed and his body.

'Of course,' he said. 'I'll see you next Tuesday.'

A successful man, thought Liz. A happy man? Of course he was. Like her, he was around fifty and had his own business that he'd started in his early thirties. He kept himself trim playing squash and tennis at the country club. Was he worth a second glance, she wondered? It was a question she could not answer. Like the mole on her shoulder, he'd been with her a long time – not quite a lifetime but a good few years. But she knew other women desired him. He'd told her so. They had no secrets from each other.

Theirs was a long-term, lasting relationship. Sex had become like drinking tea. You made it when you felt like one. It served a need. Since yesterday, her needs had changed. She felt good, better than she had for a long time. The only thing that worried her was that she hadn't told Mark. Younger men had never figured that prominently in her sex life. Most of her experiences had been with men closer to her own age. There had also been older men.

But why haven't you told him?

The question annoyed her a little, probably because it made her feel guilty.

She slammed her hands palm down on the briefcase and tossed her head. Nothing happened. That's why I've said nothing. But something is going to happen, said a little voice inside. And when it does, you're still not going to want to tell him. The reason, she realised, was that she was afraid of him feeling vulnerable, unable to compete with youthful virility.

But nothing had happened.

Liz shoved thoughts of what might happen aside and smiled as she drove into work. Fondling Ian's youthful penis had filled her with a new zest for life. Nothing else mattered except enjoying the things she loved the most.

She enjoyed the continuous changing of gear in a traffic jam, the inside of her thighs brushing together as she pushed the pedals. But she found her concentration drifting. Her gaze followed the young men striding along the pavements, running across the road in front of her. Sometimes she met the eyes of other drivers, young men young enough to be her son. Some were smart-suited, perhaps poised on the ladder to a successful career in banking, insurance or commodities. Some had a more rugged look about them, strikingly blond, gold rings glinting from their ears.

What would it be like, with him? She didn't ask herself the question every time she looked at a young man. But it was frequent enough. Although her hands were gripping the steering wheel it was Ian's firm buttocks she was feeling. Was it possible that the sensation of touch held its own memories? It felt like it.

On arrival at the office she had to wait for some thoughtless junior to be directed out of her parking place. As she waited she watched him and wondered what he looked like naked, how willingly he might submit to seduction, how he would feel beneath the sheets, up against a cupboard or over a desk. He saw her looking and smiled. She winked at the freckle-faced youngster and laughed when he winked back.

Saucy, she thought. Perhaps too young for the moment, but in time . . .

So Mark will be in Manchester for a few days. When he came back he would relate everything that had happened there. Business would not rate too high on the agenda. Sex would and, as they compared notes, their legs would entwine, their bodies undulate against each other. Each would imagine what the other had done in their absence.

Liz checked her appearance in the darkened glass of the foyer doors and again in the bronzed metal interior of the lift. She felt good: she looked good. Her blouse was of grey striped silk, her skirt a matching grey and her jacket cerise, clean cut and showing off her figure. No need like the younger girls to wear her skirt short and her heels high. Juvenile tastes were like burger bars: cheap, fast and easily forgotten. She saw herself as a gourmet meal, complete with a château-bottled wine, slowly enjoyed and always memorable.

Sleek and confident, she made her way to her office. I'm mature but not past it, she thought to herself. Experience matters. She smiled a slow, secretive smile as she thought of Ian's prick and the way it had risen to meet her fingers. How warm it had been, how quickly it had hardened. If only she had persisted, drawn aside her gown and felt its warm moist head nudging aside her curl-covered lips. Another time, she thought, and knew it would happen.

Before she reached her own office, Richard's voice broke into her thoughts.

'Liz! Can I see you for a moment?'

When she looked in his direction, he had turned his back on her. He was nonchalantly studying the sheaf of papers he was holding in his hand – as if I am of no great consequence, she thought. By the time she joined him in his office, he was already sitting at his desk.

'You wanted to see me?' She smiled as she closed the door behind her, let her briefcase slide to the floor. One hand still behind her back, she pushed the central locking device in the doorknob.

Richard's eyes slowly rose to meet hers from under dark, bushy brows. He was older than her and looked it. But the lines of life had creased his face in an interesting pattern. His jaw was square, his face weathered and his eyes were a warm dark brown. His smile could only be interpreted as extremely sensual. Besides that he was blessed with the most potent aphrodisiac of all. He had power. He was the managing director. A keen mind and a ruthless ambition had got him to the top. The trappings of the good life lay easy on his body and in his life: Armani suits, a fifty-foot motor cruiser, a Jag, a Rolls Royce, a flat in London, a cottage in Suffolk, a château in Provence.

He looked her straight in the face.

'I'm in Suffolk at the weekend. Are you?'

'That shouldn't be a problem. Mark's in Manchester until next Tuesday.'

'I'll take that as yes.' His eyes roamed over the rest of her body before he looked back into her eyes. 'What's different about you today? Tell me.'

She said nothing but merely twirled slowly like a model on the catwalk. 'Today I start living. There is nothing that I'm afraid of doing. There is everything for me to experience.'

Richard frowned. If he did understand, he didn't comment. He took a last glance at the sheaf of papers then put them down on the desk, rested his hands across his waist and leant back in his chair. Their eyes met in mutual understanding.

'If that's true, then do what I've asked you to do before.'

His eyes held hers but did not unnerve her. This

was the first chapter of the rest of her life. He was daring her to fulfil her statement. And she was looking straight back at him, defiantly – perhaps triumphantly.

'I always said I wouldn't.' It was true. She had always refused to make love in his office. Her dignity had been too important to risk discovery. Since last night, dignity no longer had a place in her life. Today she would have sex with her boss in his office.

The sensuality she had felt since yesterday seemed to flow through her veins like warm water as she walked towards him. Her eyes never left his face. Slowly, with great deliberation, she discarded her jacket. It fell to the floor. Expensive as it was, she didn't care. Clothes were not important. She undid the small pearl buttons of her blouse, rested her hands flat on his desk and leant forward. The blouse gaped open.

Still looking into her eyes, he reached for her breasts. With one hand he pulled each from its confines. With the other he pulled the stiff white lace of her bra down under them so they were still carried high, the nipples pointing directly at him. He pulled on them until they stood erect.

'I want to do everything,' Liz said, her words expressed in a long, low gasp.

The words came out so easily. They were part of the new woman, the mature woman who intended to live life to the full. Yesterday, there had been a time and a place for everything. Today, everything was made for any time, any time at all.

She gasped as Richard leant forward and sucked at one nipple. Sensations of pleasure and sexual anticipation swept over her more intensely than

15

they ever had before. They went beyond the norm; beyond wanting him to spread her legs and push it in. A feeling alien yet strangely familiar came to her mind. She had an overwhelming urge to give him more than the pink nub of flesh he held between his teeth. In an odd way she wished she could feed him, give him her milk, feel it squirting over his tongue and imagine it flowing warm and sweet into his throat. Like semen, she thought, like the white-hot milk of passion brewed deep in his groin. But sweeter, more nourishing.

He withdrew his mouth from her breast. She glanced at her nipple, noticing its length and its greater intensity of colour. A mammary erection: that was the best way to describe it.

No words were needed. Some instinctive drive that had been suppressed for years dictated what she must do next.

She straightened, then went to the large picture window behind his desk. Between the tower blocks and the spires of medieval churches, she could see the river, silver-grey in the distance. They were all tall structures, obelisks to men's power, pseudo-erections thrusting into the sky.

Shades of blue and grey glass reflected the building they were in. Did they also reflect her? A myriad reflective images of her with breasts hanging out, wanton and wanting. And how many people were looking out from behind that tinted glass and seeing her?

Previously she would have shied away from being this brazen. Without needing to look at him she knew Richard was watching her, wondering what had caused this change of heart. Age, she thought. Maturity mixed with youth.

She heard his chair squeak slightly as he turned. He remained seated. She felt his hands on her hips, stroking her, softly rasping over the silky smooth material.

Down, down, down. Under the hem of her smart grey skirt. Up, up, up over her knees and her bare tanned thighs.

I'm like one of these buildings, she thought, her gaze fixed on the London skyline. I have an intruder. He's storming my domain, tearing away my defences. She gasped as he hitched his thumbs in the strips of lace and satin that constituted her underwear.

He's stripping away my façade.

He's entering my chamber.

She moaned and closed her eyes. Who cares that the world might see and wonder what could be happening? She certainly didn't. The smell of him was in her nostrils, that stimulating mix of bottled perfume and the sort of body scent that intensified with the tightening of his abdomen, the rising of his cock.

She soaked his fingers and sucked them into her slippery flesh, felt them move inside her. Her spine flexed. Her buttocks lifted, her legs parted a little more.

Everyday life, everyday London faded away. She could not see that world. She could not hear it. The old fantasies she normally used to stimulate the intimacies of an ongoing relationship were slow to appear. Why, she wondered? Then thought of young flesh, forbidden fruit and her yearning to nip at Ian's taut young buttocks and lick his hanging balls.

17

Richard was ecstatic. 'I'm going to fuck you now, before you change your mind.'

'I won't.'

'You won't let me fuck you, or you won't change your mind?'

Last night was still in her mind: not Ian himself, but his flesh, the occasion and the fact that he was almost a son.

'Fuck me. Fuck me!'

He ran his cock along the wetness of her cunt until the entire shaft was dripping wet. Slippery with her juices, he eased the warm head of his cock into her body, nudging aside the outer lips, slithering through the inner lips, immersing his cock deep within.

She braced herself, her hands flat on the windowsill. Like a glove she had covered him, binding him round with her velvet warmth. He was her prisoner but didn't know it.

Gripped by her muscles and his own lust, he began pounding at her, slow at first, then harder, faster. Soon he would come.

And so will I, she thought. I'll soak him with my come, tremble around his shaft, his cock, his lovely big prick.

She took hold of his hand. 'Do it to me.' She placed his fingers exactly where she wanted them. Three of them covered her clitoris and the sensitive area around it. Beneath her own lingering fingers, she felt the slippery slickness of her arousal, the hot, squalid wetness of it.

'You're a naughty little girl. You mustn't touch yourself there,' her mother had said. And she hadn't, until later years: and even then, only in secret. Now there was no mother, no pristine rules left over from a past century. There was her, a mature, feeling woman. This was her time and her rules now applied.

'Will you come?' he asked her.

'Of course.'

Of course. Why would he think otherwise? And she certainly wouldn't fake an orgasm just to suit him, just to satisfy his masculine ego.

Genitals were precious. Sexual satisfaction was guaranteed if they were used right. There would be no lying, no pretending.

The occasion and Richard's technique worked well together.

This is like the first time, she thought. And it was. Losing her virginity had happened a long time ago. Now she was losing the last of her inhibitions. This was the first step, and the fact that this was so new swept over her like a tidal wave.

'Fuck me,' she said and hissed it through her teeth. 'Fuck me and let everyone see that you're fucking me!'

With great energy, he willingly obliged. Pounding force, slamming flesh rendered him as submissive to the sexual act as she was herself.

She closed her eyes when she came. It's all mine, she thought, only mine!

The effect was stupendous. It was as though her clitoris had burst into a million pieces and had spread throughout her body.

She heard him gasp, felt him tense. The crispness of his pubic hair was damp against her arse. Then he shuddered and she shivered.

When she straightened, he wrapped his arms around her. His cock was wet and spent against her naked behind.

He kissed, then whispered into, her ear, 'Liz, that was the best ever.'

'I am the best ever,' she said and meant it.

He laughed.

Because he doesn't understand, she thought. She didn't bother to explain.

Frances Porter was the next person to demand her attention that morning. Without bothering to knock, she came striding into Liz's office, all power dressing, square shoulders, a definite leftover from the Thatcher years. Totally white hair clung like a cap to her skull. Her jewellery was chunky and ostentatious.

'The Americans are unhappy,' she said. Without being asked she requisitioned a leather chair and gracefully crossed one leg over the other.

Liz looked up from the pile of task analysis forms she'd been checking. 'How tragic.'

Frances glared. 'There's no call for flippancy. This is a serious matter. There are a number of problems regarding the supply of pharmaceuticals to Parmedka. Our takeover of the company is likely to be blocked.'

Liz put down her pen and took off her glasses. She sat back in her chair. 'What the bloody hell has this got to do with me? You're International Marketing, Frances. I'm head of Human Resources. Remember?'

Frances leant closer.

Liz prepared for her to be condescending.

'My dear. The federal negotiator is not an easy man to please. But if you could convince him that training would be easily instituted, I'm sure the board would be grateful.'

Especially Richard, thought Liz. And he'd show it physically.

'When's D-Day?'

Frances had a permanently smug expression, so it wasn't always easy to recognise when she was smugger than usual.

'Friday. You're to meet him in Scotland.'

Liz stiffened. 'Why not in London?'

'His name is Robert McKenzie and he's very keen on finding his roots.'

Liz raised her eyebrows. 'Really? Trying to find out if he's related to William Wallace?'

Liz knew that Frances had neither seen the film nor knew a thing about history. But she camouflaged her ignorance and went scudding on. 'I understand your daughter – Rachel, isn't it? – is a professional researcher. Is that right?'

'She is,' said Liz.

'Then perhaps you could arrange something. I know he's desperately seeking someone to go into his details. These are his details.' She passed a business card across the desk. 'His hotel details are on the back.'

Liz was going to say 'no doubt' in as flippant a way as possible. But Rachel could do with some extra money to pay for a new flat. Researching an American's bloodline might just do the trick.

'I'll mention it,' said Liz.

Her task obviously completed, Frances rose triumphantly from her chair.

Outwardly Liz was composed. Inside she seethed.

'I'm sure he'll appreciate your inter-personal skills,' said Frances.

Liz smiled stiffly. 'I'm sure he will.'

Once the office door was closed, Liz picked up her pen, meaning to resume checking the task analysis forms. They were a blur before her eyes. Now she had to tell Richard that Suffolk was off. She'd do that before contacting Rachel.

She reached for the phone, thought better of it then switched into mail exchange on her computer. E-mail was less personal but – hell – they'd been intimate enough for one day.

Two minutes after she pressed 'send', her phone rang.

She looked at it, licked her lips then picked it up. What could he say? Scotland was company business and he was the company.

'Hello.' She kept her voice calm and even.

'Hi, Mum.' It was Rachel. 'Look, I'm off to Brentford tonight. Sophie and the gang have hired a narrowboat. We're going off up the Grand Union.'

Not Richard; Liz was relieved. 'Sounds cool.'

'I'll wear my sweater.'

'That wasn't what I meant. You can go knickerless if you like. It's your life. Your body.'

She heard Rachel take a deep breath and had an instant urge to shake her.

'Why can't you be like other mums? Why do you have to come out with such vulgar comments?'

Her daughter's statement made Liz see red. 'Because I am first and foremost a woman. And because I'm the same person inside as I was when I was twenty! What you see is what you get, Rachel.'

'But you're not twenty.'

Another dig about age. If only you knew, thought Liz. As her fingers impatiently tapped the desk, they skipped across the card Frances had left.

'By the way,' she said, 'do you want to earn some extra?'

The answer was a foregone conclusion. Rachel sounded pleased at obtaining such an assignment.

'Can he afford me?' she asked.

'He's a millionaire. Middle-aged, of course, just like your mother.'

'As long as he can pay, I don't care how old he is. I'm not going to bed or wed him, now am I?'

You don't need to, Liz thought to herself. Her daughter was attractive. She had a heart-shaped face and dark hair cut in an elfin style that framed her face and emphasised her deep blue eyes. Boyfriends were easily come by and just as easily discarded. They had all been close to her own age and all seemingly in awe of her.

But she was keen to earn from Robert McKenzie. She promised to contact him right away. A lesser antagonism remained.

After they'd said stiff goodbyes, Liz put the phone down.

The day that had started with such promise now took a nosedive. She never met Richard during the week unless they were at a business conference. He did not have the same understanding in marriage that she shared with Mark. She sighed forlornly. Tonight would be as lonely as the weekend was likely to be: just her, a quick salad and a bottle of wine – unless providence intervened.

Chapter Three

'*I* won't be seeing you tonight.' Rachel smiled as she said it, her dark eyes opening wide, daring him to question her. 'Or tomorrow, come to that. I'm going away for a few days,' she added.

Ian's jaw slackened; as though I'd just slapped him, she thought. She could almost hear him considering what to say next.

Poor Ian. In a way, she was enjoying being cruel to him. Childish, really. Perhaps, she thought, it's a perversion left over from my schooldays. A perverted education instilled by perverted tutors; some of the nuns had definitely harboured warped ideas of what constituted sin. Those of the flesh had predominated. Sex, despite their supposed celibacy, had intrigued the pallid, black-robed women. In Rachel's dreams, they had been the ones to stretch her naked on the rack, to whip her body with silver chains.

But it wasn't just a case of being cruel to Ian. Without actually saying it, she wanted to cool things off. He was a sexual partner but only for now. Rachel was not as experienced as she tried to make out. She was on the threshold of the sexual maze. There were turnings she was afraid to take, paths that could lead to places and experiences she had never known. If the words of her childhood tutors were anything to go by, she was in danger of heading into hell.

'Don't you want me to come with you?' Ian asked. He rested one arm on the bar and tapped nervously with his fingers.

Is he in love with me? Rachel wondered. It was something she didn't want.

She reached for her glass of dry white wine. As she sipped, she looked around at the lunchtime patrons of the Grapevine Wine Bar. She would only reply when she was ready. Besides, it was interesting to watch the intense young men and the vibrant young women, all talking about work while their minds followed where their eyes led. Personal as well as professional liaisons were appraised and confirmed among the clinking glasses. Hormones, as well as the smell of garlic-laced dishes, hung in the air enticing the senses.

'I'm going with friends,' she said at last. She had no intention of telling him she wasn't leaving until the following day. Neither would she tell him about the American who was taking her to dinner tonight. Why should she? It was bona fide business. Her mother had referred the man to her. He wanted to trace his ancestry and she was going to help him – and get paid for the privilege.

'And I'm not invited.'

She sensed the hurt in his voice. That wasn't what she wanted. Akin to standing over him with a whip, pushing the boundaries while getting beneath his skin aroused her. On the other hand she enjoyed his general company. Freedom to choose was great but it was good to have someone to count on. She reached for his hand.

'I have to have a little space, Ian. We're great together but don't tie me down.'

He shook his head and ran his fingers through his neatly cut hair. 'Tying you down is impossible, Rachel. I wouldn't do it.'

She stroked his fingers and looked at him over the rim of her glass. 'And I wouldn't tie you down, Ian. You know that, don't you?'

She saw him hesitate and, although he muttered that he did know that, she was not entirely sure he was happy about it.

He reached for his glass and downed his drink in one. She sensed his agitation.

'So,' he said, 'if I screwed around with someone tonight, it wouldn't worry you.'

Rachel shrugged and smiled. 'Of course not. You're your own man. One screw doesn't make a lover.' She laughed. 'Do you have anyone in mind?'

The fact that he took a deep breath, as though he'd made a sudden decision, intrigued her.

'Yes, I do. In fact, I have to say she turns me on almost as much as you do. Perhaps more,' he added.

At first, she thought light bouncing off his chrome watchstrap had added a sparkle to his eyes. But then she realised it was real. It wasn't light. It wasn't excitement or even a hint of jealousy. Intrigue, she decided. Ian, the most honest of men, had a secret. But I'm not jealous, she told herself.

26

This is not the early twentieth century. Women choose and I certainly do!

A face, a figure and a name came to her.

'Sally!' she said. 'You've always fancied Sally. I've seen you looking at her and I know she fancies you.' She leant closer. 'Do you imagine doing to her the same things you do to me?' she whispered. 'Or do you want to be rougher? Sally would like that. I hear she seduced a bricklayer from the building site across the road from her office. He tore the clothes from her body, she said. Ripped her knickers off without pulling them down. Then he fucked her. No kisses, no foreplay: just a straightforward fuck. She said it was great. Said it was the best she'd ever had.'

He looked shocked. She couldn't resist going on. 'Just thought I'd let you know that. It helps to know the standard you've got to live up to.'

He shook his head and ran his fingers through his hair. 'I admit nothing. Let's just say that you do know her and you do like her.'

She wondered why he looked away. Why couldn't he look her in the eyes? It might be Sally but she wasn't too sure.

Other names flashed through her mind. She rested her chin in her hand and willed him to look at her. 'I'm intrigued,' she said. She caught the barman's eye and raised her empty glass. 'But I won't pry.'

When he excused himself to go to the bathroom, she took a deep gulp of her drink. It hit the back of her throat and made her cough. She reddened and slammed it down hard. The barman looked at her disapprovingly. Now it was her turn to look away.

But the wine was merely a by-product of her mental annoyance.

I won't be jealous, she told herself. He's a free man. You're a free woman.

Ian stayed for one more drink. He watched Rachel leave and stared, mesmerised by her long brown legs.

But it wasn't Rachel he was thinking of. He wondered if he had the guts to do what was in his mind. He had hinted at Rachel that he would screw someone else tonight, someone she knew, and someone she liked. He rubbed each sweating palm down his trousers. He had another quick drink and took a few deep breaths. OK, it was Dutch courage. But he needed it. Stating his intentions and carrying them out were not the same thing. But perhaps it was just possible.

The chords of *Romance* played by Segovia wafted through the house. It brought with it visions of whitewashed villas, the scent of orange groves. Along with its atmospheric chords came the essence of the Alhambra, its romance, its secrets and its centuries of sensuality.

Smelling of almond essence, with her hair loose and framing her face, Liz picked up the open bottle of Fitou she had set down to breathe. After adding a glass she made her way out on to the patio. The air was cool, the sky indigo and sharply studded with stars.

She was dressed in black lace leggings and a matching baggy top. The sleeves were long and, because the neckline was wide, one shoulder was permanently exposed.

She sat down, took a deep breath and soaked in the atmosphere. The lights on the courtyard walls shone through the red and green leaves of the Virginia creeper. The first hint of autumn caressed her bare shoulder. It did not chill but merely sharpened the senses. Like anticipation, she thought.

Halfway through her first glass of wine, the doorbell rang. She took another sip before going to answer it. Through the stained glass of the Victorian-style door she could see the shadow of a man. Anticipation intensified. Wine, Segovia, oncoming night and now a man she wasn't expecting.

She opened the door.

'I hope I'm not disturbing you.'

Ian was dressed casually. Flecked lambswool sweater and faded jeans. For a split second he looked nervous. She guessed he'd been drinking. For me, she thought. He's been stocking up on courage.

'I quite like being disturbed. Would you like to come in?'

She moved to one side. The shoulder of her sweater fell halfway down her upper arm and stayed there. She raised her glass slightly as she closed the door.

'Would you like some wine?'

He nodded. 'Yes. I would.'

She led the way. Two questions sprang immediately to mind. Why is he here? Doesn't he know Rachel's gone away? A third question came to her. Do I dare seduce him?

'I'm afraid Rachel's away with friends,' she said as she poured the wine into a second glass.

'Is she? Sorry. I must have misunderstood.'

She was not sure she believed him. Or perhaps she didn't want to believe him.

Their fingers touched as he took the wine.

Liz smiled, sipped and sat back in her chair. 'You're always saying that.'

Ian raised one quizzical eyebrow. 'What's that?'

'Sorry. That's what you said the other night, when I caught you naked in the bathroom.'

Smiling, she raised her glass.

His eyelids flickered. If he had said anything, she was sure he would have stammered. Instead, he gulped the total contents of his glass. Once it was drained and back on the weathered wood of the table, he started to rise. 'I shouldn't have come.' He looked everywhere except at her.

Liz leant across, placed her palm on his thigh and gently pushed him back into his chair. Unseen, unheard but eminently discernible, a current of sexual attraction passed between them.

Look at you, she thought. I can see it in your eyes. You look amazed. Your eyes are shining. Your mouth is open as though it is waiting to be kissed, waiting to receive my tongue. Although I am not aware that you are sweating, I know you are. Subconsciously, so does my body.

Be cool. Be casually sensual, she told herself.

Suddenly, the neck of the wine bottle was very attractive. First she stroked the sweeping neck. Then slowly, one by one, she wrapped her fingers round it. At the same time, she looked straight into his eyes. 'More wine?' she said. Her voice offered more.

He nodded. She poured. At the same time she wondered how last night had affected him. You're here for me, she said to him mentally. You want to know how and why your girlfriend's mother could have fondled you like that. But more than that, you want me to do it again. And you want more, much more.

Just as he was about to raise the glass to his lips, she stopped him.

'Wine-drinking is an art – like painting or sculpting. One appeals to the taste buds, the other to the eyes. But it can be taken further than that. Would you like to sample my special combination?'

He shrugged his shoulders. 'Whatever.'

Some nervousness remained. Excitement, she decided, rather than fear.

Without taking her eyes from his, she stood up slowly. After peeling the black lace top over her head she threw it to one side.

Ian's jaw dropped slightly and his eyes opened wide, fixed on her breasts.

It's working, Liz thought as she brought the wineglass to her breast. How must he be feeling?

Pulse increased, heartbeat racing, temperature rising. Physical changes in him were easy to assess. They were mere reflections of how she was feeling. Each erogenous spot tingled in anticipation.

She went round to him, and held one breast in the palm of her hand. She dipped her nipple into his glass and offered it close to his lips.

He stared at the droplet that shimmered like a ruby as it hung there. In that moment, she knew he would take it.

Gently, he licked the wine away. She shivered. Again she dipped her nipple into the wineglass. This time he sucked greedily, his fingers holding her breast as a child would a bottle. Again and again she dipped her nipple into the wine. Again

31

and again he sucked at her, licking every vestige from her breast which he now clasped tightly between his hands.

She wrapped her arms around his head and held him close like a child. As he sucked, she rocked gently backwards and forwards, soaked in wine and the satisfaction of having given him comfort and drink as well as sensation.

'Come here,' she said. With both hands on his shoulders, she coaxed him to stand. There was fire in his eyes. He wanted her. She knew it. Old excitements sprang to mind. First kiss. First foreplay. First fuck. And what first was this? First seduction of her daughter's boyfriend? Perhaps.

His lips tasted good. His body felt good.

She ran her hands down his back, her whole body tingling because he was firm, because he was virile. As she clutched his buttocks, she remembered the first time she had seen him in the bathroom, fully clothed and peeing into the bowl.

When his hands covered her breasts, she wanted only to surrender and do all the things he might ever want to do.

I want to suck your cock, she wanted to say. I want to lick your balls and run my tongue between those firm round buttocks. I want you to possess me, to tell me everything you want me to do to you.

But she wouldn't say those things. Not yet. This was the first time. Their orgasm was yet to come. Besides, he seemed cautious and a little amazed that he was really doing this to his girlfriend's mother. And he was gentle, so gentle that the tremors of delight she felt were gossamer light. They made her feel she had to cling on to him and use her mind to assist her arousal. Fantasising was nothing new. All women did that. Sometimes it wasn't just to aid arousal. Sometimes it was to enhance the shortcomings of one's sexual partner.

She thought of the first boy who had done more than just kiss her. He'd been the first cock she'd ever felt. Fascinated by the alien creature, she had touched it before kneeling. Wide-eyed, she had studied its unfamiliar characteristics as it grew before her eyes. Trembling fingers had stroked the adolescent balls. They were white and soft as silk. His cock had jerked involuntarily. The sight had amazed her. She had wrapped her fingers around it. It had moved in her palm, twisting, pulsating like a trapped animal. Then he had come and her palm had been sticky. At the time, she had not quite understood what had happened. Later, she realised how fortunate she had been. Within half an hour, that young man had been able to make her a woman. She had lost her virginity to him. The act had been more gentle than it might have been. The joy of ultimate satisfaction had swept over her like a warm sea. That first fuck, that first lover, had never been forgotten.

Ian felt like him and smelt like him. If she closed her eyes and used her mind she could recreate that moment.

She slid her hands beneath his sweater. His chest was hairless; like a young boy's. His muscles tightened beneath her touch.

It was the waistband of his jeans she was aiming for. If she turned her mind back to her youth, that button and that zip were taboo icons, approached with a mix of fear and sexual hunger. Familiarity had replaced fear: yet, from her far youth, she

33

snatched a faint memory of it and trembled deliciously.

He gasped as she slowly slid her fingers down through his pubic hair, just as she had slid them behind his fingers, that night. His prick rose to meet them. Her grip tightened. With her other hand, she grasped his wrist and placed his hand on her waistband. He proceeded to do exactly what she wanted him to do.

Hand wrapped around his penis, she worked it with slow pulls that would be enough to get him going but not enough to get him too close to finishing.

'Lovely,' she whispered. Her delight was two-fold. The reality of his presence was a joy. But behind her closed eyes Ian had become the first boy, the first mutual masturbation she had ever experienced.

Experience had caused her to forget her surprise at how hot a prick had felt on that first encounter. She remembered gasping and did the same now. Ian took it that his technique had something to do with it.

'Like it?' he asked breathlessly against her ear. His eyes shone with excitement.

'Keep going,' she answered.

Fingers other than her own had added a hint of danger on that first occasion. The inside of her thighs had trembled as the first thrills had spread from her hard, excited little clitoris. Like a tiny cock, it had thrust up its head, glistening with juice and aching with longing.

Reviving those old sensations was something she would never have thought possible. But she was doing it and they were coming.

She pulled on his prick and felt the first throb of orgasm pump upwards.

She threw back her head, closed her eyes. Her breathing was a series of short, sharp gasps. She was coming. A cobweb of sensations spread from her clitoris. She trembled as if a high-voltage shock had spread through her system. Her flesh shook on her bones. Pieces of her seemed to fly up to the stars, explode and crash back down to earth. Like the tide racing over a sandy beach, it fanned out, reached its highest point and then receded.

It suited her intention that he came after her. She turned him away from her, yanked at his trousers so that his cock was fully exposed. He tried to pull her lips round to meet his. But her eyes were fixed on his cock. She was still pulling it, faster now. His legs trembled. His hips moved backwards and forwards. His cock slid in and out of her furled fingers. Moans became groans as the final fence came ever nearer. The tip of his cock glistened.

Liz, eyes bright with excitement, watched as his semen shot in a clear white jet and landed in spitting globules over the leaves of the Virginia Creeper.

Chapter Four

Rachel was surprised to hear Ian's voice via his answerphone.

'I'm sorry, I'm not around at the moment, but if you'd like to leave a message . . .'

She frowned. Why hadn't he said he was likely to be working late?

She switched off the mobile and slid it back into her bag.

'Not there?' Robert McKenzie smiled across the table at her.

'Not at the moment. He will be later.'

He smiled at her, as though he were analysing her makeup. 'He might be out enjoying himself.'

'Look, Mr . . .'

'Mac. Call me Mac.'

'OK. Mac. If you mean he's out with another woman, I very much doubt it. Ian's not like that. He's very loyal.'

'And very dull?' His smile remained. He raised a quizzical eyebrow.

'I think that's my business,' she replied hotly. 'Now. What was this assignment my mother said you had for me?'

Damn this man. He was making her feel uncomfortable. Perhaps she should think again about taking on this assignment. There were plenty of other researchers who could help him find his roots. Anyway, she had no intention of going out of town to do it. A visit to the British Library archives should unearth some useful details. The Scottish side of the operation was up to him.

McKenzie did not match the picture she'd had in her mind. OK, he was middle-aged. But he was no fuddy-duddy. Men of his age didn't usually have shoulder-length platinum hair, rugged features and steel-grey eyes that bored into your brain. He'd already been sitting at a table when she'd arrived. As a waiter had guided her to the table, she had met McKenzie's eyes and seen the smile playing almost sardonically around his lips. She judged him as being sardonic, never saying anything until he had thoroughly evaluated the person he was presently appraising. Being scrutinised in such a way made her feel uncomfortable. But she would not show her true feelings. She told herself she would cope with him. Backing out was not an option.

Suddenly, the colour of the drink in her glass was very interesting. She resented his implications about Ian. Ian wasn't dull. He was exactly the sort of man she wanted him to be. But the lean man with the mid-Atlantic accent sitting opposite her had struck a nerve. It surprised her that his smile was as slow and controlled as his movements. He appeared strangely laid back for such a rich and powerful man. He was relating exactly what he knew of his ancestors' family, folklore passed down through the generations. His narration was not uninteresting. Some of it was downright salacious. For instance, he was telling her about one female member who had been married off to an uncle at an early age. She had produced two children for him, after which he had promptly died. Although receiving other offers of marriage, the woman had remained alone in the old house he'd left her that was built of granite and surrounded by acres of grazing, moor and hills that were mauve with heather and mist.

Unmarried she might have been, but not alone. Three young male servants lived in the house with her, the children having been sent away for education. It was rumoured that as soon as the young men reached thirty years of age they were pensioned off and younger men hired to take their place.

It did occur to her that the story was phoney and had only been told to make her feel disconcerted. But why would he do that? Perhaps he enjoyed making young women embarrassed.

'So there you are,' he said at last. 'A brief résumé of one ancestor I do know something about.'

'Having all those servants must have cost money,' Rachel said.

'It did,' he answered. 'There was precious little to be passed on to later generations. That's why my family ended up in the States.' He smiled. 'But we managed. We started up and maintained a very good business. You can try guessing what I deal in, if you like.'

His smile was disarming and she couldn't help

doing the same. Damn the wine, she thought and looked straight at him. His blue eyes twinkled. Crinkles of amusement played around his mouth.

'The sex trade?' she said, raising her eyebrows questioningly.

'Now there's an amusing thought. But no. My business is making drill bits,' he said. 'My grandfather started the business back in the twenties.'

She hadn't asked him about his business but she prepared herself for hearing about it anyway. A debit bank balance was an excellent incentive for being a good listener. As she listened, she made notes on the pad she had brought with her.

He talked more about his business through dinner. He told her about how, when oil was really coming into its own and the demands of the automobile were increasing, his grandfather had invented a drill bit for oil exploration.

She told him about university and choosing to do historical research while she made up her mind exactly what career she intended entering.

They drank coffee in the lounge. The walls were yellow, the chairs and settees fat and very white. It was late and a Thursday night. Few people had dined and those that had had already gone home.

He excused himself to go to the cloakroom. Rachel took the opportunity to phone Ian again. This time, she was sure he would answer.

After listening to the same message as before, she slammed the aerial in and threw the phone back into her bag. Suddenly she wasn't so sure of Ian or of herself. By the time Mac came back, she was seething, but only inside. She hoped it didn't show outwardly. She hid her grimace by flicking at the crumbs that clung to her dress, a neat little black number that was only just beginning to show its age. That's why I'm here, she reminded herself. I need the money.

'More coffee?' he asked. Without waiting for her answer, he caught the attention of a waiter.

'No. I don't think so.'

Smooth as ever and extremely politely, Mac told the waiter to take away the tray and put the cost on to his room bill.

He sat back down.

She started making ready to go.

'I take it you didn't bother to explain to your boyfriend that you were going out with an older man this evening.'

She jerked her head round to face him. 'I said I was going away with friends. I am, tomorrow.' She had an urge to add that older men did not attract her. For some reason, the words would not come. You need the money, she told herself. That's why you mustn't upset him.

'But you didn't tell him about tonight,' McKenzie was saying.

The way he said it almost made her feel guilty. 'No. I didn't. Why should I?'

'No reason to. I only wondered if you were hoping to seduce me.'

Her mouth dropped open. She glared. Although the urge to spring to her feet and storm out was very great, Rachel remained seated. The cheek of this man! 'Nothing could have been further from my mind. I knew you were nearly as old as my father.' The barb was intentional.

He laughed. It was subdued but warm. 'The maiden's last refuge. Tell a man he's old enough to be her father.'

Rachel looked towards the opening where the waiter had vanished. Soon he would return to tell her that her cab had arrived. But she needn't wait for that cab. Not that she had any intention of walking home. On the contrary, it occurred to her that McKenzie might intend for her to stay the night. This man who she had just insulted would seduce her. Strangely enough, the idea was not repellent. Could she still live with herself if she did? Of course she could. But the idea was new. You've never been attracted to older men, she told herself. Why now?

She looked across the table at the handsome American. What would it be like to lie naked beside him? Would his flesh be firm? Would his stamina be up to it?

It amused her to think of what Ian would say if he found out. It might even be fun to tell him. She wondered whether he'd be jealous. Not that it mattered that much. She was her own woman, free to do as she pleased. Just as he was free to do whatever he wanted – within limitations. Ian, she knew, adored her.

She had fully expected him to be waiting for her to ring. This was yet another one of her rituals. Via the telephone, seductive words would turn dirtier. Ian would masturbate to order. She would urge him to take out his cock then tell him exactly what she wanted him to do with it. She would even tell him when to come. He loved her doing it. He'd told her so.

The fact that Ian appeared to be out unnerved her. He was predictable and she liked that. She'd heard young men boasting about their conquests:

how they'd 'given her one', had her, got her to give head, wank them off etc., etc.

The nuns had warned her that men took advantage of women's innocence. The devil, they had said, was easily roused. From the very first, she had sworn that they wouldn't talk about her like that. She would be the one telling them what she wanted.

She was so wrapped up in her thoughts that it was a while before she was aware of Mac studying her intensely. Even though he was dressed for dinner, it did not diminish the casual air he exuded.

This is a powerful man, she told herself. Can I seduce him? But the thought was still alien, even though she knew from experience that power was an aphrodisiac that few women could resist. The temptation teased her mind and excited her body. The food had been good, so had the wine: yet still she held herself in check, with a mix of pride, stubbornness and a belief that only a man of her own age could possibly excite her.

'You're becoming very thoughtful. What is it you English say? A penny for your thoughts?'

His voice is nice, she thought, warm, enticing. She couldn't resist smiling at him. Something inside began to melt. 'Look. It's been a great evening. I didn't mean to be rude about your age. And you probably aren't that old and past it at all.'

He raised his eyebrows. His mouth twitched with amusement. 'I'm glad you've changed your mind.' He rested his chin on his palm. One finger tapped at his temple where random grey hairs had come together to form one white streak.

'I'm sorry,' she said again and adopted a demure look. She knew better than to cross her legs so that her skirt drew up and exposed her thighs. An older man was drawn by youthful innocence, even if it was contrived. Seduction, she told herself, is nothing to do with it. Power, she thought. That's what was causing her to act alluring. It was about knowing that she could have him if she wanted to.

He continued to study her. She waited for him to make a move. He remained still, his eyes gazing into hers.

What he said next took her by surprise. 'This furniture is made of leather.' He reached out his hand and smoothed the creamy white settee. 'It's very cool. Think how it would feel against your bare flesh.'

She gripped the edge of the settee. Don't blush, she said to herself. For God's sake, don't blush.

It wasn't like her to even contemplate blushing. Why now? She made an effort to gain control. She tossed her head and grinned cheekily at him. 'Why don't you try it and tell me what it's like?'

His smile never wavered. 'Right now?'

She smiled too and nodded. 'Right now.'

A waiter came in and retrieved used crockery from a glass-topped coffee table that had bronze heads of corn twisting stiffly up its legs. With a rattle of cups, the waiter departed.

At last!

Fascinated, she watched as Mac undid his trousers and pulled them and his underwear down slightly. At the same time he raised his hips.

'I don't believe you're doing this!' Rachel looked around the lounge. They were alone. 'What if someone should come?' she said.

'No one can see anything.'

43

He was right. The front of his shirt and trousers were still in place and covered him.

Rachel licked her dry lips. Mac had really done it. He was sitting here with her in a very public place with his bare arse against cool leather. Although he was the one doing it, she could imagine how it felt. Not just because the leather felt good, but also because of where he was doing it. Anyone could come in.

'Does it feel good?' she asked.

He shook his head. Was he telling her it didn't? Rachel was puzzled.

'I'm not telling you. Find out for yourself,' he said.

Yet again a surprise. She took a deep breath. The threatening blush had not gone away. It might not show on her face but the heat of it had spread from her head to her toes.

He was daring her. The choice was hers. It might be defiant to refuse. On the other hand, if she didn't match his bravado, then the triumph would be his.

The decision was made.

With both hands, she reached up under her dress and pulled her purple satin knickers down over the black stockings she was wearing. Holding his gaze, she brought the skimpy garment to her lap, where she smoothed it flat. Even though her flesh was not yet in contact with the leather, her pulse was racing. With a look of triumph, she raised her buttocks and hitched her skirt up at the back.

The feel of the leather was indescribable. It was soft and yet hard, inanimate yet alive. It was cool against the hot wetness of her sex. But she controlled her expression. Her enjoyment belonged to her and her alone.

44

At last he had to ask her. 'Is it good?'

'Delicious.'

'Let me see.'

She threw him a contemptuous glare, then laid her head on the back of the settee. 'I don't show myself off purely for the enjoyment of men. I expect something in return.'

She opened her legs slightly. Not only would he notice her doing that, he would also imagine how she would smell and look underneath that dark tunnel of a skirt.

Would he do what she wanted him to do? She waited, was aware of him drawing his trousers back up. Would he go or would he stay?

Stay!

He went down on his knees between her legs. She looked up at the ceiling, as though his presence there was of no consequence to her.

Warm palms made a rasping sound over her stockings as they travelled up her legs. He raised her skirt then buried his head under it. As his tongue began licking and kissing the inside of her thighs, she held her breath and looked at the black hump that had appeared in her skirt.

This was how she wanted a man to be. This was bliss. He was now no more than the leather settee she sat on. He was an inanimate object hidden under a black veil, useful only to give her pleasure. And that was one thing Mac seemed out to prove to her.

Thumbs and fingers parted her pubic hair then slid along the slippery inner flesh. The tip of his tongue licked at her flowing juices. His lips kissed then sucked at her clitoris.

She threw back her head. Breathed deeply,

sighed and closed her eyes. This was truly pleasurable because she was giving nothing in return. All she had to concentrate on was her own satisfaction. She could let her orgasm flood over her as quickly as she liked, with the help of a few well-chosen fantasies – though they were hardly needed in a situation like this. She could hold it all in check and leave it purely to reality, the touch of his tongue, his fingers and his skill.

She threw her arms above her head, stretched her body. Robert McKenzie no longer existed. Neither did she. It was as if she were no more than a swirling mist of sensual pleasure. Body disappeared. There was only her mind and all the sensations flowing into it.

Silence is not always a deterrent to detection. Perhaps it was instinct that made her open her eyes. Unheard, a third person had entered the room.

Tray in one hand, white bar cloth folded neatly over the other arm, the waiter was staring.

Her first thought was to tap Mac's shoulder, to stop him sucking at her sex so she could hurriedly cover herself and make a swift exit. But some wickedness deep inside prevented her from doing that. For the first time ever, she had an audience to her sexual pleasure. There was no need for imagination. This was for real.

Control of her own body passed from her to the orgasm flooding over it. Like a great tidal wave it came, pushing her towards the summit, launching her into her own personal orbit.

She cried out, grabbed a tight hold of Mac's head and jerked her clitoris and her sticky flesh against his mouth until the last spasm had diminished into nothing.

She had expected him to ask her to stay the night and it had surprised her when he didn't. She had also expected him to beg to see her again but he didn't do that, either. But then, why should he? The research into his family tree would bring them together again. Still, things weren't exactly as she'd expected. In the past, she'd always regarded older men with younger women as being somewhat comical. Ageing rock stars were often spread across tabloid newspapers. No matter that their looks were gone to seed. There they were with some blonde bimbo hanging on to their arm. 'It's love, this time,' they'd say, completely oblivious to the glint of money in the eyes of their latest wife/girlfriend.

But he did escort her to her taxi.

The taxi driver was whistling as they drove and the glass partition was open. 'Had a good time?' he asked.

'It was business,' she said. The moment she said it, she realised she'd come out without her notepad. She vaguely remembered leaving it on the reception desk when she'd been waiting for the taxi.

'Can you take me back to the hotel?' she asked the driver, once she'd explained what the problem was.

It took only minutes.

Light drizzle was beginning to fall as she got out of the taxi. Droplets fluttered from her hair as she ran into the hotel foyer. The notepad was exactly where she'd left it. As she grabbed it and shoved it into her bag, she happened to glance into the lounge. Mac was still there. So was the waiter. Both were smiling. With one hand, Mac was slipping the waiter what looked like a twenty-pound note. With the other he was pushing a scrap of purple satin into his pocket.

Meaning to protest, she took a step closer to the lounge. Then she stopped, raised her hand to her cheek and felt its warmth beneath her fingers. Her feelings, she realised, were mixed. On the one hand, she wanted to confront him. On the other, she was intrigued by what he had done. A young man wouldn't think of doing something like that.

Mind whirling, she turned and walked back to the taxi. As they drove away, she looked back. Mac was getting into his car, a sleek black BMW. Experience, she thought, really counts for something.

Chapter Five

'A re you free for dinner this evening?' Richard asked quietly.

Liz looked up from her desk into the clean-shaven face that looked tanned against the stark white of his shirt collar. She hesitated before answering. Ian's body was still in her mind. She could still smell him, still see him. He fulfilled her in a way Richard could not. It wasn't just because it was Ian. It was more compelling than the mere fascination of one specific man. Youth was the aphrodisiac and the sweetness with which he had allowed her to seduce him. Her maturity, her experience, had fascinated him.

She hadn't allowed him to stay the night. That was the main rule she and Mark had agreed on. Their bed was theirs and theirs alone. But the thought of the things she could do to that firm flesh had kept her awake most of the night. In the end, she had succumbed to masturbation. But it wasn't enough. Tonight she had hoped to rectify matters.

'Is it imperative?' She looked at her computer screen and ran her finger over a set of glowing figures, as if it were their topic of discussion. No one casually glancing in their direction would know they were talking assignations, dinner for two, and sex in secret.

'I wouldn't ask you, otherwise. It's business.'

Liz looked up in surprise.

'And pleasure,' he added.

She thought quickly. Ian's office and mobile number was noted in the small red book she carried in her briefcase. She'd scribbled it there last night just before he'd left, his face still flushed, her breasts still tingling.

'OK,' she said.

'Eight-thirty. Leonardo's.'

She smiled and nodded. Once he was safely back in his office, she phoned Ian at the financial house he worked for, just to the rear of Threadneedle Street. He wasn't there. She dialled his mobile number.

'Tonight's off,' she said in an efficient manner. 'Business, I'm afraid.'

'Shit!' He said it as if he were sighing.

She felt instantly regretful. 'I'm sorry. There's always tomorrow.'

'There is?' He sounded surprised.

She frowned. 'Of course. Why shouldn't there be?'

He sighed for real this time. 'I thought you were giving me the old –'

'Brush off? Nonsense! Of course not.'

His sincerity amazed her. She glanced swiftly round the wide vista of the open-plan office. Leaning closer towards the computer screen, she cradled the phone tightly against her mouth.

'Why would I want to stop? We've hardly begun. Imagine all the things we've yet to do. There's so much I want to teach you.'

'I want that,' he said. She sensed the relief in his voice and also the pleading.

'It's a two-way street, Ian. You're giving me something, too. I've done it all but you make me forget that I have. It's like rediscovering sex all over again. I want to feel those first tingles. I want to break all those taboos I was told were bad for my soul. Will you help me with that, Ian? Will you do all the things to me that I was told to believe were wicked?'

He groaned. 'You're making me ache. You can guess where I'm aching.'

Liz smiled at the thought of what she was doing to him. What pleasure it gave her. Tightness gripped her stomach and shot down between her legs. What had been dormant there now felt heavy. Making its presence known, she thought.

'I wish I were there to kiss it better, wrap my fingers around it and relieve the tension. Unfortunately, all I can do is offer you words of comfort.'

'It won't help,' he said with a low groan.

'It will, the way I say them,' she said. It seemed a shame that he could not see her smile or the sparkle in her eyes. 'Are you alone?'

'Yes. I'm in my car. I pulled into the side of the road when you rang. I was hoping it was you. I can't stop thinking about you. What you did last night . . .'

'Undo your zip,' she said. There was only silence on the other end of the phone. She could imagine him sitting there, his mouth open as he took in what she was asking him to do. She fancied she heard the biting sound of metal teeth being prised open. 'Get your cock out,' she said softly. Sixty seconds passed. 'Have you done it?'

'Yes,' he said. His voice trembled.

'Now,' she said, 'wrap your fingers around it. As I speak, you can pull on it at will. I'm going to tell you all the things we're going to do together. Some are things I am going to do to you. Some are things you are going to do to me. We're going to explore our sexuality, Ian. We're going to try all the things we've never done before. Do you remember how cool the air felt on your body last night? It made your cock tingle. It made it stiffen, just like my naked nipples do if a cold breeze blows upon them.' She heard him groan. 'On the next occasion we meet I'm going to strip your clothes – all of your clothes – away from your body. I'm going to have you lie face down over the rough wood of the patio table. Then I'm going to kneel between your legs. I'm going to start at the crack of your arse and lick between your cheeks, push them apart and let the night air tickle your hole. I'm going to nuzzle your balls, lick at them and take them one by one into my mouth. Then I'm going to get under the table, turn round and take your cock into my mouth. I'm going to suck you out of yourself. My tongue's going to poke at that tiny hole in the tip. It's going to flick around the head. Imagine how that will feel, Ian. It's sensitive there, isn't it? So sensitive that I could make you come if I kept at it.'

'I'm coming,' he groaned.

She carried on. 'As I suck on your cock, I'm going to squeeze your balls with one hand. With the other, I'm going to scratch at your behind. Then I'm going to push my finger into you, Ian. I'm going to fuck you with my finger at the same time as you are fucking my mouth. Can you imagine it, Ian? In, out, in, out, abusing you, pushing into you, and all the time, you're pushing into me, having my mouth while I have your arse. Fucking where once we weren't supposed to fuck, but doing it anyway. Doing it, Ian. Fucking:, me fucking you, you fucking me. Do you hear me, Ian? Do you see it?'

'I ... am ... com ... ing!' His cry was strangulated, words split by a host of gasps, groans and lengthy sighs.

They'd been to Leonardo's before. It was by no means a sumptuous place, sited as it was amid a rank of small shops, most of which had FOR SALE/ LEASE notices in the windows. The street was dimly lit, the pavements wet with rain.

Both arrived separately by taxi.

Richard had seafood carbonara. She had green and white linguine in a delicious mushroom and Gorgonzola sauce. They drank Amaretto as an aperitif. A cold Chardonnay accompanied the main meal.

Liz glanced up at him between mouthfuls of food and wine. Earlier in the evening, she had promised herself that this would be dinner and nothing else. Sex was good with Richard, but not as good as it had been. Either she was going off him or her libido was striding off in another – more youthful – direction. But from the moment the dark-haired, dark-eyed waiter had brushed her breast with his arm as he'd poured the wine, it had yet again changed direction. Her eyes followed the small, tight behind as he walked away from the table. About eighteen years old, she thought, with some growing still to do. But, knowing these Latin types, he was probably already very experienced. She imagined his lovemaking included raining hot-blooded kisses on the object of his desire. Hair would cover his chest, his legs, arms and possibly his back.

How would it be, she thought, if I followed him out to the back somewhere and showed him what I really wanted?

She looked beyond Richard's head and the tangle of plants growing from terracotta pots. Where were the toilets? What better excuse for taking her leave? The waiter paused before exiting, raised his hand and smiled at a blond, broad-shouldered hunk sat in one of the other booths. The hunk waved back, his fingers waggling in an overly feminine way.

Damn!

Liz turned her attention back to Richard. Better the obtainable than nothing at all.

'I liked what you did, the other day,' Richard said, between forkfuls of food and sips of cool wine. 'Why couldn't we have done it earlier?'

Liz shrugged. 'Things change. People change. Attitudes change.' She didn't tell him that he'd never turned her on enough to do too much. He was a pleasant oasis among the daily grind and far better than a coffee break.

'So quickly?' He raised a quizzical eyebrow.

'Sudden happenings,' she smiled, and caught a glimpse of herself in the mirror on the other side of the restaurant. There were no obvious wrinkles around her eyes and no sprinkling of grey among the beige-blonde hairdo. She turned back to him. 'Perhaps it's my age.'

He smiled back and shook his head. 'A woman's perennial excuse.'

She didn't comment but felt a sudden exhilaration. She had besotted Ian and that made her feel good. The waiter too would have been putty in her hands, if only he'd been straight.

There were going to be more young men. She was sure of that. But she still wasn't sure about mentioning the fact to Mark. They shared everything. Talking about their lovers turned them both on. It excited them to think of each being desired by others. Yet she was apprehensive about mentioning a younger man. Undermining Mark's sexual confidence was the last thing she wanted to do. For now, Ian and any other young man she came across would be her secret. Or a protégé, she thought. The definition pleased her. Protégé, to her mind, meant pupil, follower. That was how she would regard her young men. It made her feel kind of special to think she was passing on knowledge, giving someone else the benefit of her vast experience.

'What are you smiling at?' Richard asked.

She looked at the other diners seated at damask-clothed tables, engaged in intimate conversations, their faces lit by candles that dribbled wax down the sides of empty wine bottles.

'I was thinking of all the experiences I've had and all those yet to come.' She turned to him. 'What we did in your office was only one of them.'

He looked deeply into her eyes over the rim of his wineglass. 'Are you telling me I have more to look forward to?'

There was an air of mockery in her glance. 'I don't know about you.' She grinned wickedly. 'I certainly have.'

His smile remained. She sensed by his thoughtful silence this evening that there really was a business element to their meeting.

He cupped his glass in both hands and looked into the yellowish liquid. 'How do you feel about experiencing some sexual adventure with our American friend, McKenzie?' He kept his eyes on the wine while he waited for her to answer.

'So you want me to get under McKenzie's skin for the honour of the company. Is that what you're saying?'

Richard grinned. 'Under his bedclothes would be adequate.'

Liz shook her head and smiled. A sudden thought had come to her. 'This reminds me of a training exercise. Get in close and get the measure of your opponent.'

'So, so,' Richard said, nodding. 'But I think role-playing might describe it better.' He looked at her directly. 'He's obsessed with his ancestors. He likes to dress up and carry out some of the things they did in their life.'

'Like what?' said Liz.

Richard waved his hand casually. 'A few of them were sea captains. Some were members of the Hellfire Club.'

'Charming!'

'But I'm sure you can cope.' Richard beamed. It was at that moment that Liz concluded their relationship would soon be over. It wasn't so much that she felt used. The opposite was true. The company was good to work for. Why not feather

56

her nest? She wondered if he had detected that something inside had changed and he was on borrowed time. For the moment, she would fall in with his plans. After all, he had been very good to her. But it didn't matter. Everything had to end, including them.

'There is a bonus,' he added. 'A monetary one.'

She raised her glass and gave him a quizzical look.

'Why are you looking at me like that?'

She drained her glass. 'I was wondering who was the biggest whore – you or me!'

His blue eyes sparkled as he smiled. Fine lines appeared at their edges. 'Sometimes it's a turn-on. Tell me, are you wearing underwear?'

She hesitated before answering. Beneath the red silk sheath she wore a lacy bra, matching briefs, suspenders and fine stockings. In answer to him, she slowly crossed one leg over the other.

'I hear stockings,' he said.

She nodded.

'Will you take it all off for me?'

She could have said no. But imagining what she could have done to the gorgeous young waiter had aroused her. Food and wine had been eaten and drunk. Sex was now on the menu.

She raised her eyes and looked purposefully around the restaurant. 'Here and now? In front of all these people?'

He shook his head. 'I'd like you to be wearing only your dress when we walk out of here.'

She hesitated as she considered. Then she nodded. 'OK. If that's what you want.'

But she wasn't interested in what he wanted. The ache of wanting still hung like lead in her groin.

The tension had to be eased, the angry need placated. It was something she too would enjoy. Liz stood up. 'I'm off to the powder room. The bill's all yours.'

He grinned and shook his head as she walked away.

In the privacy of the powder room, she removed her dress then took off every single item she wore beneath it, leaving only her stockings and suspender belt. She kept her shoes on.

Before putting her dress back on, she studied her figure in the mirrored walls. Forthright nipples stared back at her. The chill air made them jut out hard from their soft pink beds. Her breasts were still round, her belly still flat. Round, tight bottoms surrounded her. Her body was replicated a dozen times, reflected from one mirrored wall to another.

She bent to wash her hands. It was hard to resist looking into the mirror. Still bent over, she adjusted her stance. Like that, she could more easily see the dark shadow between her legs, the juicy lips, the moist opening between.

As she dried her hands she studied the reddish pubic hair that covered her quim like a cock's comb. A cock's home, she thought with a smile, would be a better description. What better retreat for a hard-nosed prick after a hard day's work than to slip into my pussy and shag me something chronic?

She put her dress back on. The silk fell like a whisper over her body. It occurred to her to stuff her underwear into her handbag. But why bother? She had plenty more at home. Instead, she hung the bra over the drying machine, the knickers over a door handle.

'Well, here you are,' she said to her reflection. 'Unwrapped and ready for action.'

With that, she turned on her heels and left the mirrors and the underwear behind her.

When they got outside, it was still raining.

He reached for her hand. 'Did you do it?' he asked, glancing at her swiftly. 'Are you wearing any underwear?'

She shook her head.

He looked at her small handbag.

Knowing what he was thinking, she smiled at him. 'I left it behind.'

As they walked, his eyes raked her body. 'You dirty bitch.'

'You love it.'

And I love it, too, she thought. I want to be dirty, tonight. I want to have a cock in me and I'm not too concerned who it belongs to.

Her body tingled. The feeling of carrying a lead weight between her legs remained. It was as if all the blood in her body had flowed there to engorge her lips and cause her flesh to be slippery.

The rain was heavier now. The wetter her dress got, the more it stuck to her body. Its coldness made her flesh tingle. Her nipples stood hard. Her belly flattened. The silk clung to her mound: a strange sensation, she thought, almost as if I am having my own erection.

She licked her lips, longing for it all to start. She glanced at Richard. He was staring at her breasts. She looked down. If there had been a wet T-shirt contest around, she would have been a firm favourite. The shape of her breasts was obvious beneath the wet silk. Her nipples and their soft surroundings stuck fast against the material.

'You whore!' said Richard.

Funny, she thought, how men dipped deeper into profanity as their lust increased. You could almost measure their lengthening cock by virtue of their contracting vocabulary.

'Round here,' he said. Grabbing her hand, he jerked her into an alley. It was completely empty. No crates, no dustbins and mostly dark. Only where a forgotten light shed a flickering flame could she see the rain running down a brick wall. He slammed her against it, his lips and his body crushing hers. The cold of the wall permeated her dress at the back. The heat of his body warmed her wet breasts and belly. The rain plastered her hair to her head.

'Be a whore for me,' he gasped against her ear. His fingers gripped her jaw as his teeth nipped at her lips.

She slid her hands around his waist and groaned with pleasure. His body felt so warm and she clasped it to her. The oblivion of sex began to take over. Sex became her master, the urge she could not ignore. This was the point when it no longer mattered who she was with. The power that had lain men low, toppled empires and crushed good intentions had taken over. There was fluidity to her flesh, a pounding in her veins. Her hips began to jerk against his as the juices started to flow.

He grasped the hem of her dress and pulled it high above her waist. She gasped as he slammed his pelvis against hers and her bare buttocks met the cold wetness of the wall behind her.

'I'm going to have you,' he rasped in a thick, lustful voice. His hands clawed at her breasts.

She closed her eyes and offered no resistance. She wanted him to have her. She wanted to give him free rein so that whatever he did was a complete surprise. A surprise was always more exciting than the familiar. Excitement was what she wanted. That's why humanity was not as monogamous as it made out. The allure of the new conquest always beckoned. Heightened passion, intense sensuality was what she and a host of humanity craved. All that there was to experience would be indulged in, despite social mores or laws set in stone.

He dragged her dress higher until both it and her arms were above her head. Both Richard and the alley disappeared behind a red veil. She felt him tangling the wet, fine material into a knot above her hands. From her breasts down, she was naked, exposed to the rain and to whatever he wanted to do to her. Only her suspender belt, stockings and shoes remained.

He pushed her back against the wall. She gasped at its wet, cold, hardness. Shivers ran over her breasts as his hands and the rain combined to tantalise her nerve ends. It was as if fine wires were threaded through her body. Along each ran a trickle of electricity. The sensations came from within. How often had she fantasised about being in a man's power? Wasn't it one of the oldest of deep-rooted desires? But she had never experienced the reality. She had never wanted to. There had been no need. And besides, the fear of things going too far had curtailed the scenes in her mind becoming fact. But there was always a first time and, anyway, this was different.

She had known Richard a long time. She trusted him as far as sex was concerned. It was only in business that she had to be as sharp as he was.

As the rain trickled around her nipples, she felt his hands tighten around her breasts. Within her red tent of silk, she gasped with delight as his mouth sucked on each one in turn. He was not unfair. Her enjoyment was evenly balanced between each breast.

Without sight and smell of him, what he was doing might have been disappointing. But her body compensated. By touch alone she was on fire. Not knowing what he would do next inspired her response. She was like a plaything, a clockwork doll that was slowing being wound up.

He slammed her more tightly against the wall.

'Open your legs, bitch.'

He forced his leg between hers. She heard his zip open and felt the coarseness of his hairs against her belly.

His cock slid easily into her. Rain and body moisture ran together down the insides of her thighs.

Her breathing was rapid. Her heart thudded against her ribs and she ached with rising climax from the navel down.

She attempted to raise her hips to meet his. He slammed his pelvis back against hers so her buttocks slapped back against the brick.

'Like this,' he said thickly. 'I want it like this.'

His fingers were like claws on her tits, pulling, squeezing, and clamping her nipples between finger and thumb. He was leaning away from her, his pelvis continually slamming against hers. Her upper body and his clawing hands were exposed.

But she couldn't see them. She could only imagine what he was seeing.

There were windows high above them. Would anyone look out from those on such a dreadful night? She almost hoped so. She wanted her body to be seen.

I'm like an actor or a dancer on stage. I'm in my own world, and yet I'm performing for the benefit of others.

The idea excited her. She wanted shame, she wanted to be used – but most of all, she wanted unseen eyes to see what he was doing to her.

It didn't matter who saw her. She had become nothing more than an object, she thought. Sex object was the phrase that came immediately to mind. And for now that was exactly what she was. But her identity was safe. Her head and arms hidden from view behind her silken tent.

Imagine how I look, she thought with amusement. A red blob above a naked body. Wet and glistening while he fucks me, does what he wants to me. And I let him. And he knows that I let him because I am enjoying it. But for now I appear submissive. I appear to be what he wants me to be.

In her mind, the fantasy and the reality of her bizarre appearance, her way-out sex, combined. A flood of pre-orgasmic sensations gathered in her abdomen, clustered around the point of contact between him and her.

Inescapable, the floodtide swept over her, made her legs shake, her belly shiver, and her buttocks tighten as her flesh absorbed the force of pure sensation.

Richard plunged, tensed, and plunged again.

'Bitch!' he rasped against her ear. 'Whore! Dirty whore!'

'Do it to me!' she shouted behind her red silk shroud. 'Do it to me!'

One last plunge, one more expletive and he stiffened against her. In that moment, she knew he had come. Also in that moment the sensations subsided. The fantasy died.

Night was the best time on the narrowboat.

The air was warm, soft against Rachel's face. It was her turn to steer. The next mooring was just a few hundred yards ahead. Her companions were sitting on the cabin roof, cans in hand, naked feet dangling over the slim windows.

The cans had only just been opened. Not enough beer had been drunk yet to make them noisy. Silence reigned. Thoughtless and speechless, they drifted past the dark water-meadows where weeping willows dipped into the water. The only light came from the cabin windows, mere slits of amber gliding gently past. It feels, thought Rachel, as if we are sliding into limbo. Her spirit began to rebel.

Something happen, it screamed. And it did.

'It's no good. I've just got to go.'

Cavan! She watched as the tousle haired Irishman made his way to the prow of the boat.

'What's he doing?' She craned her neck, raised her chin.

'What do you think?' The speaker was Nancy, someone she could reasonably call a best friend.

'He's taking a leak,' added Paul, Nancy's latest.

One of the other guys laughed and indicated with an outstretched arm and a beer can. 'He looks like a bloody mascot – complete with a water spout!'

Rachel leant sideways. As they turned slightly to the right, she could see Cavan standing up front. Sure enough a spout of water arched and fell into the canal.

'Cavan, you're polluting the waterway,' Paul shouted.

'No, he isn't,' said Nancy. 'It's a natural product. Piss is biodegradable.'

They all laughed.

By the time they pulled into the mooring, a little more beer had been drunk. Nancy and Dani, the third female member of their group, went down to prepare food in the galley.

Cavan helped Rachel tie up. As he did so, he took every opportunity to get close to her, his hands sliding over her ribs and hips as he squeezed by to fix the mooring ropes. She pushed him away. Not yet, she thought to herself. You hardly know him. All the same, his closeness, his smell, was pleasant. He was broad-shouldered, russet-haired and had smiling eyes.

'So where's your lover?' he asked.

'Which one?' she returned and hid her smile by pretending to look for whatever had made a sudden splash somewhere further along the canal.

'I meant Ian,' he said.

She fancied he sounded slightly abashed, as if his interest was purely that of a friend. But it hadn't come out that way.

'I don't know.' She glanced quickly at him. He was staring at her, hands on hips, hair the colour of dark rust blowing around her face.

As though he's trying to read my mind, she

thought. He wants to know whether he's got a chance. What will I do? Do I want him to seduce me? Do I want to seduce him?

A thrill ran through her as she imagined what he would be like between the sheets. He had a sprinkling of chest hair. She could see it in the gap left by his open shirt. Chest hair, she'd decided in the early days of her adolescence, was slightly bestial but not unpleasant. Only once had she felt the grating of profuse chest hair against her breasts. The memory wasn't exactly unpleasant, only unsettling. Even though it was a long time ago, the memory still made her feel slightly wicked.

He'd been the gardener at the convent school she'd attended and his name had been Giovanni. His name and his body were typically Italian, short-legged and broad-shouldered, dark-haired with an olive complexion.

Like all girls shielded from the normalcy of contact with adolescent men, the girls had spun stories about how the swarthy Italian looked at them, undressing them with his eyes. Whether it was the truth or no was not easy to determine. Their experience was limited to brothers or precocious male relatives.

In the darkness of their room, mostly shared with four or six others, their imaginations would run riot. Blushes hidden by the night, they had described how his naked body might look and what he would do if one of them were alone with him.

'All finished!'

Cavan's exclamation that he had finished his part of the tying-up terminated her memories.

'Do you fancy a walk in the woods?' he asked,

jerking his head in the direction of a copse of dark-headed trees.

Rachel considered, then opened her mouth to answer.

'Grub's up!' It was Nancy, her head poking out over the half-door that led to the galley.

'Too late,' she said, smiled and turned back to the boat.

Externally, she saw Cavan's crestfallen face. Internally, Giovanni faded but didn't entirely go away.

'You know I've been brought along to pair up with you I suppose,' said Cavan as he walked along beside her.

She stopped and stared at him. 'Is that so?'

He grinned. 'But there's no obligation, you know.'

Nostrils flaring, she swung her legs over the side of the boat. 'No, there isn't, so don't hold your breath!'

She didn't see him shrugging his shoulders and grinning, yet she knew he was. This was the first time they'd met and she couldn't say she wasn't attracted to him. You don't have to fuck him, she said to herself. It was one of her rules. Like him first, then fuck. But woe betide the guy who took it for granted.

The fact was, she did like him. But something was niggling at the back of her mind. She couldn't shake off thinking about Mac and what he had done. He's too old for you, she told herself. Who wants a sugar daddy, anyway?

The idea appalled her. She knew girls who did have older boyfriends and had always viewed them with an element of pity. None of them went with them for their money or power, so they said, and yet they appeared besotted. Were power and money really the aphrodisiacs they were made out to be? Or was it a case that they had good sex with experienced men?

She did her best to shake the thoughts from her mind. Older men were not an option on this boat. Everyone here was around her age. They had lots in common – at least, that's the way it seemed.

As she drank, ate and laughed with her friends, she exchanged glances with Cavan. She recognised attraction when she saw it and she liked him. But something was holding her back. Was he as intrigued by her as she was by him? And yet he appeared casual, uncaring whether they got together or not. But at least they were being friendly with each other.

'I hear you research people's genealogy,' he said between mouthfuls of pasta. 'I'll have to get you to do mine.'

'Would it be worth it?'

He looked hurt, though she fancied it was put on. 'Of course. Don't I go back to the Kings of Ireland?'

'No,' Clem, one of the other guys intervened. 'You go back to your Dad's pub in Dublin. Spit sawdust and pints of black beer. Disgusting stuff!'

'Oh, how can you say such a thing! It's disrespectful, so it is.' He leant close to Rachel's ear, his voice still loud. 'Take no notice of my friend, Rachel – sorry – ex-friend. He's a first-class moron.' He shoved at Andrew's shoulder.

'Some friend!'

They started talking about their youth, Cavan in Ireland, Andrew in Bristol.

Rachel watched and listened. It wasn't so much that their biographies were so gripping she had to listen. It was because Giovanni was still drifting around in her mind and so was Mac, a man she was trying her best not to find attractive.

But then Cavan did something to take her mind off her own confusion.

Lit by gas, the cabin got hotter. Cavan took off his sweater and tossed it to one side.

A thread of excitement seemed to twist itself in and out of knots in her stomach as she eyed his chest and caught the faint whiff of male hormones. And his chest was hairy, just like Giovanni's had been. Her mind drifted as she sipped at her wine. Although the company in the narrowboat cabin was good, sex was invading her mind. Old memories came flooding back with the whiff of Cavan's maleness.

'So when was the first time for you, Rachel?' It was Andrew's voice that broke into her thoughts.

'What?' She'd only caught snatches of their reminiscences. Her own memories had been too compelling to ignore. Even now she felt hot between her legs. But she wouldn't let on. If the chance came, well . . .

'When did you lose your virginity, darling?' asked Nancy, wineglass held high, mouth open and buttons undone.

Rachel hesitated. For a moment it occurred to her that they'd been reading her mind or she'd been voicing her thoughts aloud. But she hadn't. Sexual experiences were something she kept to herself.

They were stored-up treasures she used when reality was not giving her the turn on she deserved.

She slowly surveyed the eager faces. Eyes shining, lips moist with wine and expectation, they really were expecting her to unload. Only Cavan sat quietly in the corner, head bent forward slightly by virtue of the overhanging cupboard behind him. His eyes were fixed on her face and a hint of amusement played around his mouth. As if he knows what I'm going to say, she thought. What is he, some kind of mind-reader?

'I don't play to a public gallery,' she said.

'Private thoughts and private talks,' said Nancy and raised her glass.

'That's right,' said Rachel, getting suddenly to her feet. 'And not right at this moment. I promised to phone Ian. How far is it to the pub?'

The pub was about half a mile away. Cavan offered to walk with her. The others had their own plans. Rachel surmised that, by the time they got back, all four were likely to be in bed, probably all in the same one. Somehow she didn't want to be part of that. She wondered if Cavan also knew they would do that. Perhaps that was also the reason why he was silently walking with her. He did not attempt to touch her. Neither did he attempt to make overtures that might also lead them into throwing off their clothes and leaping on each other's bodies.

Light from hooded brass shades brightened the grey stone of the waterside pub. Gold lettering on a green background advertised the fact that fine wines and good food were always available. Printed in Victorian lettering, THE JOLLY BOATMAN it said above the wide door.

The bar was straight ahead. Rachel quickly took in the flagstone floors, the walls packed tight with old pictures, artefacts and things that only an interior design team would want to hang in a bar. A sign above a door to her right told her where the phone was located.

'Will you have a drink with me, while we're here?' Cavan asked. 'I'll get it while you do your phoning.'

'Yes.' She said it quickly before moving off to her right.

The phone was situated in a deep alcove halfway between the loos. The alcove had brown painted wood to a dado rail and yellow painted wallpaper from there to the ceiling.

She dialled. It rang six times before he picked up the phone.

'Where were you?' she asked.

He said, 'Oh,' as if surprised to hear her.

'Am I interrupting something?'

He paused, stammered slightly. 'I've just got out of the shower.'

The picture was clear. She could almost imagine how he looked. And his scent, crisply clean from the application of a luxury shower gel for men, the sort he always went for. She could smell that, too.

'I phoned last night. Where were you?' She tried not to sound demanding. After all, she didn't like anyone asking where she was going or what she was up to.

'I was with an old friend. I bumped into him in the wine bar on the way home.'

An old friend. He'd said 'him'. A male friend. She smiled to herself. He had made sure she knew it was a male friend, probably someone from his school or college days. But she wasn't going to ask details and risk being bored.

She curled herself tighter into the cubicle.

'Are you wearing your bathrobe?' she asked.

'No.'

She closed her eyes. Ian's clean flesh, slightly tanned and very firm, came easily to her mind.

'Is your cock clean and wrinkled from the shower?'

'Yes.' He said the word softly, similar to a sigh.

'Take it in your hand. Pretend it's my fingers around it. Imagine me pulling on it. Can you imagine that?'

'Yes.' He sounded breathless.

Rachel leant against the wall. Why did it thrill her so to do this? She had asked herself that question before. At this moment, she was in the throes of dictating to him what she wanted him to do. It was no time to dwell on considering her sexuality. Like him, she was riding along with it. The difference was the pleasure. The vision was in her mind. His reality was her fantasy.

'Pull on it,' she said in a breathless voice. 'Pull on it slowly. Are you doing that?'

Silence.

'Are you?'

He gasped. 'Yes. Yes. I am.'

She sighed. The cock in her mind was pulsing, growing inch by steady inch. That was how it was when she did it to him slowly. Each fold of flesh would become smooth. The tip would become shiny and his body would tremble. Doing it slowly could almost be torture.

'I've got your drink.' It was Cavan.

Rachel opened her eyes. He had surprised her.

72

She put her hand over the receiver. 'I'll be right there.'

He nodded and went back to the bar.

Her lips moved closer to the phone. 'Faster,' she said. 'Do it faster!'

Ian groaned. 'More,' he said suddenly. 'More!'

It wasn't the usual response. But she wouldn't question. If he wanted more, she would give him more.

'Pull it,' she ordered. 'Pull it faster and faster. Do you feel your come rushing up to the surface? Do you feel your balls bunching up into your body? Do you feel it, Ian? Do you feel it?'

Groans mingled with cries of delight poured out of him faster and faster until that final exclamation that told her it was all over. His showered body was no longer as clean as it had been.

'Have you come?' she asked.

He paused before answering.

'Ian?'

'Yes. Yes. Of course I have.'

For a moment she was disinclined to believe him, but she didn't know why.

'I'll see you when I get back,' she said eventually.

As she put down the phone she wondered if she could ever get an older man to do what she had just done to Ian.

'Over here,' Cavan called to her. He was sitting at a table in the corner. A pheasant in a glass case sat on a shelf above his head. Well stuffed, she thought, and smiled.

Without meaning to, her eyes met those of other men in the bar. Some were near her age and were easily ignored. It was the older men she was suddenly drawn to. What was going on behind those confident smiles, the appreciative twinkle in their eyes? They were upmarket men, the sort that younger women were drawn to. Regular workouts obviously kept their bodies in good order. But what about their sex lives? she wondered. Could she ever see herself having sex with an older man? At some stage she would. Mac had intrigued her. She was curious to find out what an older man could offer. But, for now, she had Cavan.

She looked into his face and smiled. 'So tell me all about yourself,' she said.

'You mean you weren't really listening earlier to what Andrew and I had to say? Really, Rachel. You disappoint me greatly.'

'It's been a nice evening,' Cavan said to her on the way back to the boat. 'I'm glad you sought my company.'

Rachel stopped in her tracks. 'I *sought* your company?'

Moonlight picked out the features of his face and the sauce of his smile. He stood with his hands in his pockets, head held slightly to one side. 'Of course. Why else would you opt for walking to the pub to phone your boyfriend when your sort always carry their mobile around with them?'

'My sort?' She stopped and stood with her hands resting on her hips. The cheek of this man!

'Sure. Truly Miss Dominant: The sort that always likes to be in touch likes to be in control. Isn't that the case?'

She didn't like his description. If he hadn't called her that, perhaps she would have allowed him to lead her into the long grass of the water-meadow, where an owl hooted from some far-off barn. But

I'm not domineering, she told herself as she strode off back to the boat. I'm not!

Later, in bed, she wished she had had sex with Cavan. It had been a definite case of biting off her nose to spite her face. She ran her fingers down over her belly and felt the moistness between her legs. Bringing Ian off from a distance had left her wanting. But she was too proud to slide off her single bunk and snuggle close to Cavan. In a way she wanted him. But her pride was too much to overcome. Besides, she still had Mac to think about. Should she allow herself to be seduced by an older man or should she keep to her own peer group? The question would stay with her until the moment came when a decision had to be made. Perhaps he would come to her flat and things would get hot there. Perhaps she would take it into her head to go along to his hotel room and offer herself there and then.

In the meantime, she let her fingers weave in and out of the familiar crisp hair that covered her sex. She enjoyed the silky feel of her inner lips. The pleasure was twofold. Her sex responded to the touch of her fingers. Her fingers responded to the feel of her sex. The delight started to happen and would result in an orchestrated orgasm. And, of course, she would help it along.

A familiar fantasy began to take root in her mind. A man – any man – was telling her what to do in the same way she had Ian.

'Open your legs, tap at that little nub of flesh that gives you pleasure, sink your fingers into yourself, then run your moisture between the cheeks of your arse. Push your moistened finger into your anus. Let me hear you squirm with pain and with pleasure. Open your legs wide. Let me see every detail of your sex. Let me see you pleasure yourself.'

The man had no face, yet she had seen him before. No matter who she was with, it was always he who used her as he wanted in the depths of her mind. No matter that he was male, in actuality he seemed to be part of herself.

'Bring me off,' she wanted to shout. But her words only echoed around her mind.

'No,' said her imagined mentor. 'I want to see you bring yourself off. I want to extract pleasure from watching you giving yourself pleasure. Perform for me. Use your body for me.'

Like a marionette dancing to his tune, she did as he said. She played with her sex, stuck her finger into her juices then stuck it up her own anus. Her hips jerked against her own fingers. Her buttocks went up and down, her anus sliding over the invading finger.

'Filthy bitch!' he shouted at her. 'You're enjoying that, aren't you! You like doing that to yourself, because it makes you feel you're in control. But it's me that's in control, whore. It's me and me alone!'

He's telling the truth, she told herself. He really is in control – and she smiled. In effect, that man was merely an extension of her alter ego. He was a product of her imagination. Therefore he had become her. That meant she really was in control.

Chapter Six

When Liz came out of the bathroom, she saw that Ian had shed his robe and was standing naked, his cock proud and as stiff as it had been earlier. When he saw her, he put his hand over the phone receiver he was holding. The guilty look in his eyes was sweet to behold and whatever had caused it must also have contributed to his stiff dick.

'What's brought this on?' she said. Her voice was husky and meant to beguile. But she was no fool and had no need to ask him the question. There was another woman on the other end of the phone. The thought of tantalising him while he listened to this woman was too good to resist.

He flushed slightly but did not answer and kept the phone close to his ear.

She ran her hands over her round breasts, the gentle rise of her belly and the triangle of pubic hair nestling at the confluence of her thighs.

She saw him gulp. His hand was no longer over

the phone. He said little but whoever was on the other end must be hearing the quickening of his breath, the unrestrained groans of delight.

Liz took a deep breath. Although they had made love just an hour before, she wanted him again. By the looks of his erection, he was ready to take her on.

She moved closer and ran her hand down his belly, her fingers tangling in the dark nest of hair from which his cock rose. She breathed in his freshness, breathed in his maleness.

'You're good enough to eat,' she said, close to his ear.

Then she looked into his eyes and saw the sparkle, the unspoken plea for her to continue.

Slowly she slid to her knees.

She didn't care that he was murmuring the odd word to whoever was on the telephone. In a way, she wanted him to be distracted. That way she could study him more closely.

Pleasure him. That's what she was going to do. At the same time she would be pleasuring herself, fulfilling a desire she had briefly entertained not so long ago.

By sliding her hands between his thighs, she forced him to open them a little wider.

His cock was in her face, warm against her cheeks, her nose and her lips. It wasn't easy but she resisted the urge to take him into her mouth. Sucking him was only part of her plan.

Firm hands clutching firm buttocks, she nuzzled his cock and his smell seeped into her nostrils. Still on her knees, she moved behind him. She parted his buttocks, licked in between and nipped where the flesh was hardest.

And he's groaning, she thought. No matter who might be on the other end of the phone, he cannot control what he's feeling.

What pleasure it was to make a young man do that. It was like having a performing seal or dog. The creature would dance to your tune if you gave it the right commands and rewarded it accordingly.

Just as she had imagined before, she pushed her face between his thighs and licked at his balls.

Peach soft. Velvet soft. And warm.

She nudged closer, her nose taking in their scent, the soft unseen hairs tickling at her nose.

Like this, she thought. I'm going to make you come like this.

His knees were bent now to accommodate her shoulders. He was saying 'yes' to whoever was on the other end of the phone.

Yes. Yes. The word revolved in her mind. Yes! Yes! Yes!

She took one whole ball into her mouth. It was just possible – just possible – she could hold both at the same time.

Concentrate. Eat his sweet peaches.

Opening her mouth as wide as she could, she sucked in the soft outer and the hard inner of his most secret flesh.

Apricots, she decided. That's what they resembled.

Borrowing from her own moistness, she brought her left hand over her head, ran the wet finger down his buttocks and into his rectum. With her right hand, she took hold of his cock.

Whatever he had meant to say to his caller was drowned by cries of lust and submission. He was moving to her direction, his body rocking backwards and forwards as she dug into his backside, pulled on his prick and sucked and chewed at his balls.

When he came, it was similar to the previous evening except there was no Virginia Creeper to blemish with his semen. Instead, he was happy to shoot his load all over his own body. Liz was amazed by the amount that jetted out, and wished she could have captured the moment on video, to replay over and over at her leisure.

A little spice had been added because he'd come while talking on the telephone. Liz didn't bother to ask him who it was. Judging by Ian's monosyllabic responses, the other person had done all the talking.

He insisted on driving her to the airport. She didn't put up too much resistance. In fact, she thoroughly relished the fact that he wanted to be close to her. It gave her such a feeling of – power? Not entirely. Not the corruptive power usually coupled with material matters. It was more a case that being desired by a younger man instilled in her a new vitality, a new confidence. It had occurred to her that he might just be using her as a way to get to Rachel. But he'd had Rachel sexually. Their relationship didn't appear to be that serious, not in the emotional sense. That meant he found her attractive. *Her*. Liz Carr, who was fifty years old and blessed with an understanding of what sex, men and love were all about.

She glanced at him. Their eyes met for a moment before he looked at the road ahead. The traffic was coming to a halt before a set of lights. A taxi dived into the space in front of them.

'Professional drivers!' he said with disdain.

Once he'd braked, their eyes met again. His fingers seemed to tighten on the steering wheel.

If we weren't in the middle of this traffic jam, she thought, I'd have him here and now – and he wouldn't resist. He's hot for it. I can see it in his eyes.

'Why are you with me?' she asked suddenly.

His lips parted slightly. He smiled. 'Because I want to be. Anyway –' he glanced at the traffic, which was just beginning to move '– at least I'm taking you through the side roads. A taxi would have taken the main route, taken longer and charged you more money.'

'How much are you going to charge me?'

He touched the brake slightly and smiled. 'Whatever you're prepared to give.'

'You still haven't really answered my question. Why are you with me? What attracts a younger man to an older woman?'

He looked confused. He shrugged his shoulders. 'I don't know that I can answer that.'

'Don't say it's because I don't look my age. You know Rachel, so you know my age. Is it because I remind you of my daughter?'

There! It was out. She hadn't meant to voice her suspicion, but it couldn't be helped.

To her surprise, he burst out laughing. 'What's so funny?'

'You're nothing like your daughter. Perhaps that's the reason. Anyway, why are you attracted to me? You have a husband and could have as many lovers as you wanted, I shouldn't wonder. And all rich, worldly men, not inexperienced novices like me.'

She smiled and rubbed his thigh affectionately.

The muscles bunched beneath her touch. What else was hardening? His cock, too, I shouldn't wonder.

'You make me feel good, Ian. The years fall away and I'm young again.'

His hand covered hers. 'I read somewhere that women are like wine. Some take time to get to their best.'

'Thank you.' She smiled. It was slightly corny, but she liked it.

He squeezed her fingers. She squeezed his thigh and ran her fingers beneath them. At the same time she wondered if she could catch a later flight. It wasn't that she felt any great affinity to Ian for himself. His youth and his body attracted her. She wanted to feel it again, wanted to feel his hardness penetrating her body.

Running her hands over him was like retracing old memories, resurrecting all the sexual encounters she'd ever had in her life. Feeling him was like pressing a button. Passion was instantly aroused. Present scenarios would be stored like all the rest and become one of her personal fantasies to be used at leisure.

They were now travelling on a dual carriageway and the traffic moved more freely for a while before coming to a standstill again.

'More traffic, I'm afraid,' said Ian. 'But we've got time. We won't be late.'

Liz sighed and turned to him. 'Positive thinking is called for. Let's take advantage of a negative situation.'

'What?'

She said nothing but merely smiled at him, then glanced down. His eyes followed hers. They both watched as her fingers curled and uncurled over his thigh then slowly crept over his belly and down to his crotch.

'Not here!' he gasped. 'You can't do that here.'

But you won't stop me, she thought, and that makes me feel powerful, as though I am the puppet master and am pulling your strings.

She merely smiled at him and lowered her head.

The traffic remained static.

Ian stared directly ahead, his chest falling and rising in time with his rapid breathing.

She felt his stomach muscles tighten beneath her touch.

Liz's fingers lingered over the chrome stud that fastened his waistband. Next the zip, the metal teeth snarling and stopping intermittently until it was completely undone.

Before going further, she looked at the growing mound pushing against the cloth of his trousers. She took it into her palm.

His cock formed a subtle bow against the constraints of his trousers and underwear. Liz eased the material away slowly. His cock leapt free and stood upright.

She glanced at Ian. His eyes were glazed and fixed on the traffic ahead. His Adam's apple twitched as he swallowed.

No words were needed.

Burrowing under steel zip then cool cotton, her fingers enclosed the base of his erection. Coarse hair made a slight rasping sound. Above her curled fingers, his cock pulsed in time with his blood flow.

Blood was passion. She knew that. But it was also death. Funny, she thought, that both could be so casually combined. If I were a man, I would stare at this longer. But it's not enough. I want to smell him, touch him, and taste him on my tongue.

Regardless of the crowded road, she lowered her head. Closing her eyes, she rubbed him against her nose. Smell matched touch. Both were warm, both somehow comforting and obviously inviting.

She kissed it gently, savouring the subtle taste, the soft texture on her lips. It's just as soft as my lips, she thought, velvet soft.

A thrill ran through her: perfectly normal for her body to respond to the sensation of being close to a man. But what about his responses?

How did it feel to have balls hanging between your legs? To a woman familiar only with hair-covered lips and a responsive clitoris, hanging flesh seemed a burden. And what about his cock? Strangely enough, its pulsing, its rearing away from one's body seemed far easier to imagine, even to envy. OK, the clitoris was known to harden and stand proud like an immature penis, but its presence was nothing compared to a penis. One day, she would strap on a false one and see what it was like to have such a protrusion sticking out from her body. It was a plan for the future.

And now, she thought. What about now?

In her mind she became him. The feel of his cock between her lips was soft, pleasant, but obtrusive, heavy on her tongue. Did her tongue and mouth feel slippery to him, as slippery as the flesh that lined the passage to her womb?

She began to slide her mouth up and down his length. He was fucking without moving, the sensations similar to those when she rode a man and he lay there staring at his cock as it disappeared and reappeared as she went up and down.

His buttocks tensed against the seat. She felt his thighs harden, his cock pulse in her mouth.

'The traffic...' he began to say. But the words were mangled in his throat.

His right foot went down on the accelerator. His left rose from the clutch. They were moving. Liz was not troubled. She was absorbed in what she was doing. Sucking on such a fine young rod was better than staring at slowly moving traffic. Indulging herself in public, while her subject was otherwise engaged, doubled her enjoyment.

When the car stopped again Ian's hand slid down beneath the white cotton shirt she wore and cupped her breast. It fell into his hand as if waiting for him. He squeezed and she squirmed and got closer. Opening her legs slightly, she moved her hips backwards and forwards. All that flesh between her legs suddenly felt very heavy.

Amazing, I've grown a penis, she thought.

But she knew that wasn't the case. The vestige of woman's penis was nudging against its restraining lips, seeking satisfaction, and seeking sex. No penis met its lusty arousal. No plying fingers reached into her white lace knickers to ease the steady throb.

She moved her body, buried her head more deeply into his lap and curled her hips under her. At last she found what she wanted. Her throbbing sex met the round head of the gear stick. Its touch was electric. She jerked her hips, rubbed her sex against it. It did the job. Unyielding, it heightened her enjoyment and finally gave her relief.

Ian groaned. His body tensed. He could have been just another piece of the car itself, an automaton manufactured to drive it forward. That's how he became as his climax shot through his body.

Semen spewed from his penis and smattered his belly. Some of it hung like pearls in Liz's hair. She sat up and ran her fingers through her hair, spreading the fluid through it like some kind of aromatic gel.

Little of the journey remained. They drove in comparative silence until he swerved into a parking space immediately outside the departure facility.

'Will I see you when you get back?' Ian asked, just before she got out of the car at the airport.

'No doubt.'

He got out of the car himself.

'Let me help you.'

Liz took her bags from him. 'I can manage.'

He looked slightly hurt. 'I can wait with you until your flight is announced.'

'No,' she said. 'I can manage.' She kissed his cheek. 'I'll see you when I get back.' She turned swiftly away and knew he watched her walk all the way across the honey-coloured floor to the check-in terminal.

She didn't look back. 'Porter!' She chose a young black guy with a shaved head and a range of gold rings hanging from one ear.

What a torso, she thought as she eyed the broad shoulders and the hint of well-worked-out arm muscles bulging against the restriction of his uniform. Imagine how hard he is. Going to bed with him would be like cuddling up to a piece of mahogany.

He smiled broadly down at her. 'Can I be of assistance, madam?'

She smiled back at him. 'For a start, you can help me with these.'

He took her bags from her and obediently followed where she led.

'Can I help you, madam?' asked a young man with red hair at the check-in for Scottish Air. He wore a badge stating that his name was Patrick.

Liz took in the straight nose, the twinkling eyes and the sensually chiselled chin. About twenty-three, she thought. My, but it was amazing how many nice young men were around. And it wasn't taboo for a woman of her age to think of touching him, kissing him and perhaps even . . .

And of course, he was so willing to please, perhaps in more ways than one.

She smiled brightly at him. 'Do you have a private departure lounge? I have some business documents to attend to.' She held up her briefcase.

'Certainly, madam.' He turned and reached for a set of keys, then turned back. 'Would there be anything else you'll be needing?'

Liz smiled and raised an eyebrow alluringly. 'We'll discuss that when we get there.'

The young man grinned secretively. She guessed what he was thinking: another lonely woman in need of male company and a damned good shag, and he was her man. He'd soon see her all right.

He led her into a corridor that ran down to the main departure lounge. He stopped at a door, inserted a key and turned it.

'I hope this suits madam,' he said as he reached for the light switch.

Liz caught his wrist. 'I prefer a more subtle light. A table lamp would be nice.'

He looked down at her. Their eyes met as their

bodies brushed together. She saw him swallow, then lick his lips.

'As you wish, madam.'

He crossed the room and stooped to click on a table lamp. Her eyes fixed on his bottom. Nice, she thought, rounded but not too large.

At that point she became aware that the porter was close to her shoulder. She turned quickly, in time to see a grin disappear from his wide, sensuous mouth. She turned her attention back to Patrick and his firm buttocks. The truth was obvious. The porter had seen her eyeing Patrick's behind. She looked over her shoulder and looked up at the dark-skinned young man.

'Where would you like it?' he said, quickly regaining his composure as he held up her overnight bag.

She said nothing but smiled slowly.

Patrick joined them. With a puzzled frown, he looked from one to the other.

'Is anything wrong? Is there anything else I can – we – can do?'

Liz pointed to the door. 'Close that and I'll tell you.' She nodded towards the open door. The porter lost no time in closing it, then he snapped his fingers at Patrick. Patrick, still looking puzzled, didn't immediately take up on what the porter was asking. Obviously, thought Liz, he was quite prepared to stay and keep me company but thinks that two is a crowd. Does he have some learning to do!

'The keys,' the porter explained. 'The lady wants privacy.'

Still obviously uncomprehending, Patrick looked from one to the other. The porter took the keys from his hand.

'The lady is in need of our services. *Both* of us. Are you staying or do I have to take care of her all by myself?' He stood poised by the door, key at the ready. Just to clarify matters that much more, he rubbed the flat of his hand down over his crotch, then he reached out and ran it over the breast nearest to him.

Patrick blushed. 'You mean . . .'

The porter merely raised an eyebrow. Liz admired his cool. She'd made a good choice in him. Patrick, she was sure, would follow suit.

She was proved right. His eyes sparkled. By the time the key turned in the lock, the porter's lips were already on hers. One hand crept to her breast. He touched her softly, as if mindful that fierceness would automatically earn an instant rebuff.

She sighed with pleasure and closed her eyes. Patrick came round to her other side. Their bodies were firm against hers. Their smell was like a veil or mist covering her. And she welcomed that smell. Imagine, she thought, being smothered by it. Imagine drowning in its exquisite masculinity, its hint of sex before the act itself had fully started. This was what drew the woman to the man. The smell was what chemical attraction was all about. Sometimes, without knowing it, a woman picked up the scent of a nubile, sexual man. This – not always his looks – was what aroused her. This was what demolished her defences, drew her close and made her give herself, body and soul, to whatever he wanted to do.

They stripped her to the waist. She moaned as their fingers explored her breasts. When their lips sucked on her breasts, she threw back her head. One of them kissed her throat.

Truly, she lost herself when both were sucking on her breasts. Her nipples lengthened and the sensations created there ran over her stomach and settled in her groin.

It made her wish she'd had the experience of twins taking nourishment from organs designed to feed, to give life. In a way, these two sets of lips were also taking life from her. The touch, the feel of her body was igniting in them the most powerful urge in the world. Their cocks were responding to the touch of her breasts against their lips, the feel of her soft ripeness beneath their fingers. Such feelings made her feel powerful.

She knew how it would be. She knew they would only stop to strip off her skirt and her panties. Stockings and suspender belts were merely a garnish to accentuate the flesh they left unrestricted.

Still with her eyes closed, she ran her hands down over their erections. My, but young men were so easily aroused. They had no real need of excessive foreplay or way-out fantasies. Their urges, their world and their jobs forgotten, because a woman had offered herself willingly. And because that woman was more experienced than they were, their excitement, their curiosity was increased. Experience also meant that she could read them well.

They were young men, so their method of giving her pleasure was also relatively predictable. They bent her over a table and although the porter, who stood behind her, rubbed his hands over her buttocks and ran his fingers through her cleft and into her body, he did not linger. Ruled by his cock, he lost no time in unzipping his trousers.

It was like, thought Liz, opening a surprise

parcel. She wasn't sure what she was going to get, but whatever it was, she knew it would be good.

It fitted well, tight widthways and long enough to make her gasp. Not that she had much time to cry out. Patrick too had unzipped. Warm, covered in softness yet hard, he entered her mouth.

I am full, she thought. I have more than some women ever have.

Whatever thoughts of masculine bravado they might be experiencing were of no consequence to her now. Men could be charming or exciting while preliminary seduction moves were being made. But once she was being fucked or she tasted their bodies, individual characteristics were forgotten. They were men and she was enjoying their bodies. She had lured them, sucked them in. And now she held them tight, one between her lips and one gripped by her abdominal muscles.

They thought they were having her. In reality, she was having them.

Chapter Seven

The October evening was drawing in by the time she arrived at Castle Cael, McKenzie's rented pad during his stay in Scotland.

Stark towers jutted into a silver sky where grey clouds chased across an early moon. Slits of amber light fell from castle windows on the first and second floor.

'If you'd like to follow me, madam.'

The chauffeur carried her luggage and preceded her to the double oak door that was set in a stone archway.

The reception hall was round. A staircase swept up from both her left and her right to meet on the same open landing, situated directly ahead of her.

The walls were painted a deep red, a rich background for the gilt-framed paintings that hung from brass chains at varying levels. She averted her eyes from the glassy-eyed stags. Such animals were better appreciated complete with a body and still alive.

'Quite a place,' said the chauffeur, whose origins were obviously somewhere in the Caribbean.

'Only if you're into blood sports and historic barbarism,' Liz exclaimed as her gaze roamed over the motley collection of claymores, axes and cruelly barbed spears. 'Only a moron would call it tasteful.'

'Then perhaps my name should be McMoron instead of McKenzie!'

Liz started and upturned her face to the landing. Her natural confidence took a nosedive. Robert McKenzie was looking down at her, his face like thunder. He was wearing full highland regalia, brass buttons, and a red kilt. She spotted a dirk in the long grey socks he wore.

Liz rallied quickly. 'No disrespect was intended, Mr McKenzie. After all, it isn't your castle.'

She could see by his face that her apology had had little effect.

His grip on the handrail turned his knuckles white. His eyes glittered. 'I cannot say you have impressed me, Mrs Carr. I would expect more tact from someone who expects to do business with me.' With a swirl of plaid pleats, he turned away.

She stared after him, unsure whether to smile or swear. Was it her imagination, or had he been feigning a Scottish accent?

Once in her room, which was circular, spacious but lacked an en suite bathroom, she regained her composure and reminded herself why she was there.

This is a business trip. You have to suck up to this guy in order to keep his business. Remember that. Forget it at your cost.

She slumped down on the bed, spread her hands

behind her and threw back her head, rolling it from side to side to ease the tension in her neck.

How do I make amends? I can't foul the negotiations simply because of a chance remark.

She listed the possibilities.

Number one, be nice to him.

Number two, show him how clever you are.

Number three ... bearing in mind what Richard's already hinted at ...

She got up on to her elbows. Her gaze travelled to the open door of a huge mahogany wardrobe. Slinky and shimmering, her favourite dress hanging in its plastic covering seemed to throw her the answer.

You look good in blue. Seduce him.

Not a bad idea, she decided. It would hardly be a tortuous occurrence. He was ruggedly good looking, younger than her, but not much. He had a chiselled, straight nose, a strong jaw, and deep set eyes. A shock of prematurely white hair hung to his shoulders and was tucked behind his ears. On the whole, he looked the epitome of a medieval Scottish laird, the sort fantasies are made of. Traditional socks had covered strong calves. When he had turned angrily away from her after hearing her tactless comment, his skirt had swirled and she had caught a glimpse of firm thighs.

Why not seduce him? If it went some way to mending bridges and getting a firm up on the contract, then so be it. And of course she would enjoy it. Hadn't she always enjoyed a new conquest?

Sex in youth had been new territory to be explored with caution. Sex in maturity was coloured by experience. Everything had been tried and only new conquests added the piquancy once experienced in youth.

The blue dress came out of its cover. It had a plunging neckline and long sleeves. Skilfully created darts made it seem a mere sheath of a thing that clung to her body, without being vulgar. She wore a black basque beneath it that lifted her breasts high, its suspenders crossing her white thighs to connect with black silk stockings.

'Right,' she said as she surveyed herself in the mirror. 'You look like a whore: now go ahead and act like one! Your career depends on it.'

More oil paintings lined the stairs down to the dining hall. Her eyes took in the stiffly formalised poses, the milk-white, barely concealed breasts, the rough beards, and the sturdy legs.

They fascinated her only until she saw the young man waiting outside the double doors that she guessed opened into the dining hall.

He was russet-haired and strong-faced and his fair skin was childishly pink on his cheekbones. His shoulders were broad and he stood with his hands behind his back, his legs parted as though he were standing astride a tumbling stream. Perhaps on the orders of McKenzie or perhaps in homage to patriotism, he wore a dark green kilt, white shirt, black waistcoat and the all-important sporran.

'I'm James,' he said and blushed as he smiled. 'I'm here to be of service.'

'Like the porter and Patrick,' she said with a slightly wistful air.

He looked puzzled. 'I'm sorry?'

She shook her head. 'I'm sure I will find you

95

very satisfactory, James.' She smiled as he opened the door and she passed through.

Richard and Robert were already in the dining hall.

The former immediately stepped forward, ready to play whatever part he had to. Richard was a corporate player through and through. Liz knew this.

'Liz. I don't think you've met Robert McKenzie.'

She thought about lying, then about telling the truth. McKenzie stepped in first.

'Delighted,' he offered her his hand. They shook. He had a firm grip. She fancied it might have been a warning not to offend him again.

Not once during dinner did he refer to her earlier comment. But she could tell he was bristling. Even Richard was struggling to push their case. Every time he put forward a feasible suggestion, McKenzie found fault with it. It was like a sparring match that neither her nor Richard could win. McKenzie was going out of his way to trip them up, to make things awkward for them.

She thought about challenging him and apologising for speaking out of turn earlier, but she didn't want Richard to blame her if the contract was lost. Besides, Richard was drowning his exasperation with more whisky than was normal. Perhaps it was the fact that he was treating the aged malt as if it were a blend. The amber liquid was quickly going to his head and his head was swiftly failing to control his body.

At last he succumbed. As he struggled to his feet, he stumbled, grabbed at the tablecloth. A glass tumbled. A plate fell to the floor.

'I'm sorry . . .' he began.

'Please . . .'

McKenzie signalled for his manservant, the same man who had acted as chauffeur. With the help of James, Richard was led from the room.

Both of them watched as the three men made their way across the room, two sturdy and steady on their feet, the third leaning heavily on their arms.

The door slammed, the sound echoing around the vaulted ceiling and the panelled walls before fading away.

A pregnant silence remained. There was chilliness to it but also a crackling heat, as if threatening to burst into flame.

Liz wished she could fade away like the echo had. What could she say to this man to make him more amenable to what they were offering?

Whatever he wants, you have to give, she told herself. But was he that approachable?

Seduction had seemed a justifiable and pleasant option, back in her room. Now, she resented the notion. Why should she bare her body to this man? Were the contract and her job worth such a price?

She picked up her wineglass as she considered her next move. The wine swirled in her glass, rising and falling, sometimes red as blood, sometimes a deep blackcurrant.

The silence was oppressive. He made no attempt to break it. Again he had hit the ball into her court. Now all she had to do was make her play.

She eyed him over the top of her glass. She sipped slowly. Wine clung to her lips. Thoughtfully, she ran her tongue along her top lip then the bottom one. He was looking at her, but she could not tell what he was thinking. There was no expression on his lips or in his eyes. It was like trying to read the thoughts of a stone statue.

He's playing with me, she thought and it's not entirely to do with business. He wants to make me feel awkward, to force me to play the hostess, the fawning woman half begging him to seduce me.

Well, damn him! Suddenly, her mind was made up. She'd play his game. Who knows where it might lead? Perhaps she'd enjoy it. Two clever, successful, handsome people pitting their resolve against each other. Experience and stubborn resolution made her want to triumph over this man.

Look at him, she thought. Sitting there so self-assured with that closely shaven jaw, those deep-set eyes staring into mine. Yes. He's daring me all right.

For the briefest of moments, his expression changed.

Was it her imagination, or had his eyes flickered? Yes! They had!

Inwardly, she smiled in triumph. Although barely perceptible, his gaze had briefly left her face and taken in the details of her body. It was enough to boost her confidence. It was also an opportunity to reach out to him or to have him reach out to her. Either way, she knew his dark mood was growing lighter.

'Why a castle?' she asked behind her raised glass.

She half expected him to answer, 'Because I'm a moron. You told me so yourself.'

'I like history. That's why I asked your daughter to look into my family tree. I want to know everything about my family. I want to know about their decadence as well as their virtues and, from what

I've heard from family members, plenty of decadence happened in the far and distant past.'

'That still doesn't explain hiring this castle. It never belonged to your family did it? Besides, what's this castle got to do with decadence? It might well have belonged to some really down-to-earth farming types who never beat their servants and never undressed with the candle still burning – if you know what I mean.'

He smiled, half in wishing, half in longing, and rose from his chair. 'Come with me.'

The dark blue jacket he wore rode up above the leather belt of his kilt as he stretched out his arm, palm upwards. He didn't say, 'Take my hand,' and didn't need to. The broad hand, the thick, strong fingers invited her to slip her hand into his. His fingers closed tightly over hers, trapping them there. But the feeling of being trapped was short-lived. His hand was warm and reminded her of snuggling naked between warm blankets.

'That door,' he said, nodding to an arched oak edifice that must have measured at least four feet wide, 'is the door to the ramparts. And that one,' he said, indicating a much narrower, nail-studded door, 'is the door to the cellars – and the dungeons! Which do you wish me to show you?'

He waited for her reaction as well as her answer. She saw the hint of amusement, the hope she might tremble with fear.

She looked him straight in the face. 'Are we talking ancient or modern dungeons?'

'Your pardon?' He looked puzzled.

Liz held her head high and chanced a hint of scorn. 'This is Europe, Mr McKenzie. We have a much more liberal attitude to sex than you colonial pilgrims, though we don't advertise it too much.'

'Oh, come on,' he said, his accent thicker, his words less measured than they had been. 'Who are you kidding? The Scots are a dour lot. Isn't that the word, dour?' He looked pleased to have thought of it. 'Sex in a cold climate means diving under the quilt for a quick fumble in the long dark of winter.'

Liz, her hand still in his, took a step towards the door. 'Modern dungeons have central heating, Mr McKenzie. And besides, I'm not Scottish. I'm English.'

But she sensed he hadn't really meant what he said. Instinctively, she knew he had surveyed those dungeons and been fascinated by them. What sort of man was this? What sort of family had he descended from?

She let his hand go and walked purposefully to the narrow door that he indicated led to the dungeons.

She ran her hands over the aged oak. It made a scraping sound, as her painted nails scratched at the uneven surface.

'It's very old,' he said. 'And very strong. It had to hold back secrets as well as prisoners.'

'I sense you wish you could use them now,' she said with a bemused smile. 'Perhaps incarcerate a few muggers or car thieves?'

McKenzie studied his nails. 'Too good for them.'

He was being flippant. Unwittingly or not, it became his dramatic appearance, his white hair, his tanned skin.

One arm stretched above her head, and one graceful hand resting on her thigh, she looked at him. As she smiled, she ran her tongue over her lips.

'Well, Robert. Is this secret place of yours too good for the likes of me, too? Will you show me the dungeon, or do I have to slip into its darkness alone?'

A flicker of interest crossed his face. She could see she intrigued him, and why not? It was her turn to dare him to step forward. She was also telling him she was unafraid of anything he might show her, anything he might want to voice about this dark, subterranean place of his.

Without her needing to ask him, she knew he discerned her as an experienced woman who was not afraid to indulge in the more perverse aspects of sex. But she sensed he was the sort who wanted to be in control. That was something she found hard to tolerate. Equality in sexuality was some-thing rare or difficult to achieve. She and Mark had grown into it. The jealousies of youth had been lain behind them. Contempt comes with some long-term marriages but, in their case, understanding themselves and sexuality had come with long-term togetherness.

Men like McKenzie were unlikely ever to under-stand that. No matter! He was never likely to be long-term with her or anybody else.

Liz watched with interest as his massive hand closed over the iron ring that formed the door handle. He pushed. The door opened smoothly, as though someone had kept the hinges well oiled – perhaps because of frequent use?

A tingle of apprehension made Liz raise her left hand to rub at her right arm. Because it's cold, she told herself and, indeed it was. But the apprehension remained.

Stone steps led down into a blanket of blackness that was only dispersed each time Robert McKenzie found a light switch. They seemed to be placed at regular descending intervals on the curving walls.

'Here. You must be freezing.'

Without her mentioning her feeling of cold, McKenzie had taken his coat off. He placed it around her shoulders. The warmth left by his body was pleasant.

She was just about to thank him, but the sight that met her eyes struck her dumb. She hadn't really expected to find a real dungeon, either ancient or modern. But here, it was full of devices she had seen many times before. But McKenzie wouldn't know that. What man alive knows anything of a woman's mind or her sexual fantasies?

'As you can see, we have the real McCoy, Mrs Carr. This is, I believe, authentic and very old. Wouldn't you agree?'

Liz didn't answer. In fact, she could quite easily forget he was there and, what was more, she wished he wasn't there. She had a tremendous desire to throw off his jacket and her dress. The fantasy that had fired many an orgasm was there before her in reality. If he hadn't been there, she might have thrown off her clothes, stepped into one of the metal objects and closed its iron arms around her. A shiver ran through her body, as if she could feel the chill touch of the metal contraptions.

'Fascinating, isn't it?' she heard McKenzie say.

But she didn't answer. Her eyes were full of the

objects of torment. Her mind was absorbed with possibilities.

She walked to where an iron cage hung on a chain from the ceiling. The bars were rough beneath her touch, but still hard, still as cold as they'd ever been.

Just touching such a device evoked a response in her body. She felt heaviness between her legs. In her mind, she wanted to be naked inside this contraption. She wanted to be at someone's mercy but, up until now, she had never acted out the scenarios created by her mind.

'Imagine the poor devil locked up in that,' said McKenzie. 'Must have starved them to death.'

'No,' she said as she eyed the rest of the implements. 'The muscles wasted. The limbs became bent after years of being confined in the same position without exercise, without sunlight or good food. But, of course, we don't know for sure whether that was what they did down here. Nothing is rusty. Everything looks cared for – as though these objects were respected, even revered.'

Her voice was like a dream. It was as if she were seeing something the American could not possibly see. The feel of the place had seeped into her flesh more quickly than its chill. And it didn't matter whether McKenzie had noticed or not.

But she realised he must have noticed when she felt his hand on her shoulder. She started and turned round, her eyes wide with surprise, as if seeing him for the very first time.

'Are you still with me?' He looked intrigued. His eyes glowed. His lips were slightly open, as if in surprise.

Blinking as if he had rudely awoken her, she

looked up at him anew. She'd seen the likes of him before in every fantasy she'd ever experienced. She'd seen the dungeon, too. Sometimes it was hard to distinguish between fantasy and reality. But it had never stopped her using her imagination. The mind was the key to true sensuality. In her youth, the images in her mind had troubled her. Experience had taught her not to deny them.

McKenzie obviously saw her odd expression. He frowned as though he were seeing her for the first time. Perhaps, she thought, he is only now realising the possibilities of this place. But why? Am I suddenly glowing because I can feel its wickedly sensual past seeping into my flesh? Is he sensing the fact that my flesh is tingling because of the pictures in my mind?

'It's been a long day,' he said. The warmth of his hand seemed to burn into her back. 'Perhaps you should go to bed.'

Perhaps it was the wine, but she didn't remember being led into her bedroom. Too many images of naked bodies writhing with pleasure were in her mind. She could almost feel the dank air, the harsh metal bands around her wrists and her ankles, the chains around her body pressing her breasts against her ribcage. And they were doing things to her. She did not protest but merely mewed as though she were too weak – or too enthralled – to resist them.

She yearnt for unseen fingers to handle her body, to pinch her nipples, to knead her breasts. At the same time, she imagined other hands running down over her belly, other fingers pulling apart the outer lips of her sex, flicking at the most sensitive spot, dipping into the fluid that told her she was willing for whatever they might do.

But she wasn't in the dungeon. She was in her room, yet it was unreal as though a mist hung over everything in it. Were the sexual fantasies she had used all her life becoming reality? Had they played their part and now returned to claim their due: her body, or perhaps her soul?

Only the smell of apple logs burning on the fire invaded her senses, that and the hands of the man with her.

'Let me help you,' she heard McKenzie say.

His fingers fumbled at the zip at the back of her dress. She didn't protest. The warmth of his palms was pleasant; the touch of his fingers was cool. The cold, forbidding eroticism of the dungeon and her own imagination made her abandon any will she might have had. The dress slid with a hush over her belly, her hips and down her thighs until it lay at her ankles. Only the black basque, the stockings and shoes remained. But she wanted them off. She wanted it all off. This man would give credence to the acts she imagined in her mind. It didn't matter whether he enjoyed it or not. This was her body, her sensuality, and her fantasy.

Robert McKenzie's lips kissed the curve between neck and shoulder. The fingers of one hand caressed her ear lobe. The other brought her breast out.

Suddenly, the cool air she craved was caressing her body. From out in the corridor. The door is open. The thought was fragile, as if some other mind and not her own was voicing it.

She heard Richard's voice.

'Sorry! I didn't mean to . . .'

He sounded a little more sober then he had been.

McKenzie looked round. 'I believe Mrs Carr was turned on by the dungeon.' He turned back to her. 'Is that right, Mrs Carr?'

She barely acknowledged him. Although infused with eroticism brought on by what she had seen both in the castle and in her mind, she knew what had to be done. There was a part to be played, a scene to be acted out. How could she play her part if he broke into her thoughts? Encouragement! Both he and Richard needed encouragement. And hadn't McKenzie been upset by her rudeness? This was the goad she would use.

'I was overcome with remorse for insulting you earlier. I realised that I deserved to be punished like that. Naked and vulnerable. That's how I should be. Apologising isn't enough.'

She looked up at him. She saw his lashes flicker slightly and knew he had interpreted the meaning of what she had said. Soon he would not be able to resist carrying out the things she wanted him to do.

'Imagine how it felt,' she said her voice husky and quivering slightly. 'I have sinned, committed a punishable offence. Perhaps I have not done my work as I should. Perhaps I have spoken out of turn.'

Opening heavy eyelids, she gazed momentarily at McKenzie before shutting them again.

'Perhaps I'd better go,' she heard Richard say.

'No!' He had to stay. There had to be two men, like there had been at the airport. It didn't matter that one of them was more sober, more dominant than the other. She needed them both. This was her fantasy. She selected the players.

The door remained open. She could almost feel Richard's eyes burning into her. The effects of the whisky would be wearing off. His cock would be resurrecting somewhat and pressing against his pants, aching to fuck her mouth, her cunt, her arse, any orifice where he might get satisfaction.

'We all go,' said McKenzie. 'She spoke out of turn earlier this evening, when she first arrived. I think it only just she should be punished for calling me a moron. Don't you, Richard?'

'She called you a moron?' He sounded genuinely shocked. Quite touching, really.

Yes! She had them eating out of her hand and they didn't even know it.

Richard came closer. She heard his breathing and knew he had indeed sobered up a little. He breathed like that when he was aroused. He would go along with everything McKenzie suggested. In turn, McKenzie would be dancing to her tune.

She opened her eyes to see him untying one of the silk ropes that held back one of the bed-curtains. It was red and dark as blood.

He pulled her arms behind her back. She struggled – just enough to make it interesting. He shouted at her. 'Keep still, you bitch!' He turned to Richard. 'Give me a hand, will you?'

Richard, who had been as a statue, now grabbed her head, cupping her face between his hands. He stared. Liz looked up at him, her breathing heavy, her mouth slightly open. She saw his amazement. Her eyes were reflected in his. They were sparkling, shinier than she had ever seen them before.

Suddenly he seemed to enter the spirit of the thing. With a smile, he slipped his thumbs into the corners of her mouth. She licked her lips in response, her legs weak with excitement at the game they were about to play.

McKenzie twisted the rope around her wrists one more time. Her wrists were secure behind her back.

His face came close to hers. She saw the flush of his cheeks, the glint in his eyes. 'Now we'll see who's a moron,' he said.

Richard started towards the door.

'One moment,' said McKenzie with a sneer. 'I think we need to get her prepared for what's coming.'

Richard looked puzzled. But a thrill ran through Liz's body; the submissive object in this particular scenario knew and wanted what was to come.

McKenzie slid his hands into the cups of the basque and pulled her breasts up above the stiff lace. Her nipples stared straight ahead.

Richard gasped. 'What a sight!'

Somehow, the look on his face annoyed her. 'Close your mouth, Richard. You look like a fish!'

McKenzie stared at her in a mix of horror and delight. 'More bad-mouthing? We can't have that, can we!'

He took off his tie. She struggled a little more as he bound it around her mouth.

'Now we are ready,' he said. 'She'll take her punishment in silence.' Suddenly, he took out a pen and notepad from the tight-fitting black jacket he wore and began to scribble. 'Get these items from the kitchen on the way down,' he said.

Richard's eyes nearly popped out of his head. Mouth still open, he gaped at Liz, then at McKenzie. 'Right,' he said, his voice quivering.

Although the passage leading down to the dungeon was cold and the steps were of stone, Liz was burning. The Lord of the Manor had spoken. The woman who had insulted him was about to get what she deserved and she couldn't wait!

The dungeon was as cold as she remembered it. Her flesh erupted in goose bumps. A shiver ran down her spine. And yet she burnt. Her blood raced. Her heart thudded.

Richard returned holding a carrier bag. She wondered what toys McKenzie had sent him to find. There was no time to dwell on it. Robert McKenzie pushed her into the middle of the room. She made sure she stumbled and went flying on to the stone floor. Her shoes flew off. Her stockings were laddered.

McKenzie, Richard just behind him, came forward. He reached down and fetched his dirk from next to his calf.

'First,' he said, 'some humiliation.'

He cut the sides of her lace pants and ripped the tattered remains away.

Suddenly she felt truly vulnerable. There was no hiding the bits of her that were usually hidden from business acquaintances. Her most private parts were exposed. Her breasts were perched above the stiffness of her underwear. And there was nothing she could do about it. Her hands were tied – literally.

'What are you going to do now?' Richard asked. His face was flushed. He looked almost frightened, unsure as to whether he should be stopping McKenzie. At the same time, he couldn't stop himself.

McKenzie smiled as he looked around him. 'Seeing as she likes this place so much, she's going to try each gadget in turn.'

'She might get angry,' said Richard and looked genuinely worried.

Please, Richard. Go along with everything. Everything! She would have screamed the silent thought if she could. Her gag prevented that.

McKenzie was obviously on the same wavelength as she was. 'She won't. I expect, if the truth were known, she's actually enjoying it.'

He heaved her to her feet. 'Right. Let's make a start.' He ran his hands over her buttocks. 'Nice arse.' He pushed her up against a wall and used both hands to separate one buttock from the other. 'Nice hole, too.' He turned to Richard. 'Has she ever let you go in there?'

Richard shook his head. 'No.'

'Ah!' said McKenzie. 'Then it's time she did. And this looks just the right implement to hold her while you try it out.'

Liz struggled, as required. What was he going to do? Was she fighting enough to fire up his enthusiasm?

Heaven, please don't let it flag! Not now we've got this far.

Not many men had let her down and been unable to perform. Those that had disappointed her were in the long distant past, when she hadn't been so sure of herself.

But she needn't have worried. She had judged them correctly.

He lay her face down on what looked something like a medieval rack. A metal collar went over her neck and held her fast to the main beam of the contraption. He placed her astride the wide wooden beam so that her feet just about touched the floor. The rough wood scratched her belly and rasped against her pubic hair.

'Good Lord!' Richard exclaimed.

Shut up, thought Liz.

'Did you bring a cushion?' asked McKenzie.

'Yes,' Richard replied.

Get on with it. I want it. I want it now! Liz thought.

There was a sound of rustling plastic while the cushion was taken out of the carrier bag.

'You hold her up. I'll slip it underneath her pelvis,' said McKenzie.

Feel my cunt while you're at it, Mac, she silently pleaded. Run your fingers through my pubic hair and get the juices flowing. And don't forget to give my clit a little tap on the way. Make it rise. Make it erect. The way I'm feeling it might even ejaculate, if it had the necessary bits with it.

She knew he'd do it. Flesh that was no more than a cover for the more sensitive bits beneath was prodded and pushed aside. He tapped at the little button set like a jewel at its centre. He ran his finger along the increasingly slippery flesh and dipped it into its source as if he might plug it and stop the juices flowing altogether.

She wriggled her bottom as delicious thrills emanated from his fingers and gripped her stomach like iron pincers. Yet her sex was open. So was any other orifice they might give attention to. And that's what she wanted. Their attention, a mere adjunct to her own long-experienced fantasies.

'Now?' asked Richard. Liz heard the sound of a fly being undone.

Richard, you are so green at times!

'Of course not.' McKenzie sounded irritated.

111

'You might injure yourself. It's a very tight hole, you know. Best to prepare it first. Give me the carrot and the oil.'

Liz closed her eyes. This was it. She was going to get something hard and unyielding in her arse. The oil would ease its insertion. But it would be a tight fit, an intrusion into the unspeakable. And the fact that the hole was taboo would make it even more arousing. Wicked, according to some; adventurous, according to others.

Every nerve in her body was burning with lust. Anything was possible and she wanted it all.

She heard the bag rustle again.

'I see you like your vegetables to be on the large side,' said McKenzie. 'Give me the oil, first.'

Liz played her part. She struggled and lifted her pelvis off the cushion. She muttered unintelligible sounds against her gag. It was futile and she was glad it was futile.

'Keep still!'

Just as she'd expected, McKenzie slapped one buttock, then the other. This was ecstasy. This was the fantasy that had always given her the most pleasure.

'We need a little docility, first,' she heard McKenzie say.

'You mean . . .?' said Richard. She could almost hear him slavering with a mix of excitement and amazement as the American slid the thin leather belt out of his sporran.

'Six of the best should do it,' said McKenzie. 'Six from you and six from me. Do you want to go first? After all, it's you that's going to fuck her arse for the first time. You want her just right, don't you?'

'Well, yes. I suppose so.' Richard replied. He

didn't sound too sure. In fact she couldn't remember him ever dithering like he was now. But it had been there, she told herself, just beneath the surface. Perhaps that's why she had gone off their one-to-one relationship.

The belt stung, but only pleasantly. Her bottom jerked towards it. With the second stroke, she felt a warm glow spread from the strike area. With the third, her pale rear got warmer still.

'Wait,' said McKenzie suddenly. 'I think we're doing this all wrong.'

'Whatever you say,' said a breathlessly excited Richard. 'Whatever you say.'

'Let's get her prepared for what you're going to give her. Give me the oil.'

'Do you think I could do this?' Richard said. His voice trembled.

'OK. I'll hold them open,' said McKenzie. 'You put that tube from the bottle and let it trickle inside and out.'

She stiffened as the coolness of the oil seeped inside her and trickled between her buttocks and tickled between her legs.

The carrot came next.

Stiffer than a penis, she thought. She tensed. And colder. Perhaps Richard had got it out of the fridge. I wonder, she thought with amusement, whether Richard had thought McKenzie was going to have him make a salad. She tried not to laugh but it wasn't easy. Luckily the gag muffled it.

Imagine what Richard was thinking. He had always considered himself such a man of the world, an uninhibited stud of inexhaustible knowledge. Yet, because he lacked perception, he was severely lacking. He knew nothing of her fantasies. Unlike other

113

men, he had never asked her whether she fantasised he was someone else when they made love.

Made love. When you fucked him, you mean. When the boredom of the boardroom became too much and you wanted some distraction. Be honest: he was merely convenient.

McKenzie, with Richard's assistance, continued their game.

Wasn't making love really a pseudonym for playing games, giving pleasure? Wouldn't it be more accurate to say they were just having fun? Laughably, it was actually more accurate to call the whole thing physical education. Somewhere, she thought, as she wriggled her bottom suggestively, there must be a considered syllabus on the subject. If there wasn't, perhaps she should write one!

Although the chill air caressed her body, she did not feel cold. On the contrary, a warm glow seeped over her flesh. She kept her eyes open now. She had entered her fantasy world. This was a real dungeon, where untold pain had once been inflicted. Times had changed. Torture had been replaced by tantalisation. It was no longer a place of incarceration but had become something of an erotic pilgrimage.

'She's ready,' she heard McKenzie say.

She wriggled her bottom again and mumbled against her gag.

'No good struggling, woman. You'll have what you're given!'

Then get on with it!

Why was it men had no sense of timing? There she was her bottom hot and her body ready and there was McKenzie misinterpreting the subtlety of her actions.

Or was he?

Silly girl, she thought to herself. He damned well knew she was impatient to get on with it. After all, it was her game and he knew that the dungeon had fired her imagination. He had seen her react to the cold walls, the dark shadows and the forbidding atmosphere. The psychology of a sensual mind substituted pleasure for pain. She had the security of knowing no real torture would occur. No blood would be drawn, and those participating, including herself, were doing so of their own free will.

Although she murmured against the leather gag, it came out more like a groan as if she really were in pain instead of ecstasy.

Richard removed the carrot and entered her, the tip of his penis soft at first against the tight stricture between her buttocks. What followed was firmer. Inch by inch, it invaded and her muscles held it fast. Her legs trembled as his fingers gripped her pelvis and raised her on to him.

But where was McKenzie?

She needed to know where he was, so she could fit him into the right spot in her mind. In a way, it was like directing a play, perhaps with real people – or maybe in the same way as Victorian cardboard theatres, where the actors were agitated by small sticks glued to their backs. This was what it was like with these two men. She was the prima donna. They were merely the supporting cast.

'Let me know when you've come,' breathed McKenzie. 'I'll work on her tits and, if she resists, I'll use her mouth.'

Resist? Why the hell should she resist?

She raised herself slightly to accommodate his hands.

That's it. Cup them at first. Then squeeze them. Oh yes! That is so good. So torturously good! Hairy loins against my arse, a stiff prick in it, and another guy's hands squeezing my titties and fingering my nipples. If this is torture, give me more!

And she certainly knew how to get more.

She struggled against Richard's hands, as if she hated every minute of it. She bucked against Richard as if trying to throw him off – an impossible act, seeing as she was impaled on his cock.

But, just as she'd surmised, McKenzie got the message.

'Struggle, will you? Well, just for that you can accommodate my cock. Here it is! Now, what do you think of that?' He pulled up his kilt and there it was in all its lengthy glory.

Kingsize! That's the only way I can describe it. Definitely more than a mouthful, but then, I've got more than one place to accommodate something like that.

He held it like a quill pen, traced the edge of her face with it, rubbed it against her nose so she could smell its maleness, its aching need to have her in whatever way possible.

She craned her neck so the tip of his fine appendage touched her lips.

He laughed and tugged it away from her. 'Impatient bitch!'

Too right, she thought. Let's get sucking and then we can get fucking.

She'd judged him well. His eyes glowed. His cock throbbed and, despite the leather that lay over her tongue, he entered her mouth.

Deep throat! Had such a woman existed? If she had, she'd have choked on this guy.

But Liz wasn't so stupid as to expect too much and she knew by the movements and noises that Richard was making that McKenzie wouldn't be in her mouth for long.

While he was there, the experience was pleasant. It was like satisfying a long-lasting hunger. Soft-skinned but hard as iron. That was the best description possible for a man's dick. The taste seemed to radiate around her mouth and yet, in a way, it wasn't a taste but just an intensity of smell.

Just as she had guessed, Richard was not long. He stiffened. He tensed. He cried out and, for that moment, she dragged her thoughts away from the cock in her mouth and clenched the one in her arse as though she were squeezing the life out of it. At the same time, she jerked her buttocks against Richard's thrusts until the final spasm, the final cry of relief and triumph.

'Don't be greedy,' said McKenzie.

He jerked his cock from her mouth.

Bastard! Give me it back.

But of course she knew he wouldn't. Yet she hadn't come herself. She wasn't ready yet. She had not had her fill. They must know that.

But she needn't have worried. They lay their hands on her and she sighed. The next act of their play was about to be enacted.

'Help me turn her over,' said McKenzie to Richard.

Richard's answer was breathless, as though he had run a five hundred-yard sprint. But he did find the energy to do as the American said.

Prepare yourself. Now for the big one.

And she knew more or less what position she would be put into. She glanced at the manacles that were hanging from hooks in the ceiling either side of her feet. When she looked at McKenzie, he was looking back at her, a faint smile playing around his lips. The gleam in his eyes seemed brighter.

I know what you're thinking, she thought. I know what you're going to do.

She heard his words and saw his outrageous smile as he lifted her leg and fastened the rusty manacle around it. But she didn't care what he was saying. He was merely a tool, a slave carrying out her pleasure.

The other manacle was a couple of feet away from the first one. It was a little looser than the first manacle, but she crooked her toes over it to stop her foot slipping off.

McKenzie stood between her legs, eyeing her exposed flesh. At the same time, he stroked his cock: preparing it, no doubt, for what was to come.

Richard stood behind him and, although he had only recently been satisfied, he was salivating anew.

'What now?' he asked McKenzie.

McKenzie frowned and looked at him as though he were stupid. 'I'm going to fuck her, of course.' Then he looked thoughtfully back at her. 'But she does look a bit uncomfortable. Untie her hands. They're still behind her back and must be a bit stiff by now – though not as stiff as me, mind you.' And he laughed.

Richard did as he said but was surprised when she began to lash out at him with her freed hands.

'Use that!' shouted McKenzie nodding in the direction of a lump of iron that had a ring and a length of chain in the top of it. 'Drag it over and place it on the floor underneath her head.'

Richard obeyed. He didn't need any more orders but grabbed her flailing arms, ran the chains up from the floor and fastened more manacles around her wrists clipping them to a metal ring just above her head.

A perfect position. Now for that dick. Put it in me, you bastard. Don't keep me waiting. I want it! I want it!

Now it was her turn to salivate.

Her eyes went to the length that was now approaching her wide-open pussy. She noticed that Richard had pulled up a chair behind McKenzie and would have a good view of him entering her.

Imagine, she thought. I'll be hearing those hanging nuts slapping against me, that slurping as he slides in and out. Richard will actually be seeing McKenzie's nuts hanging and swaying.

He teased her. He stroked her moistness with the tip of his cock. He held it between his fingers and ran it up and down her cleft. And she murmured against the leather that sat on her tongue. She was wet and getting wetter. She was aching to be filled with him, to be pressed against the wood she lay on, for her breasts to be flattened against her by his weight.

Bastard!

He kept running the tip of it along her slippery lips. She closed her eyes to savour the moment. Behind her closed lids, she tried to imagine how he was seeing this part of her body, how he smelt her.

Like the sea, she thought. He would be invigorated by her smell, sucking it into himself. It would course through his veins and fire up every extremity. Heart would beat faster. Blood would surge and warm his flesh. His balls would feel heavy. His cock would dance as the blood pulsed in time to the unseen tune.

And if he paused to look at her, he would see those lips he sucked. Deep pink, purplish in places, it would make him think of a flower, possibly a rose. Drops of dew, her dew, would make it glisten.

Ah, but it was good to know what was in his mind. Good to know he could read hers too.

It didn't matter in what way they might come. Whether he fucked her arse or her cunt, or whether he licked her to orgasm, the game had been played. The players had been well matched. There was no victor, only a pleasure in knowing that something had been done very well.

Chapter Eight

Rachel was glad to leave the chill waters of the Grand Union behind her and return to the city and her own place. It wasn't so much that she had tired of her companions but she couldn't bear not knowing what Ian was doing. Perhaps it could be called possessiveness, not that which derived from jealous love. No, it was more like wanting to make sure your car was still in the garage or your most comfortable shoes still under the bed.

Besides that, she still had the research to undertake for the intriguing Robert McKenzie, the man her mother was meeting in Scotland. So far, she had avoided contacting him, even though he had left messages on her answerphone. He was sexy, sure, but his public behaviour was a little – bizarre. Even so, she could have coped well enough with that and even been attracted to him. But he was older than she was. She didn't want to be thought of as an older man's plaything. Old man's darling – wasn't that the correct phrase?

Of course she still thought about him and what he had got her to do. Sitting on a leather settee with no knickers on left a kind of after-effect. It gave her goosebumps every time she remembered the cool smoothness of the cowhide against her skin. A moist secretion had also caused her to make a sucking sound when she'd got up. A stain must have been left there. Would anyone have smelt the evidence of her presence and her nakedness when they came to clean it? Someone must have wiped it away afterwards. She'd never know. And it didn't matter. Only the memory of what she had done really mattered. Thinking of him made her smile and, although she tried to deny it to herself, she wouldn't be averse to sleeping with him. It would be an adventure. She couldn't deny that.

But she didn't want him to think she was putty in his hands.

I don't want to be your baby doll.

That's what she imagined herself telling him.

OK, it's been fun. But it has to be a mutual thing. I want you to know that.

Pride was part of it. She wanted to keep him at arm's length for a while and show him her professional side. Research was what he had asked her to do and that was what she was doing. Playing games and indulging in sex must wait for opportune moments.

She was also glad to get back to her new apartment that her father had so kindly given her the deposit for.

The apartment she had decided on was in a converted warehouse down an old cobbled street in Tooting. Up until its conversion, the Victorian brickwork and arched green doors had been business premises for bottom of the barrel businesses, such as rag and bone merchants and dealers in scrap metal. Like a phoenix newly risen, the brickwork now shone and the paintwork gleamed.

Her apartment was on the third floor, just high enough to see over the rooftops opposite towards the mainline tube to the city.

Honey-gold floorboards were complimented by no-nonsense furniture, some from IKEA and some she had made from bits and pieces rescued from skips. Rachel was like that. She didn't like waste and didn't believe in expending unnecessary energy on domestic duties. This included dusting and vacuuming. Hence her no-nonsense approach to interior design. The less ornamentation, the less cleaning there was to be done.

Before leaving for Scotland, Robert McKenzie had given her a tin box containing a lot of old papers given him by an aunt who had driven a US army staff car during the war. She had met and married an English army captain and had remained in England until her recent death. Robert had browsed through some of the stuff, he told her, but not all.

She sat at her pine plant table with the box before her. It squeaked like a trapped rat as she opened it.

There were the usual old photographs, old letters and diaries. The earliest covered the years when the aunt had first met her intended husband. From these, Rachel deduced that those years had sometimes been lonely and Betty Jane, his aunt, had taken to writing her diary and looking into her family history.

For some reason this came as a surprise. She hadn't expected things to be this easy. It always was easier if some antecedent had thoughtfully undertook the spadework.

Rachel had not expected to become so intrigued with the family history. After all, without exact details, such things can merely appear like a list of those born, who married who, how many children they had and when they died.

But this was different. Betty Jane had obviously harboured a love of history plus a burning curiosity for the unique and the salacious.

She had found out a lot of things about her forebears and not all of it was entirely respectable. Love and lust figured high on the agenda.

Rachel, her nose nearer the paper, ran her finger along the neatly squared off writing.

One character description above all others took her eye.

Duncan McKenzie was something of a rake that tired of Scotland's provincial society and headed south. He had lands, he had looks and he also had the strength of character and glib tongue that gained him entry to the upper levels of London society.

However, those he fell in with were of as rakish a disposition as himself, members of a hellish club where depravity was the norm and decadence encouraged.

Orgies occurred, where much drink was consumed and women were encouraged to set aside their morals and their corsets in pursuit of pleasure.

To a large extent, it seems the men dominated and set the agenda for these wanton displays. Dominating them all was Duncan

McKenzie. It is with some embarrassment that I learnt more of his disposition and what he got up to. Surely a man of my family, ancestor to many upright American citizens, couldn't possibly have played with women as if they were toys! Where was loyalty? Where was fidelity?

Rachel paused and smiled. The turn of phrase reminded her that this was a woman from a former generation speaking. A hint of Puritanism ran through the writing. All the same, Rachel could not resist reading more.

Although I felt bashful about asking for the book yet again, I found myself being drawn to the British Library at every opportunity. I wanted to know more about this man and these poor women who were ruined by him. Few women of that time would have had the courage to face up to him: yet, to my surprise, I found that one woman did. Her name was Caroline Standish. She proved to be the making of him and to some extent, his undoing, for he was never the same again. The process by which she did this has unnerved me. Strange as it may seem I feel echoes of that process will stay with me for the rest of my life.

Rachel rested her back against the beige canvas of the chair which had 'director' printed on the back. Betty Jane intrigued her. She could almost feel the palpitating of the dead woman's heart all those years ago as she had read heated extracts from the book she had mentioned. And all around her would have been silence, the matt dullness of wood panelled walls and blacked-out windows. In contrast, wild orgies would be taking place in her mind. Years had separated Betty Jane from Caroline Standish. Yet, across the centuries, the exploits of one had greatly impressed the other. She could tell that just by the change in tone of the writing. And now it was making her heart race, too.

So this book, Rachel thought, as she skimmed through the pages, is in the British Library.

I must have it!

She flipped backward and forward through the crisp pages of the diary.

Where is it?

It occurred to her that Betty Jane had merely scribbled the title on a scrap of paper then thrown it away, once her research was finished.

Please no!

Her persistence paid off. After flipping back closer to the beginning, she found what she was looking for.

A Concourse on Depravity, Decadence and the Pursuit of Fleshly Sins. The title was written in surprisingly small block lettering, as if, she thought, Betty Jane was afraid of knowing its title, let alone reading it.

Rachel smiled as she imagined the hot blush flowing over Betty Jane's cheeks. I wonder if she ever told her husband about it, she thought. Doubtful.

Typical of the eighteenth century, the title was anything but glib. Did it still exist? Very likely! The archives of the British Library were immense.

Someone there might be able to find it. She picked up a pen and wrote down the title.

Next, the library. Was there enough time? She glanced up at the wide face of the old school-house clock. She'd arranged to check on her mother's house and to meet Ian there but it didn't matter if she was late. Besides, she had enough time. From there, she'd go over and pick up Ian. Then back here for supper. His turn to cook. Bolognese, crusty bread, butter, salad, wine and cheese. Not too demanding.

The British Library was no doubt a lighter place than it had been in Betty Jane's time. All the same, when she asked for the book, it took some time to find.

'I'm afraid it does not appear on our computer system,' said the young man, after he'd tapped a few keys.

'It has to be here,' said Rachel. 'It's a classic dating from somewhere around 1780. According to my research, it was here during the war, so it must be here now.'

She flipped over the pages of her notepad and kept a straight face, as though she were researching something more earth-shattering than the sexual exploits of some eighteenth century super-stud.

'But if it's not on the system . . .' He covered his mouth as he coughed. She suddenly hated freckle-faced people with receding chins and tangled orange hair. And they certainly shouldn't be working in a library if they looked like him and couldn't find the book she wanted!

But she took a deep breath. 'Are you absolutely sure?'

'Oh, yes,' he said with a condescending smile

that made her feel as though her brain was pea-sized. 'The system covers everything. If it's not on the system, it isn't here.'

Enough was enough.

'Fuck the system! It's an old book and if you can't find the bloody thing, then get me someone who can!'

His mouth dropped open. He glared at her silently before recovering. 'I'll see what I can do,' he mumbled.

When he came back, a man with a shiny head, gold wire-rimmed spectacles and a smattering of snow-white hair above his ears accompanied him. His legs, she noticed, were slightly bent, as though he'd been perched on a stool for far too long.

'What can I do for you, madam?' he said, his pink face glowing beneath the sharp glow of the spotlights. His smile was kind.

'I want a book. It's old but I think you still have it. It was last out, as far as I know, during the war years.'

The old man beamed steadily at her, as though he had not heard. She briefly wondered whether he'd been incarcerated in some dusty corner of the place and was only brought out when people asked for something really old with covers of vellum or pigskin.

But he had heard. After sliding his spectacles up over his forehead, he glanced down at the title that had been written down by freckle-face.

'Ah, an English comparison to the Marquis de Sade – only my humble opinion, of course.'

'You've read it?'

The younger man went off to deal with someone

else. The eyes of the older man twinkled. Was that a hint of lust she detected?

'This isn't on the computer system. Because of its nature and age, it is only listed on the old cardex system, which is maintained by me and me alone. Follow me.'

He took her along many corridors, down many flights of stairs, forever twisting and turning. It was as if they were journeying towards the centre of the earth.

Eventually they were in a place of cobwebs and dark panelling, the sort of place – without the cobwebs – that might have been familiar to Betty Jane.

He turned on the light then sighed and looked around the room before moving again. As if he was remembering the place, she thought.

The old man pulled out a set of Regency-style library steps that wouldn't have looked out of place in the Brighton Pavilion. They squeaked as he pulled them into place then creaked as he stepped on to the first step, then squeaked again as he mounted the second and then the third.

Rachel wiped her palms down the thighs of her jeans. She was impatient and might have shown her impatience with anyone younger. But the man had been kind. She constrained her impatience to her mind.

Get on with it. Get the damn book down and don't be so slow about it.

She watched as he heaved a heavy tome from a shelf near the ceiling. Slowly, he descended the library steps. Eventually both feet were back on terra firma.

'There. No problem,' he said as he turned round to face her. 'Found in a jiffy.'

Your definition, not mine, she wanted to say, but the book was in front of her and time no longer seemed so important.

She had expected the book to be thick with dust, just like most of the other items sat shrouded in time and cobwebs on the dark wooden shelves. But to her surprise its covers were red and bright and the title etched in gold gilt still gleamed. As if, she thought, someone was taking good care of it.

'Take care of it,' the old man said as if reading her thoughts. 'Many would condemn its contents. Few have savoured it in the spirit of enlightenment.'

His fingertips brushed against hers as she took it from his hands. It was hard to take her eyes off it.

'I shall leave you to your studies,' he said in a voice used to being polite. 'I am sure this publication will be even more than you expected it to be.'

He chuckled as he left. But she didn't hear him.

The librarian's presence was no longer of any importance. She had already opened the cover by the time he had closed the door. Betty Jane's diary had whetted her curiosity for this book – purely in the interests of research, she told herself. She assured herself that she would be immune to its erotic content because she had been born into a permissive society where sex was uninhibited and freely indulged in. At least, that was how she perceived things, until she opened the book and came face to face with the frontispiece. An instant flush coloured her face.

The drawing was of ink. The woman was naked, a pile of white flesh with small breasts, large hips and heavy thighs. The woman had a voluptuousness that was fashionable at the time, definitely larger than a size sixteen.

She appeared to be partially lying down, leaning against the man behind her. The man's face was full of lechery. His hands were on her breasts, her nipples peeking through his fingers.

Rachel touched the paper and caught her breath. This was a flat drawing; a black-and-white line etching that had no real depth, no real artistic merit. And yet it fascinated.

The woman's naked body was contorted slightly, the leg nearest the reader held high to show the fact that her buttocks were being pierced by the man's prick. At the same time, another man was standing between her legs, his cock half buried in pubic lips that the man was holding apart with his fingers, so he might better view the object of his attention.

The etching did not stop with the woman being penetrated back and front. Another man stood at the woman's head. He was pinching her nose between finger and thumb so she had no option but to keep her mouth open and accommodate the length of cock that sat upon her tongue.

Rachel sat back in her chair. The need to catch her breath surprised her. After all, wasn't she the modern Ms who knew all there was to know about sex and had lost her virginity the moment she'd turned sixteen? This was ancient stuff, the sort of thing that had titillated previous generations but should be tame meat to the likes of her. But it wasn't tame meat. It wasn't that it was purely the stuff designed merely to arouse. It was more as if she were being shown a mirror and it was reflecting some aspect of her deepest desires. The truth flooded over her. In an odd way, she was that woman. The fact that she could contemplate such a thought brought a flush to her face and shame to her heart. No woman wanted to be raped – and wasn't rape the subject of this picture?

She took a deep breath, sat forward and swiftly turned the page. The Hellfire Club, it said at the top of the page in blurred lettering, was an organisation of gentlemen who pursued the sins of the flesh with the greatest of fervour. Below were printed a list of members. One of those was Duncan McKenzie. In the interests of research, Rachel read on.

Some of it was too unpalatable to take. She began skipping passages relating to torture, to animals and the blood-letting of innocent strangers. Duncan, thankfully, had had little to do with this side of things. It appeared that his appetite was restricted to sexual lust, not blood lust.

She found an entry supposedly written by him.

Most whores are willing to take on three of us
if the price is right.

So it wasn't rape. The woman on the frontispiece had been paid for posing.

I think my favourite moment, besides that of the final spasm of sexual release, is that moment when her clothes are being removed. The scent of her body wafts up over me, then clings to my senses, inviting me to lick, suck and fuck every orifice of her soft white flesh.

It is better, of course, if the woman is not a

paid whore but one who is intrigued by our secret society, or enamoured of one of our members. A woman will do anything if she is in love with him who asks her to do so. If he pleads with her to let one of his friends fuck her, she does so willingly. Such is love! And there he stands, the object of her fixation watching the spectacle, prick in hand, its head in the mouth of a keenly sucking whore.

If such a woman is willing, then the scent of her body clings in a subtler way than that of a whore. It is as though one senses her fear of what men are capable of forcing her to do. Such is the power of her emotions. Yet this kind of woman can sometimes submit with little encouragement, as long as her love pleads with her to do so. She cannot know at first what will be required of her. When she finally finds out that more than one man will be savouring the delights of her body, fear creeps into her eyes and is only calmed by sweet words of encouragement from her lover. She will do what is required because she wants to please. And that is all we want of her. We want her to please us. We will have her mouth if we desire. We will delve between her legs to that well that is the centre of her being. Or, if the fancy should take us, we will tie her up, whip her buttocks and then force our way into her smallest hole. Whether she gets any pleasure from the experience is of no interest at all.

Again Rachel took a deep breath and sat back in her chair. This was enough to turn the most feminine of women into a raging feminist overnight. What right did a man have to think that way? It was as Betty Jane had commented: the women were mere playthings, adjuncts to the sexuality of men, a slipper in which to slip their cocks when the need arose.

And yet it wasn't just anger she was feeling. She placed her hand over her pounding heart. Inadvertently, she touched her nipple. It rose to meet her finger, surprisingly hard, surprisingly aroused.

She snatched her hand away, shocked at how treacherous her body could be. It was somehow demeaning to be aroused by the self-centred views of Duncan McKenzie. He had been an outright chauvinist, an insensitive moron of the highest order.

She thought of Mac and of how he had manipulated her in the hotel lounge that night and she had taken off her knickers. Wasn't that similar? Had she felt used, that night? No. She was adamant about that. She had not felt used at the time, because she had enjoyed the experience. Even when she had seen him slip the waiter money and push her knickers into his pocket, she had not felt used even then. Why was that?

She rested her chin in her hands as she considered the problem. There was only one reason. Pleasure. She had enjoyed carrying out his dare. She had enjoyed the added piquancy of knowing the waiter had watched.

Personal pleasure was the reason, she thought, and coming to that conclusion made it easier to read on. And besides, this book was relating incidents and attitudes of a previous century, when women had no status except as sex objects or mothers. Things had changed a great deal since then.

Think clearly, she said to herself. She sat back and slapped her hands on her thighs.

'This is research and you're being paid for this,' she said out loud. Her words echoed around the panelled walls, the high ceilings and the china lampshades. They were barely post-war, by the looks of it. Somehow they had escaped the attention of modern innovation.

Back to the book she went, and began reading the next line.

Sometimes we play games. The whores (I shall call them that from now on, because most of them were) were naked and wore dog collars around their neck, to which a chain leash was attached. We made them crawl around on all fours. Some of the men crawled around with them, each sniffing the other's rear orifices as such creatures do. After some licking and sucking of teats and pestles, a man would mount his chosen bitch and fuck her until he was satisfied. Those men then took the places of the masters holding the leashes and the bitches would be mounted again until all the men were satisfied and all the women lying exhausted.

Much more went on. Rachel read all that written by Duncan McKenzie. After reading descriptions of countless orgies, it finally came to an end. By this time, Rachel was red-faced and slightly confused: not at the book, but at her reactions to its contents. She should have been thoroughly disgusted, and yet she was not. On the contrary, her body seemed strangely alert to what it was capable of and what it could do with impunity. Duncan McKenzie, despite the chauvinistic slant of his writing, had given her pleasure. She smiled. He probably wouldn't have approved – or perhaps he would have been equally confused to find that his exploits had made her tingle. It might never have occurred to him that women could actually derive pleasure from such a scenario.

Because she had come to the end of the piece written by the man she was researching, she would have closed the book then and there. But, for some reason, she flicked through it. As though preordained, the book flew open at one particular chapter. She was about to close the book completely but something familiar about the chapter heading caught her eye.

Caroline Standish, it said, *Her Thoughts on the Frailties of Men and the Cunning of Women.*

Caroline Standish. Wasn't that the name of the woman Betty Jane had said had changed the life of Duncan McKenzie? But how had she done that?

Rachel glanced up at the fading light coming through the pavement level window. Soon the library would be closing. There was little time to read whatever Caroline Standish had written and yet she was desperate to do so.

She looked at the book and then at the copious brown leather bag she carried around. It contained everything a thorough researcher might need, but there was still room for one more item.

Did she have time? She glanced at the clock. Could she get out before the librarian came to remind her that both he and she had a home to go to?

There was no time to dither. Without doing up the buckles, she flung her bag over her shoulder and made for the door.

She told herself not to panic but her heart was thudding against her ribs. Hell: if she got caught, she'd just have to say it was an oversight. Perhaps she'd get a fine. So what?

She climbed the stairs two at a time and came to an emergency exit door on a bend in the flight. Good enough, she thought, hit the escape bar handle, and felt the evening air chill against her face.

She was out and the book was out with her.

Godfrey Peltman smiled as he reached for the light switch of the secret archive. What luck, he thought, that young Winston had fetched him to sort out the young woman's enquiry. There were some books that had never been entered on the computer system. No one knew they were down here and had been since World War Two. Erotic books had always been stored and listed separate to everything else, especially back then. People's minds might be broader now, but Godfrey had never relinquished control of those that recorded the more lascivious side of the nature of man. Man might be lower than the angels but was most certainly above animals. What else would explain the imaginative ways he sought to satisfy his desire?

So Godfrey had clung to the old ways and old systems. This wasn't just a secret archive, it was a treasure house of erotic history. Sometimes, at close of day, he would stand in the silence of this room with his eyes closed. If he concentrated really hard, he could almost feel the sheer vibrancy of the genre, the energy of life itself.

He glanced at the bulbous-legged refectory table over which many a scholar of erotica had perused literature hidden from the outside world. What wonderful stories that table could tell. It was big and wide enough to hold two. How sweet was the thought, sweet enough to bring a tear of regret to his eye. If only he could turn the clock back: but time travel was a figment of fiction. The coupling of a hungry man and a lonely woman was not.

He glanced at the shelf. There was a gap where the book had been. He smiled. Like many of her predecessors, the young lady had taken the book with her. No doubt it would be returned. But he wasn't unduly worried about that. Age was catching up with him and so were more liberated attitudes than he had faced in the past. The book deserved to be outside the stone prison in which it had resided for a very long time.

Again he glanced at the table. When he was younger, that book had cast a spell over him. Of course, so had the pretty American girl who had come to read it. She was looking for her roots, she said, and he had helped her find them. He had also helped her come to terms with her own sexuality and that of men in general. She hadn't really learnt that much from him. He had just been the man around at the time. Awakening Betty Jane's sexuality had been down to Caroline Standish – and what a woman she must have been. A good deed well done, he thought, as he reflected on his memories before switching off the light.

* * *

Ian was already at her parent's house when Rachel got there.

'You turned up, then,' she said tartly.

'Why shouldn't I?'

'Well, you haven't exactly been easy to contact since I've been away.'

'I've been working.' It sounded like the truth but she sensed something was bugging him.

'Evenings as well?'

'Sometimes. Does it worry you? Do you care?' he said.

'No,' she snapped. 'Is everything all right here?'

He nodded as he opened the front gate for her. 'No burglaries,' he said.

'That's not funny.'

Once they were inside, Ian took her by surprise. He reached for her quickly and held her close. 'I'm so glad to see you. How was the canal boat?'

She frowned, considered shrugging him away, then thought better of it. 'Fine.'

Previous to going away, she would have eluded his kisses for a while, enjoying the knowledge that he was most likely hard for her. Denial, she had always believed, would only make him get harder. Seeing him almost salivating to seduce her also gave her a feeling of power. It was the most pleasant thing she had discovered on becoming an adult.

But today, things seemed different. She felt more aware of the warmth of his hands through the white cotton shirt she wore. The smell of him seemed more intense, more masculine than usual.

All thoughts of denying him left her. She was on fire and she didn't know why. What was he doing to her? What was so different about him? What was so different about her?

She made one last attempt to resume the status quo. 'New aftershave?' she asked after they'd kissed and his hands were cupped around her face.

'No.' He said it breathlessly, as though he had no time for words. His hands, his arms, his lips were all over her, pressing, kissing, rubbing, and caressing.

One hand closed over her breast. Her nipple tingled, hardened and rose to meet it.

This is going too fast, she thought. Why can't I stop myself? She gasped for breath but couldn't stop herself. She was suddenly helpless; suddenly wanting whatever Ian wanted to give her in any way he wanted it.

He ripped her breasts from her bra and bent his head to kiss her breasts. At the same time, her bag slid from her shoulder and landed heavily on the floor. Suddenly, she knew the reason why she could not control her lust. The words written by Duncan McKenzie were still in her head. Scenes enacted over two hundred years ago were alive again in her mind and she was the woman about to get fucked in any way that she could.

Disgusting, thought the old Rachel. How can you think like that? How can you even contemplate letting a man – or men – do all that to you?

She refused to acknowledge that her own generation might be wrong in believing that there was some equilibrium in sexual desire. A woman should not let herself be used. That was the uppermost thought in her mind. Perhaps it was the fact that her own inexperience was leading her to the wrong conclusions. It didn't matter. Suddenly, she had to do something about it.

'Stop it, right now.' She pushed him away.

'But I want you.' He came back for more, his arms wrapping round her as they had before, his lips seeking hers.

'Stop that! You will not force me into this. I won't let you!' She kept pushing him and kept shouting. 'Stop it!'

This time, she swung her right fist. It connected with his chin.

This time, he got the message. He stood arms hanging at his sides, a sad hangdog expression in his big, brown eyes.

For a moment, he looked as if he were going to cry.

Suddenly, she wanted to submit to his kisses again, but she wouldn't let herself. She shoved her breasts back into her bra. Her nipples were long now and red. She stifled a gasp as she shoved them into their hiding place.

'You'd better start dinner.'

He smiled and reached for her.

My God, he's coming for it again!

'I'd prefer to eat you. I'd prefer to lick your pussy and nibble your tits.'

She could easily have given in. But something inside of her stopped her dead. She glared at him. 'Don't speak to me like that! You know I hate it when you talk like that.'

She pushed his hands away. Again, he looked hurt, and she didn't really want that either. You're so confused, she thought to herself. The book. I wish I'd never read that damn book! It's turning me into a whore.

But she had read it and, in some odd way, it had changed her. But its effect was two edged. If men could impose their will on women, then the reverse must also be true – at least, in this century it was.

'Take your clothes off,' she said suddenly.

Ian looked mightily relieved. 'OK.'

He began to hum the first lines of 'The Stripper' as he peeled off his clothes. Each discarded item was flung on to a growing pile on the floor.

Rachel was transfixed. She wanted to laugh. She also wanted to tell him to stop acting the fool but the words didn't want to come. He wasn't to know about the book and how it had confused her. Duncan McKenzie's chauvinistic statements still rang in her head. And yet she was aroused. Nothing in the hallway existed except the smell and look of him. Everything around him was no more than a frame for his body.

'Take me!' Ian finally cried, arms outstretched, legs apart and cock pointing straight at her.

If he'd have grabbed hold of her there and then, things might have been different. But he'd given her chance to think and let the mix of anger and guilt take over. She smiled engagingly. Beneath her cool veneer she seethed.

'Come on then. Up to bed.'

She took his hand and led him up the stairs to her parent's room.

'Go on,' she said, indicating with a quick jerk of her head that he should enter first.

What a nice bum he has, she thought as she walked behind him.

He turned and smiled once he was in the room. His eyes twinkled. He looked around him as though the room was far more luxurious, far more intriguing than it really was.

Rachel's eyes alighted on his cock that swayed from side to side as he moved.

It's nice, she thought. Really nice. And I would like to have it. Perhaps later I will.

Normally, she might have set some significance by what he next said. But lust had deafened both sound and suspicion.

'This room smells of your mother.' He closed his eyes and took deep breaths. For a moment, it seemed as if her presence was forgotten. When he opened his eyes again, he looked at her as if suddenly remembering she was there. He blushed and began to stammer an explanation. 'It's just that your mother always smells so nice,' he blurted. 'Not like you do. I mean, different than you. Different, that's all I mean.'

But Rachel wanted to get out of the room before she gave in to her lust and ravished him to bits. She slammed the door. Luckily the key was on the outside. She locked it. Then she frowned. Why had he been so taken with the smell of her mother? And why had he been at odds to explain his obsession away?

She shrugged. Ian was a sweet and willing boy, but perhaps a little immature for someone as sophisticated as her. Perhaps, she thought with a smile, Robert McKenzie is the man I should be with.

It wasn't the first time she'd thought of the wealthy American within the last few days. Likely as not, it wouldn't be the last. What a contrast, she thought. An immature predictable young man and a mature and outrageously exhibitionist older man.

She began to walk away.

'What are you doing?' he called from the other side of the door. 'It's cold in here.'

'Good,' she said. 'You could do with cooling down.'

'Rachel,' he called out as she made her way back down the stairs. 'Rachel! Where are you going? Come on. Let me out of here.'

He was easy to ignore. The book that sat in her bag drew her like a magnet and, in particular, Caroline Standish.

She sat down and opened it at the relevant chapter. Her heart began to flutter and something deep inside seemed to burst into wakefulness as she began to read.

I truly cannot remember who it was who suggested I attend a certain club that catered for the more lascivious side of a gentleman's nature. However, the gentleman concerned pursued me most fervently, the main reason being, I believe, that he mistook my soft voice and girlish looks as a sign of virginal innocence.

Accordingly, I accompanied him to this place and was mightily intrigued by what I saw there. A woman of dubious profession was being ridden by one man (by that, I mean he had inserted his member from behind) while another gentleman was taking full advantage of her wide mouth.

The woman was naked, her breasts full and her belly a little ponderous: not that the spongy consistency of the latter worried them at all. They were far too absorbed in their own sensations and the orifices she had made available to them to worry about her less than perfect body.

The man I was with invited others to join him, and I could tell from the look in their eyes that they intended forcing themselves on me, whether I liked it or not. Rape was what they wanted, but this was not to my liking. I was sufficiently aroused to want satisfaction on my own terms.

Having been endowed with a quick mind, I planned exactly what I wanted them to do and how I would go about it.

'First let me see what size weapons you are offering me,' I said. 'It is not enough that I can see those bulges at the front of your breeches. You could be carrying a bunch of quince and a carrot, for all I know.'

They laughed at my bravado. I knew then that I had lessened their desire to wilfully overcome me. Unbeknown to them, I had put them into competition with each other. Once men are competing, especially about the size of their staves, all thoughts of unity are swiftly forgotten. Accordingly, they undid their breeches and slid their members from the warmth of their groin. With a smile on my face, I viewed each in turn, tapping and stroking wherever I fancied. Suddenly, my potential rapists had become puppy dogs, each one trusting that their cock would be the one unto which I would show the most favour.

Oh, what fools those men were. Once their cocks were out, their brains left their heads. Their egos had become enslaved to a mere slip of a girl who had every intention of using their bodies to satisfy her own lusts, her own satisfaction. And that girl was me, dear reader.

As I said, I smiled at each of them in turn, stroked their cocks, merely tapped the more undeserving, but gripped and pulled at one I particularly liked. I looked into his face. Ecstasy was written all over it. Pride was there, too. After all, hadn't I just favoured his splendid rod above all others?

'In size order,' I said. 'I shall have you in size order.'

The man with the biggest cock beamed, obviously assuming that his would be the first to enter my portal. But I turned away and went to the smallest.

'I like to build up slowly,' I said. I tickled the man under his chin. 'You first, then the next size up, then so on and so forth, until . . .' I smiled provocatively at the man with the biggest one. 'Until I am ready to take that splendid monster.'

Immediately, without them knowing it, I had destroyed their masculine unity. They argued amongst each other as to who had the next size in line. They were each in competition with each other.

I then loosened my stays and pulled my bosom into view. 'Now,' I said as I lay back on a stack of comfortable cushions and gathered my skirts well above my thighs. 'Let us begin.'

Well, my friend. It was a delight. Can you imagine what it was like? Each entered in turn and, as I lay there gasping with orgasm after orgasm, a gentleman lay to either side of me, massaging my breasts and kissing my stiff little nipples.

They did try and kiss my lips, too, but I would have none of that – at least, not until I had duly surveyed the next entrant to my lushly watered gate.

Once the next prick was doing homage to my quim, I welcomed the kisses. What woman wouldn't? Imagine, one man ploughing my furrow, two more massaging my tingling breasts, while another kissed my lips or put his cock close to my mouth so that I might taste its piquant flavour.

Rachel sat back. Her knee hit the table as she crossed her legs. She clenched her thighs tightly together.

'Wow!' she exclaimed. 'What a woman!'

She attempted to resume her reading. It was no use. The ache between her legs was in danger of becoming an orgasm.

Suddenly, she wanted a man. She looked towards the ceiling. Ian was pacing backward and forward. There had been other sounds, though she hadn't taken too much notice. All her concentration had been fixed on Caroline Standish.

After slamming the book shut and burying it in her bag, she got up and went up the stairs.

Her heart was hammering against her ribs. Her 'quim', as Caroline Standish had so cutely called it, was throbbing. If she didn't plug the hole shortly, the juices would be running down her legs and into her shoes!

She unlocked the door to the bedroom and went in fully expecting Ian to be sat shivering or even cowering under the bedclothes. What she actually saw made her stop in her tracks.

'Ian!'

The bra he was wearing was purple. So were the skimpy knickers and suspender belt. His cock bulged like a pound of fruit against the fragile material. *A carrot and some quince* ... But Rachel knew Ian's bulge was for real.

The stockings were black fishnet and the shoes high and red.

Eyes wide, she looked him up and down. 'Where the hell did you get those?'

Ian blushed. He pointed at the low-level chest of drawers that stood beside the full-length mirror he had been admiring himself in.

'There,' he said. 'They're your mother's.'

She looked him up and down again. 'My mother doesn't wear things like that.'

Ian smirked. 'Then whose underwear is it? Your father's?'

This was disgusting. She continued to tell herself that her mother would never wear such things. Mothers wore comfortable things. And they were secure in their relationship. Her parents' marriage had lasted a long time. Why would her mother need to wear such decadent underwear?

The sight of Ian's rear reflected by the mirror drew her attention. A strip of purple material disappeared between his buttocks. Had her mother ever actually worn a thong? She couldn't believe it. After all, only women who wanted their arses fucked wore garments like that. It accentuated the buttocks and invited entry to the gap in between, didn't it?

She snorted angrily. 'They're appalling. Get them off!'

Ian's fingers went to the bra first. He began to peel the straps from his shoulders.

Rachel stood and watched.

You should leave, said a voice inside her head. But she couldn't leave. Her legs felt like lead. She wanted to watch him. In fact, it suddenly occurred to her that she wanted to enjoy him in just the way Caroline Standish had enjoyed those men at The Hellfire Club.

An idea came to her.

'No!' she snapped. 'Stay as you are.'

He stayed still. His hands, which had been fumbling with the bra, fell to his sides.

Rachel, her hands trembling, began to undo the buttons of her blouse.

I loosed my bosom above my stays and hoisted my skirts above my hips . . .

Once the top few were open, she brought her breasts out above her bra so they were trapped there on view and staring straight ahead. Then she slid her knickers down her ankles and kicked them away.

'Lie on the bed,' she ordered.

'Anything you say,' said Ian.

If excitement could be measured by breathing, its sound filled the room.

Her gaze went to the chest of drawers where Ian had got the underwear. Definitely not Marks and Spencer, she thought. Crisp white cotton would surely have been her mother's choice, she thought, not this sexy stuff.

The drawer was already open. Slowly, she reached out and touched the silky garments that were mostly in black but also in red. Satin and lace were cool beneath her hand. She took hold of a bra, pulled it out and held it before her eyes. It was an odd item, the cups cut away so the nipples were left exposed and vulnerable.

She turned and looked at Ian. His eyes were bright and she was sure he was only barely controlling an excited trembling.

'Your mother's got some lovely things,' said Ian.

Rachel looked at him. 'You seem to think so. Aren't mine just as good?'

'Sure,' he stammered. 'Sure, it's just that . . .'

'Do you fancy my mother?' Rachel blurted.

A hint of pink appeared on his cheeks. His gaze dropped to her breasts. 'She's a lovely woman,' he said.

'She is,' said Rachel. 'We'll stop talking about her. Mothers and sex don't mix, do they?'

He didn't answer. His gaze stayed fixed on her breasts as if afraid to meet her eyes.

Was it possible he was fantasising about her mother? The image of a slim, mature woman with silvery blonde hair and deep-set eyes fixed itself in her mind. Yes, she thought. As a woman, I suppose she is worth fantasising about. The revelation surprised her. But why should it? You're naive, she thought. Why shouldn't men – even men young enough to be her sons' – fantasise about her?

Wicked man. Naughty Ian. Well, she would certainly show him a thing or two! Just like Caroline Standish had done.

Smiling, she walked over to him and trailed the garment up and down his belly.

'You're going to be my whore,' she said to him.

His cock jerked against the thin material. 'I'll be anything you like, Rachel. Anything at all.'

'Good,' she said slowly. 'Now put your hands above your head, like a good little whore, and I will tie them together.'

He was putty in her hands. Of course he put them above his head, and of course she tied them there. She did the same with his ankles.

'Wow,' said Ian. 'If I'd known we were going to do this, I wouldn't have got dressed up.'

Rachel turned swiftly and glared at him. 'I don't want you to say things like that!'

Somehow, the sound of his voice tarnished the vision in her mind. It was difficult to put into words and she had no intention of trying, but she wanted Ian to know how it felt to be a woman being raped by more than one.

'Things like what?' He sounded amused and that wasn't a requirement either.

She got a pair of panties from the drawer. They were of red satin trimmed with matching lace.

'You putting them on?' he asked. He sounded excited – like a child at Christmas.

'No,' she said. 'You are.' With that, she stuffed them into his mouth leaving the satin crotch flapping over his chin like a long tongue.

He was not at all prepared for what he did next. After disappearing into her own old room, she brought back a long, greased plastic tube, a large doll with one leg and a five-foot-high foam sponge pink panther.

She pulled the panties down and hooked the elastic beneath his balls. Cock and balls bulged outwards and upwards.

151

With vivid enjoyment, she watched the amazement in his eyes as she slid his cock into the tight confines of the tube. Wonderful, she thought, what imagination could do, when she followed this action by lifting her skirt over the tube so it was hidden from view.

To all intents and purposes it was her fucking him, riding up and down, her breasts wobbling. The tube was cold against her but her clit didn't care. As if it had a mind of its own, it rose and made the most of it.

Through her skirt, she held the tube with both hands, jerking her hips against it and mewing with the first stirrings of pleasure.

What a sight, she thought as she eyed this man who was being raped by a plastic tube!

He struggled and amused her more. How could he not, lying there dressed in women's underwear – including a bra he couldn't fill. But the plastic tube was being filled and that was all that mattered.

'Hm,' murmured Rachel as she rubbed herself against the tube. 'I think this one's finished.'

She got off and when she came back, she was holding the doll in front of her. This time, she slid his prick into the hole where a leg should have been, held the doll in front of her and went on to jerk up and down as she had with the tube.

He squirmed against it, jerked his head from side to side and cried out unintelligible words against the red silk that filled his mouth.

Last came the sponge animal. Ian would not know, but she had cut a hole in its crotch. His prick fitted in easily and, like before, she began to move, except that this time she had eased a portion of the creature's tail into her body. Like the real thing, the appendage was firm but softly covered. Wonderful, she thought, and proceeded to thrust her hips and bounce up and down, the sponge animal bouncing with her and its tail eliciting the desired result from her saturated sex.

How convenient, when the time came, that the creature was absorbent.

Rachel cried out with glee and closed her eyes when she came. Because Ian was inert by virtue of his bonds, she seemed alone with her orgasm. She guessed he'd come but made no attempt to confirm the fact. No mess to clean up before leaving the house and going back to her flat.

Although he had ejaculated, Ian was a little quiet on the drive to her place and the food waiting to be cooked.

'What's up with you?' she asked.

'Nothing that a good fuck wouldn't cure,' he answered as they made their way from the street to the door to her place.

'You've just come. Be grateful,' she said as she swung the door open and left him to catch it.

'I would be,' he replied moodily, 'but isn't a guy supposed to put it into a woman?'

Chapter Nine

*I*an wanted to stay over later that night, but Rachel wouldn't let him. Firstly, she wanted to read more of the adventures of Caroline Standish. Secondly, she was still shocked to think her mother could even contemplate wearing the kind of clothes she had found in the drawer. Somehow, the fact that Ian seemed to enjoy silky fabric against his balls and the constriction of a bra about his chest didn't worry her.

However, in view of what seemed like adoration for her mother, she had to ask him one question before he left.

'Ian, did you know that I once caught my mother watching you peeing?'

His hand was already on the door handle. He looked at her, startled. 'No,' he said, once he'd cleared his throat.

Rachel smiled. 'She couldn't see anything much, mind you. You had your jeans on and your flies open. I think you just fired her imagination. Isn't that something?'

Again she saw a blush colouring his features.

'Yes,' he said. 'Yes. It is.'

Once he had gone, she stripped off and settled herself down in bed. The book was already on the bedside table and the sheets were cool against her naked body. Everything was ready for her to enjoy.

Then the telephone rang.

She eyed it speculatively. Surely not Ian begging her to let him come back in and stay the night?

She patted the book open at the page she wanted to resume reading, then picked up the phone.

It turned out to be Mark, her father.

'Hi, darling, just to let you know your mother's decided to stay on a while in Scotland and I've got to do a quick trip to Amsterdam. Is everything all right there?'

'Sure,' replied Rachel. 'I checked out the house. Nothing's out of order.'

Except the underwear, she thought. Should she tell him what she thought of her mother wearing such items? He was her father. She just couldn't bring herself to do it. Instead, the image of them playing games and having sex sprang like a new idea into her mind. Of course he would know if his wife wore sexy underwear. It was probably for his benefit and he must therefore approve of it.

'That's good. I wouldn't want to put you to any trouble. Neither would your mother.'

'It's no trouble. Business is business.'

'Business? Oh, your mother's finished with the business side of things. It's purely for pleasure. She wants to do some sightseeing. How's the research, by the way?'

155

She glanced at the yellow-edged pages of the open book before answering. 'Overall, some of Robert McKenzie's ancestors and contemporaries make interesting reading. I've learnt quite a lot I think.'

'That's good. When do you see him again?'

'Two days. I think he gets back from Scotland in two days. I shall see him then.'

She did not immediately go back to her book when she put the phone down. In two days, she would meet Robert McKenzie again, and this time she wanted to call the shots. But what sort of scenario would he be unable to resist? It would take some thinking about. In the meantime, she would read more of Caroline Standish. Perhaps she might give Rachel some ideas.

Robert McKenzie was surprised that Liz was unwilling to accept his invitation to stay a bit longer.

'But I thought we could play a few more games downstairs,' he said to her over breakfast, before Richard appeared. 'I'd like to keep you naked in that cage a while. Perhaps stretch you on that rack contraption and tickle you all over with a bunch of feathers, or run an ice cube over your nipples, then watch it melt between the lips of your cunt. Would you like that, Liz? Would you like that? I know I certainly would.'

Although the thought of him doing that made her wriggle deliciously in her chair, Liz gave him a forthright look. He was a good-looking guy, she'd give him that. But arrogant!

What was she thinking? They're all arrogant, aren't they? All of them seem to think they're doing you a real big favour and you should be grateful for them poking you.

'I'm not so playful, today. Besides, I want to do some sightseeing. I'm going to head up into the Highlands and find some little bed and breakfast place. I might even be lucky enough to find some little cottage – croft, I believe they call them – for rent.'

He blinked only once as her rebuff sank in. 'Leave when you wish,' he said eventually.

Richard, too, was surprised.

'But I thought we could have stopped off on the way back,' he began. 'I really fancied a fuck in the Highland heather.'

'Stop!' Liz held up her hand and looked from one to the other. 'We've had fun, very adult fun. But don't read anything into it that isn't there and don't think I'm going to do a repeat performance just to satisfy you. I satisfy myself. I'm mature enough not to get uptight about it.'

They didn't like it. She could see that. But just look at the glint in Robert's eyes, she thought. Obviously the contract for which she had come to Scotland for was in the bag. She had given him a memory to be cherished at some future time, when he was sitting in a rocking chair, alone with his memories.

'I can't order you to stay,' said McKenzie, so I won't. 'But there'll be other times. I shall make sure that there are. But don't say no too often. You might regret it.'

Oh, really, thought Liz, and hid her smile. Mc-Kenzie had reverted to being the laird he thought he was. Perhaps somewhere in the past there had been such a person. She wondered what Rachel had found out. All in the family, she thought and was comfortable with it.

Richard exited the dining hall with McKenzie. Both were returning to London.

'We'll take our leave,' said McKenzie. He paused and looked deep into her eyes. 'You've surprised me, but wait yet and I might surprise you.'

With that, they were both gone.

Unlike them, Mark was already aware of her plans. He had phoned her the night before to ask how she had enjoyed herself. She had told him about the dungeon.

'That's one of your favourites,' he said with a laugh. 'My, what a lucky girl. How was it? Did the men match the moment?'

'Never you mind.'

'Come on. Tell me.' His voice dropped an octave.

Liz licked her lips and cradled the receiver more closely, as if her husband might be nearer that way.

'What will you be doing while I'm telling you this?'

He laughed. 'I take your point. Give me a minute. I'll get her out of the bathroom and on to her knees. I'll sit on the edge of the bed. Will that suit you?'

'Only if you don't have your pants on.'

'I've got nothing on,' he returned. 'My balls will be resting on the bed, my cock will be hanging over the side. Just wait a minute.'

All went quiet on the other end. She covered her mouth with her hand as she imagined Mark calling his latest lover out of the bathroom and getting her on her hands and knees between his legs. Before she started telling him about what she'd experienced, his cock would already be in his mistress's mouth. Like Richard and any other male Liz came into contact with, the other woman would never know that the services she rendered were known to her lover's wife.

Mark came back on the phone.

'Can you repeat the details of the meeting?' he said.

She heard him sigh and knew he was ready. Every word would be couched in a businesslike manner.

'I did everything,' she began. 'I was half-naked and slippery with my own juice and a surfeit of vegetable oil they'd fetched from the kitchen. The chains were cold and heavy but worthwhile. I almost felt I could have eaten each of those men, opened my legs and swallowed them whole.'

'A big task,' he said. 'Were all your dealings up front or were some behind –' he paused for effect, also to sigh because his mistress was doing a reasonable job on him '– behind the scenes,' he said.

She knew exactly what he meant. 'Each and every hole, darling. You know how tight my arse is. That's what the oil was for, to get me ready for their intrusion.'

'I shouldn't think you had need of that,' he laughed. 'You're very experienced in that particular field.'

He stifled a groan of pleasure, under the pretence of clearing his throat. The mistress would think this was to protect her presence. In fact, it was to protect the fact that his wife was turning him on and she was merely an accessory to the fact.

'They played their parts well. I enjoyed what they did. I was the imprisoned lady and they were

159

the evil laird and his wicked jailer. The latter was useful when it came to fetching things from the kitchen. You know Richard. When he's sober, he's great. After a few whiskies, he's not always up to scratch.'

'Vegetarian food at the meeting?'

'The usual root vegetables, hard and well grown.'

'Yes. I can see another meeting might be quite advantageous. Their performance might very well improve. Is another similar conference likely to occur?'

'I wasn't going to stay here for that. I thought I'd do some sightseeing while I'm up here. There is so much I haven't seen, unexplored places of interest I would like to examine further. I think the subjects might benefit from my mature experience. Young men with hard muscles, lusty bodies and wearing skirts!'

There was no need to tell him too much more. She was familiar with his voice and familiar with his sexual performance. He had come and the woman with him had reaped the benefit of it – with his wife's help, of course.

Anyone who saw her would say she was in no hurry to leave. The white satin robe she wore reached her ankles. Its touch was cool against her flesh. Her nipples jutted into it. An expectant tingle ran over her body. There was something she had to do before she left: something she was looking forward to.

When the knock came at the door, she was looking out of the window to the parkland and the mauve hills beyond.

She turned, ran her fingers through her hair, then

opened her robe a little more to show the inside curve of her breasts.

'Come in,' she said.

The door creaked and James entered. 'When do you want me to take your bags, madam?'

She smiled at the innocence of James Campbell, the young gillie who worked on the estate during the day but waited on table at night.

His voice was deep, surprising for one so young. There was something seductive about his phrasing. He could just as well have asked her if she wanted him to remove her underwear, though at present she wasn't wearing any.

Today he was wearing corduroys, leather boots and a flecked fisherman's sweater. At night, he wore a kilt that swung like a series of waves around his hips.

A beam of sunlight filtering through one of the high, leaded panes touched his hair and turned the red mane to gold.

Liz smiled and approached him. 'Would it be that inconvenient if I stayed a wee while longer?'

She fancied she saw a blush steal across his youthful features. 'Sure, no, madam.'

'And would you be willing to wait on a woman alone tonight at dinner?'

'It would be a pleasure.'

She smiled and nodded appreciatively. Yes. It very well could be a pleasure, much more so than he could imagine. With obvious purpose, she used both hands to sweep her hair back from her face. Her robe fell open, almost fully revealing her breasts.

'And in the meantime, I will build up my appetite,' she said. 'Where would you suggest I walk?'

His mouth dropped open. His gaze stayed firmly fixed on her breasts. It was almost a surprise to her when he found his voice.

'To the village, perhaps?'

She looked towards the window then walked slowly towards it, her breasts still half exposed.

'What about those hills? Could I walk there?'

He hesitated before answering. She could almost feel his desire reaching out to her, like unseen hands aching to rip off her robe.

And once it was ripped off, his rough, strong hands would squeeze her breasts and his muscular thigh would force her legs apart.

'The hills are a fair way, but I could drive you up there, if that would suit.'

She turned quickly and caught him unawares. His eyes were fixed on her buttocks; their shape was easily seen through the gleaming white satin.

'I think that would be a good idea,' she said smiling.

It was no big deal to persuade him to join her.

'It's pretty up here,' he said, nodding towards a steep path that led up through pine and thick gorse.

It was her lust that forced her to agree. By the time she got to the top, she was breathless, but the view compensated. So did the company. It was a turn-on to see his chest heaving and it was hard not to reach out and touch his pink cheeks. But she did not wish to frighten him off. On their walk up, he had done most of the talking, telling her about the scenery they passed and what the birds were flying high above them. She had been content with that, partly because she wasn't used to steep climbs and partly because fixing her eyes on his buttocks as he climbed the high path brought her great pleasure. The landscape was secondary.

'Do you not think it's beautiful?' he said.

'Well worth the climb.' It was difficult to say more than that. She was still catching her breath. 'Warm work,' she added. 'But a great view.'

He grinned. She fancied he knew what she meant. 'Then I'll take you on down,' he said. 'There's the path. There's a pool at the bottom.'

There was indeed a pool and, unseen from above, a waterfall gushing into it.

'I swim here,' he said. 'Each time I come here I feel the same. I can't resist.'

She tossed her hair away from her face and smiled up at him. 'Then give in to temptation.'

He raised his eyebrows questioningly. 'Are you tempted too?'

She echoed his look but with a hint of sheer wickedness. 'Oh yes! Very often.'

She caught that bashful look again. He was shy but she knew instinctively that he was interested. Just as with Ian, she was flattered that a younger man was responding to her presence, perhaps even imagining what it would be like to lie naked against her full breasts, her firm, ripe belly.

'Then I suppose we might just as well give in to temptation,' he said and looked directly at the water as he said it. But the meaning was there. She knew he was willing and she was feeling hot.

'OK,' she said.

She peeled off the red sweater. Her bra was black.

He glanced then took off his sweater and the T-shirt he wore beneath it.

It was hard not to stare so she didn't bother to refrain from doing so.

His body was just as firm as she'd expected. His chest was hairless. Although sweating slightly the smell of his body drew her to him.

He turned his broad back to her and stood looking at the greenish pool and the tumbling white waterfall.

Even without touching him, she knew how hard he would feel. The yearning to run her hands over the thickly muscled shoulderblades, the knotted curves of his spine, was hard to resist. She wanted to kiss those broad shoulders and run her hands over every inch of him. The thought of exploring his body and seducing his youth was too beautiful to ignore. Paradise, she thought, was a place where virile youthful angels like him pleasured languid, jaded women like her.

Carefully, she trod the slippery rocks, drawn on by the sight of his back, and the heady mix of masculine scent, natural surroundings and the erotic fantasies provided by her mind. He filled her eyes. She had to touch him. He was so young. So beautiful.

Hardly daring, yet not being able to resist, she reached out.

He started and turned round in amazement.

His trousers were undone. Her eyes dropped to the thin line of hair that disappeared into his underwear.

'I'm sorry,' she said breathlessly. 'I just had to touch you.'

He blinked. She could see his tongue moving over his pearl-white teeth as if he were searching for the right words to say. Would he reject her, or would he take advantage of the situation and the mature woman standing before him?

What do you do? she asked herself. Keep apologising and lose this chance? Or do you throw caution to the wind and become the femme fatale who ensnares men with the promise of heaven she holds in her eyes?

'There's no need to be sorry,' he said at last.

Those were the words she'd been waiting for. She stepped forward, her heart fluttering, and her blood hot in her veins.

You're mine, she thought as she ran her hand down his chest. His body tensed beneath her touch. His breathing quickened. Her fingers slid into his underwear. She sighed when she reached the throbbing warmth of his cock. It leapt into her hand.

How quickly youth could rise to the occasion she thought. And how hard it was, how full of the first thrusting curiosity with which only a youthful prick was endowed. The feel of it almost made her want to growl with delight. Lengthways and widthways, it would fill her. Hard as iron, it would press against the soft flesh of her inner passage. And she would cling on to it. Her muscles would tighten in their desire to keep him thrusting and filling. In a way, she would be taking his youth, sapping his energy. The ache of anticipation was too much to bear. If only she had never discovered Ian and her effect on him. Perhaps then, she would not have to suffer this longing. But it's life, she told herself. It's the throbbing, thrusting urge of life and you cannot deny it. Have his body. Have him fuck you and have any other young man you come across do the same.

She voiced her feelings. 'A thing of beauty is a joy for . . . every woman of sophisticated taste.'

Clever wording, she thought, then changed her mind as a hint of guilt drifted into his eyes. Perhaps sophisticated was the wrong word. It was a mature word, a connotation connected more with her generation than his. Oh, God! Why had she said that? Don't panic. For God's sake, don't panic!

The fear of rejection made her think quickly. How to keep him interested. How to keep him hard. A list of possibilities ran through her mind. Massage his ego. Tell him he's handsome tell him he's strong. One term of flattery above all others sprang to mind.

'You have a very large cock,' she said looking purposefully into his eyes, then lowering it to his proud, lengthy erection. 'In fact, I think it's the best I've ever seen. Will you let me stroke it? Will you let me look at it more closely?'

Any misgivings he might have had swiftly seemed to dissipate. She knew men; she knew all the signs.

You've hit the mark! Now there was pride. Didn't every man want the biggest and best? Didn't they all want to be a stallion?

'Do you really want to do that?' he asked.

She looked deep into his eyes as she gripped his cock. 'I want to worship it. I want to pay homage to its length with my lips. I want to feel the weight of your balls on my tongue. I want to lick the head of your cock until it's shiny with my spit.'

His eyes opened wide. His lips parted and he nodded slowly. 'I see,' he said. 'Well if that's what you really want, lass, then so be it.'

And that indeed was how she wanted it. That

indeed was how she was feeling. With a young, beautiful man, there was no need for fantasies, dungeons, outrageous characters and dangerous situations. The urge to touch him and worship his youth and his looks overrode any need for dramatic scenarios.

She shivered, raised her gaze from his cock and looked into his eyes. This was a moment to be savoured.

'That's what I want,' she said softly. 'But let's not rush things. Do you want to swim first?'

He paused and looked at her with a hint of wonder before nodding. As he looked, she stripped off her clothes. She did it slowly. Each item was peeled away and dropped with slow purpose. That, she reasoned, was the right way to do things. Take clothes off languorously, so as to heighten the anticipation of the one watching, the one you intend seducing.

The air was chill upon her naked flesh. The breeze kissed her nipples and ruffled her pubic hair. A few stray leaves fluttered across her stomach and tufts of wild corn whipped at her calves.

James licked his lips. Even if he had not done that she could have read his thoughts. Remaining clothes were discarded. Like Adam in a chill, Scottish Eden, he was naked before her.

Suddenly she felt weak. Something deep inside screamed, I want him at any price, in any way, in any place!

Desire, so familiar, yet so exciting, spread over her body. At times, the ecstatic tingles felt as though they were just beneath the surface of her skin. At other times, they were like a crisp sugar coating, clinging to her breasts and her belly.

Desire had also taken hold of the young man with her. No matter who she was, what she was, his cock pulsed ferociously. As if, she thought, it is so full of desire, it has every intention of leaving his body, and embedding itself in this one.

The time had come. Swim first. Sex after.

As she held her hands slightly behind her, she smiled at him.

'Are you ready for this?'

His red hair blew around his face. 'Yes.' He said it in a breathless hush, so the word itself was almost lost on the breeze.

Naked, they both dived in. Liz gasped. The water was cold enough to take her breath away but became warmer, the more she swam.

He swam beside her, his strong legs kicking. He passed her with considerable ease and reached the other side of the pool before she did.

When she caught up with him, he had hauled himself up on to a rocky ledge and was sitting there, with his feet dangling in the water. Despite the chill of the water his body was flushed.

She eyed him on her approach and swam more slowly.

What do I do now? she thought. How do I maintain his interest and ensure I have the full benefit of his erection?

Her hair was wet now and plastered to her head. The water she swam in caressed her body. She might have felt cold but was too busy judging him; assessing what she should do next occupied her mind.

My young Adonis, she thought, and smiled at him above the rippling water.

He was looking at her, his hands folded sedately over his private parts.

Private! What a quaint term that was. And wasn't it amusing, she thought, that younger men were more inclined to hide their assets than older men? She remembered that Ian had done exactly the same thing when she had first attempted seduction.

Thinking of her daughter's boyfriend added something to the occasion. First moments with a new man always did. First kiss, first fondle, first fuck.

It was his youth that inspired you, she told herself. You wanted him and the memories that came with it. In your youth, your sex-drive was far more intense than it is now. Fantasies were unnecessary. Playing games the same. Thinking back, even the smallest thing was enough to turn you on. Remember the first kiss? The first holding of hands? The first grope in a dark and lonely place, when neither of you could stop yourselves and both of you longed to know what it would be like to feel what the other one had? And that ripe moistness that occurred between your legs, remember that? How wet you were. How curious you were to know how it would feel to have his prick inside you and his hands rolling your breasts.

Prick. The word itself had made her wonder. Greek gods, goddesses and the myths she had learnt as a child came back to her. Pan had been the horny, hoofed god of fertility and all things sexual. He had also been called Priapus, thence any male organ of large size was priapic – prick. And cock – stiff, strutting, upright, and dominant.

Neither might not have been the true explanation, but it suited her.

She saw him looking at her and dived beneath the water, her rear breaking the surface behind her. The memories went with her.

When she surfaced, his hands had moved to either side of him and he was looking a little worried. Obviously, she'd been under quite a while. But she always had been able to hold her breath. It was a skill that came in useful in certain circumstances. Who was it said that the worst thing about oral sex was the view? His hands shot back to where they had been before.

Shit! That was the last thing she wanted. Again, she dived beneath the surface; but this time, when she came up, it was between his knees.

He gasped.

'I've come to take a closer look,' she said, her hair flattened against her head.

As she rose higher between his legs, he moved his hands. He rested them behind him and leant back.

His cock was wet and cold but his erection had not diminished.

'Such a pretty thing,' she said as she wrapped both hands around it. She heard a sharp intake of breath. 'My hands are cold. I'm sorry. But don't worry. Mouth to cock resuscitation might be a good idea, don't you think?'

'I can't believe –'

She didn't give him time to comment. Her mouth closed over his flesh. She closed her eyes. It was better like that. She could smell his pubic hair but not see it. Not that she disliked the view. On the contrary, she quite enjoyed studying the frizzy locks that curled so close to the body.

She took him in. His crown nudged against the back of her throat. She didn't gag. Long as it was, broad as it was, she mustn't do that if she was to enjoy this experience to the full. He was young and highly impressionable. She had no wish to put him off such a delicious pastime as this.

She pushed on his stomach. With a groan, he lay back on the soaking rock. There was no longer a man beneath her. There was merely an appendage that represented pleasure and life itself. Perhaps because of its smell, its taste, its strength, she was overcome by the urge to cram the whole thing into her mouth: cock, balls and all. It was as if she wanted to eat it, as if she could only truly worship it by taking it into herself, by making it part of her. Of course, her mouth was too small and his organ too big to do such a thing.

Moans of ecstasy mixed with the sound of the crashing water. I want to hear more, she wanted to scream. I want to hear you cry out that what I am doing is good, that experience shows, that you will always remember this day.

But his moans were enough to tell her all was well. The kissing and fondling continued. His flesh was sweet on her tongue. She sucked and licked it and around it: his belly, his thighs, even the narrow slit behind his balls. She opened her eyes, cupped the whole object, and pulled it.

She feasted her eyes upon it, rubbed her nose around it, and swiped it over her cheeks and under her chin. She trapped it between her breasts and sucked on it, as if it were a third teat.

My, but youth is so sweet, she thought. I could

eat it forever. It is my new interest – no, fetish. I want to change boys into men. I want to be remembered by them for the rest of their lives.

And all the while he moaned, this red-headed Adonis who lay at her command while she sucked on him, adored him and pleasured herself because she was pleasuring him.

And all around the waters crashed and the shadows of dappled sunlight played through the sparkling water.

When she sensed he was too far gone to refuse her, she heaved herself out of the water, sat astride him and lowered herself on to his upright cock.

Purposefully, she rested her hands on his chest and leant forward. Her breasts swung before his eyes. He would not be able to resist them. Just as she had planned, his hands folded over them. His penis slid into her body and she sighed long and low until her pubic hairs were matted with his.

He dressed in the kilt for dinner. She got out a neat black dress, the typically classic item that never fails to impress on any occasion.

On this occasion, she wore sheer black stockings, shoes with high gilt heels and a gold collar around her throat. Her underwear was purple satin, a great favourite with her and her lovers.

Perfume had been applied in all those places she wanted him to sniff: under her arms, behind her ears, down her throat, between her breasts, down her spine, between her buttocks and down each inner thigh. His nose would follow. So would his lips. Then his tongue, his hands, his body and that staunchly erect obelisk that lurked between his legs.

She sat alone at the table. Its polished surface reflected the light from the iron-framed chandeliers hanging above her.

He served the soup. His hand shook slightly as she touched his knee.

'Nice to see you are dressed in a traditional fashion, this evening,' she said as she smiled up at him.

'Entirely traditional,' he said, without meeting her eyes.

When he served the next course, she explored the territory above his knee. His thigh was firm. Her stomach tightened and she clenched her thighs.

'I have to know,' she said as he served the dessert.

She looked into his eyes. He looked down at her.

'Madam?'

She smiled. Despite his feigned ignorance, he knew full well what she meant. She could tell. 'Underwear. Are you wearing underwear?'

'I told you, madam. I am dressed entirely in the traditional manner of any real Highlander.'

They held each other's gaze. She raised her hand higher. Her fingers touched his balls. Delicious! They hung warm and bare, except for a covering of peach-like hair.

'Would you like dessert, madam?'

She smiled at him but did not answer. Just as she'd hoped, he put the dish down on the table.

'All mine,' Liz said and saw the excitement in his eyes.

She lifted his skirt. There was something extremely arousing at seeing bare balls hanging above bare legs, rather than having a cock peer out from between the zip of a pair of trousers.

Liz was transfixed. 'A sight for sore eyes,' she murmured and dropped the skirt over her head.

The taste of what she had eaten mixed with the taste of him. She wrapped her arms around his thighs, hugging him tightly to her, burying his cock in her mouth and her face in his pubic hair. She clutched at his buttocks. She dug her fingers between them, pulled them apart, squeezed them and ran her hands down to pull his balls back towards his arse.

The kilt hid her from the outside world and hid the outside world from her. Nothing else existed. Nothing else mattered. But it didn't last.

'Mrs Carr, you are a liar!'

She froze. McKenzie was back! The kilt drifted down over her face as James retreated. Her hair was left in wispy disarray over her face.

She brushed it back, then looked to where Robert McKenzie stood in the open doorway. Richard stood just behind him.

They walked slowly towards the dining table. Liz was only vaguely aware of James slinking back into the shadows.

McKenzie and Richard looked directly at her. The former looked furious; the latter was merely flushed with excitement.

'You said you were leaving, Mrs Carr. Yet you've taken further advantage of my hospitality, when you specifically stated you were going off sightseeing.' He glanced deliberately at James. 'I think I know the sort of Scottish sights in which your interest lies.'

When excuses won't work, tell the truth. That's what she told herself. Besides, she had no option. With an air of casual indifference, she got to her feet and again smoothed her hair away from her face.

'OK. I admit it. I fancied a young stud. Do you have some problem with that? If it's OK for you guys to fancy younger women, then the reverse is true, surely?'

'Come on, Liz,' said Richard. 'This was a business arrangement. That young man over there is not part of the deal.'

'Besides which,' said McKenzie, 'you have taken advantage of my hospitality. If I were an hotelier, I would charge you a suitable rate for bed and board.'

'OK. Then charge me. Will Visa do?' She reached for the small black bead bag she'd brought downstairs with her. Of course, her credit cards and such like were not in it, but she was merely trying to prove a point. Everything had a price.

McKenzie looked at her thoughtfully and nodded. 'OK,' he said slowly. 'I'll buy that. You can pay. But I don't want money, Liz. I want your body. I want you to be my plaything for a little while longer.'

Somehow I knew that, she thought. Oh, well. So be it.

She adopted the sexiest pose possible, one hand resting on the table, one on her hip. Everyone's body looked good in that pose.

'Sex? So that's what you want.' She said it casually as though she paid for everything that way.

'In a way,' said McKenzie. 'But, be in no doubt, I want you to feel demeaned by the tasks I set you. I want you to feel used.'

She wondered what he meant. What deviation could possibly demean her that much?

Richard licked his lips and glanced quickly between her and McKenzie. His enthusiasm for another session in the old dungeon was no big surprise and it didn't worry her. What the hell? It was fun and games time and if James wanted to join in as well, three men were better than two and much better than one.

McKenzie looked her up and down. It made her feel uncomfortable. Somehow she knew things were not going to work out quite how she wanted. What sort of games did he have in mind?

'Do what anyone has to do if they haven't got the wherewithal to pay the bill. Wash the dishes.'

No, she thought. Not that! Not domesticity, for God's sake.

'Go to hell!' she screamed.

McKenzie turned away. 'That could be a mistake, Mrs Carr. After all, I'm only exacting my dues.'

A worried-looking Richard stepped forward. His voice was low. 'Look, Liz. You've got to go along with this. Remember what we're here for.' He caught her accusing glare and blinked. 'What we're really here for.'

A sex orgy would have been far more agreeable. But dishes? She hadn't done them for years.

No way!

She folded her arms and tossed her head. 'Doesn't this place have an automatic dishwasher?'

'Yes,' McKenzie replied. 'You.'

Her eyes were full of fire, her face warm with anger. 'I don't want to do this.'

Panic entered Richard's eyes and he frowned. He seemed about to say something, then looked at McKenzie, as if awaiting his permission. His mouth stayed shut.

McKenzie stepped close to her. She smelt his hair. His breath was warm on her cheek.

'I think you might enjoy it,' he whispered.

She looked into his eyes. They glittered.

She glanced at Richard and James. Richard was frowning. James looked openly curious. Neither, she realised, had heard what had been said.

McKenzie's mouth stayed close to her ear. 'Please. I want you to do this. Please. Do it for me.'

There was no mistaking the pleading in his voice. So far, he had given no reason as to why he had returned. Now he didn't need to. She knew why. He had seen her eyeing James. No opportunity had arisen for her to seduce him. He had guessed she would stay. And he had wanted her to stay. Although he did not show it, he had been deeply affected by what had happened in the dungeon. In that scenario, he had acted at being the master. In actuality, she had mastered him. He was back for a replay, but this time in the kitchen.

From the business standpoint also, she knew she had to give in. That particular fact was written all over Richard's face. Chances were, she might not have a job if she didn't go along with this. But Richard was not perceptive enough to know how deeply she had affected McKenzie.

The menial task assigned to her now took on a different perspective.

'OK,' she said shaking her head as she prepared to fit into the part. 'But I warn you, washing dishes isn't exactly my field of experience.'

'Right,' said McKenzie turning back round to face her. 'Let's all go down to the kitchen and get this set up. James, you collect these dishes and bring them down with you.'

The men led the way. She was forced to follow on like some lowly servant.

The kitchen was Dickensian. There was a high dresser running the entire length of one wall. Three sinks, all deep and all manufactured from glazed china clay, lined one wall. The taps were made of brass and a range of copper cooking pots hung from a row of iron bars above a large pine table that stood on a flagstone floor. An Aga warmed the kitchen from the alcove of a bricked-up fireplace.

'Where's Little Nell?' sniffed Liz.

McKenzie raised a quizzical eyebrow. 'Who?'

'She means it looks like something from Dickens,' Richard explained.

McKenzie smiled. 'I don't think any Victorian novelist could ever imagine the sort of scenes this kitchen is about to play host to.'

'Hm!' Liz exclaimed defiantly and turned away. She hid her smile behind her hand.

James came in just then with the dishes from upstairs and put them on the draining board, a large wooden affair that had been scrubbed to a mellow honey colour over a number of years.

McKenzie addressed James. 'Mrs Carr is at present improperly dressed for washing dishes.'

They all eyed the slinky black number she was wearing.

'There are overalls in the cupboard,' said James.

McKenzie's look was enough. The young man opened the door and retrieved a ghastly pink and white checked overall. He offered it to McKenzie.

'Not to me. Give it to her.' He nodded at Liz.

James handed it to her.

With a sigh, she started to pull it on over her dress.

McKenzie grabbed her wrist. 'Just the overall. Take the rest off.'

'All of it?'

'All of it.'

Although a shiver of excitement ran down her spine, she tried not to let it show on her face. Instead, she slipped out of her dress. Richard took it from her and draped it over his arm. Goosebumps broke out all over her body as she stood there, wearing nothing but the flimsiest of midnight blue underwear.

'All of it,' said McKenzie, just as she attempted to get the overall over her head.

The request was something of a surprise. She had thought he would want her to keep her underwear. It was exactly the sort most men liked. The cups were cut low; the panties were no more than a strip of lace at the rear and a triangle at the front. Most men would have considered her suspender belt and the stockings they held up to be a big turn-on. McKenzie obviously preferred flesh to be unfettered by decoration. OK, if that was what he wanted. The bra was discarded; so were the knickers. She was just about to unhitch the suspender belt when –

'Not that. Leave that on.'

Her hair fell forward and hid her smile as she hitched the hook back into the eye. He'd just proved her point. Men were predictable.

The overall was of a cotton polyester mix and cool against her skin. She kept on her shoes.

Sex scenes in kitchens had never featured very strongly in her fantasies or her games. There had always been something too domestic about such a scene: something allied to the submissive role expected of women in the past. But her instinct was to go along with the game. He had almost pleaded with her to play. Judging by that and the look in his eyes, he was also making her a promise. Trust me. I'm sure you'll enjoy it. Let your imagination run free. Forget the surroundings. Forget domesticity.

But still she seethed. I'm the servant, she thought. He wants to make me squirm. He wants me to be submissive. All right. I'll go along with it, for now. My career depends on it. All I can do is get as much pleasure out of it as I can.

But I will still want revenge, she thought, and at some stage the right opportunity will arise.

Lust and apprehension mixed together inside her. Don't show it, she warned herself, but it wasn't easy.

Play your part. That's the best way to control what you are feeling.

'Let's make a start,' she said. Warm water trickled from the brass tap optimistically marked HOT in blue lettering on white china.

She could almost feel McKenzie's energy, Richard's excitement and the amazement of the young, beguiling James.

Ah! James, she thought. I was truly looking forward to having you to myself. But sadly, you must be part of the team. You must take your turn, but you are the one whom I shall favour above all the others. Just thinking about how his body had felt against hers would give her the strength to get her through this.

The sink filled. She piled the dishes to her right and added the suds. Because of her heels, she had to stoop slightly.

McKenzie came up behind her. He forced his leg between hers.

'If you stand with your legs wide open, you won't have to stoop.'

She did as instructed. It was a logical move. Keep the woman occupied and available. What a marvellous combination! Now she had to add her own contribution to sexual arousal.

'Excuse me while I test the water before putting the dishes in,' she said.

She heard a gasp – probably James, she thought – as she undid the top buttons of her overall, exposed her breasts and dipped them in the warm, sudsy water.

'Help her, James,' said McKenzie.

'What do I . . .?'

'Use your imagination,' said McKenzie. 'Start washing. Enjoy them, and I don't mean the dishes!'

This was better than she could have hoped for. Out of the corner of her eye, she saw James rolling up his shirtsleeves. Suds and fingers covered her breasts. She eased herself out of the water and saw they were shiny, globules dropping from her nipples and back into the water.

'They still look dirty,' she heard McKenzie say. Somehow she had known he was going to say that. She was aware of James hesitating, so turned her head slightly and looked into his eyes. Then she directed her gaze to the nylon brush lying on the edge of the sink. He picked it up.

'Are you sure?' He sounded afraid.

She could say nothing to reassure him. In a situation like this, for her to speak would break the spell. He had to play his part. She had to play hers.

'Get on with it,' said McKenzie.

Richard said, 'Do you think I could . . .?'

Liz did not hear the rest of what he said. If she were to retreat into herself and enjoy this, as she should, then the rest of the world must go away. She felt a hand on the back of her neck and she was pushed forward. She gasped as her breasts were again submerged in the water before she was raised again, her breasts again dripping with suds.

'Scrub her,' said McKenzie.

James hesitated then began to run the brush over her breasts, between them, under them and around her nipples.

She moaned. It wasn't unpleasant. The bristles of the brush left a tingling sensation. On contact with her nipples, the sensations were more intense. Some might have thought that the use of any sort of implement and any sort of sexual game was perverse. But sex was eighty per cent pleasure and twenty per cent procreation. No, she thought. Ninety-nine per cent pleasure, one per cent procreation. Sex was fun. Sex was games between consenting adults – and that didn't necessarily mean just a pair of people. Group sex and group games had their advantages.

The sudden sound of chairs being scraped across the stone floor intruded into her thoughts. What did McKenzie want to do next?

'James. Come here. Liz, stay where you are.'

She heard them whispering. Half of her wanted to spin round and confront them, ask them what the bloody hell they were whispering about and why wasn't she included? The other half was aching to know what sexual exploit was now in store. Perhaps they would lay her out on the table and garnish her body with food; cream on her breasts, jam on her belly, and a very large banana firmly wedged –

Or perhaps they would tie her wrists to the overhead pan rack, lift up her overall and smack her bare behind with a selection of kitchen instruments. The flat head of a spatula would feel good, she thought. A wooden spoon shouldn't be too bad. They'd already done the root vegetable thing and, if nothing else, McKenzie was a man of some imagination.

What she hadn't expected was the order McKenzie gave her.

'Scrub the floor,' he said. 'We'll be back in fifteen minutes, so make sure you're on your hands and knees.'

With a whirl of naked breasts and soapsuds, she turned from the sink. The door slammed. She heard the key turn in the lock. She stared at the door for what seemed like a full minute. Then she turned to the sink, grabbed the nylon dish-brush and flung it at the door.

'Like hell I will!'

They'd taken her clothes so she couldn't put them back on. But she rebuttoned the overall and seethed.

Well, if they thought she was going to skivvy around while they were upstairs enjoying themselves . . .

She sat on one of the chairs she had heard them drag out into the middle of the floor. She was still sitting there when they got back. Eyes glaring, she sprang from the chair and turned to face them.

'If you thought I was going to –'

Then she stopped. McKenzie and Richard were exactly as before. But James was naked, his youthfully muscled body gleaming with the application of oil. His eyes, too, shone. Probably, she thought with the application of malt whisky.

'You haven't scrubbed the floor,' said McKenzie with an amused grin. 'There's no reward, either monetary or in kind, if the servants do not obey their master.'

She hardly heard him. Her eyes were fixed on the beautiful young man. Desire had rushed headlong to hang like lead between her thighs. My clit weighs a ton, she thought, and if I don't have that guy in every way possible, I'm pretty sure it will burst.

'Get on with it, Liz,' said Richard. 'Or you won't get the bonus we've prepared for you.' His eyes were glittering with excitement. He sat himself down next to McKenzie on one of the two chairs in the middle of the room. James stood between them, his cock erect, his lips smiling and his eyes looking straight into hers.

Like a zombie, she filled a bucket and found a scrubbing brush. She dropped to her hands and knees, knowing she would do anything they asked, as long as she could have James.

She hadn't done much before Richard got up from his chair and stood behind her. She felt a draught as he lifted the hem of her overall with the toe of his shoe.

'Don't stop scrubbing,' he said. He folded it up to her waist and fixed it with clothes pegs, but only after he'd pinched her bottom with one or two of them.

Her anger lessened as his fingers slid between her legs. Her juices flowed. For the first time since she and Mark had decided to free up their sex lives, she felt used and no longer in control. She wanted James. They knew she wanted James and they would enjoy dangling this particular carrot. And carrot, she thought, was the right word.

Richard ripped open the top of the overall, rolled the material away from her breasts and pegged it back. She felt exposed. She felt vulnerable. It occurred to her to get up and refuse to do anything else. But James was involved. What were their intentions? She could guess – and if she was right, then she couldn't possibly leave. Her yearning to possess the young man was hard to resist. Obviously, their actions so far were designed to arouse James as much as her. They were setting the stage for an outstanding performance. She and James were the performers. McKenzie and Richard were the spectators.

It wasn't difficult to imagine how her appearance would affect a virile young man. The overall, like the suspender belt and stockings, was a trinket to adorn her body. She was like a sacrifice being offered to him. He was a sacrifice being offered to her. All right, she thought, I'll go along with it – for now.

They all watched a while. Richard, sounding full of whisky-induced bravado, asked James how he liked the view.

James almost choked on his words. 'I've never . . . I really want to . . .'

'I think you should,' said McKenzie.

Just as expected, Richard came to her side and got her to her feet. He took the overall from her.

'Lie on the table,' he said, then with a grin, added, 'feet towards us.'

Now she knew what the chairs were for. The

dirty little sods were going to watch James put it in her. And after watching that, they would be so aroused they would want to do the same themselves.

She glanced quickly at James. My, but his cock was standing proud. She lay out on the kitchen table, knees bent, legs wide, her feet resting on the corners. James came and stood between her legs. Richard took his place immediately behind him in the chair beside McKenzie. From there, they would have a great view of balls slapping against her slippery flesh.

She arched her back as James put it in. He leant over her, his eyes bright. His hands groped for her breasts, his lips kissed her mouth. In a straight-forward sexual game, she would not have allowed that. But in this instance, she did. As their bodies blended together, it was almost possible to believe they were alone rutting, groaning, thrusting and groping.

She stroked his back, felt him shiver. She dug her fingernails into his buttocks and felt the muscles tense. Like her, he continuously closed and opened his eyes, as if he too wanted to forget that two more men, both business colleagues, were sitting watching them fuck.

Well, let them watch, she thought. Let them feel their cocks getting harder in their pants. Let them imagine what James was feeling. Let them antici-pate getting into me themselves.

There was a beauty in their fucking. If two souls became one when people fell in love, then surely two bodies could become one when they fucked? Each, by instinct, moved to elicit the best from the

186

other but also to give of the best. A fair exchange, she thought.

Not once did she glance at Richard or McKenzie. She didn't want to see their lascivious looks, their tongues drooling around their mouths as they gazed at the coupling they felt they had orchestrated. Their cocks would be big with anticipation by now. James was tensing, his thrusts intensifying. Something between her legs was coiling like a spring, as though all her nerve ends were twisting into tight knots.

I'm flying, she cried within as the tight knots exploded and reverberated up over her belly.

I'm coming, I'm coming, I'm coming . . .

James's hair fell forward. He closed his eyes and tensed his body. The final thrust came. The last gasps of orgasm raced on his breath. His chest stiffened then heaved, as if with endless pain.

Then his face softened, his whole body relaxed, and he took deep breaths. There were no more thrusts, no more pounding against her juicy wet sex, she had had him again and he had had her.

She stroked his damp hair away from his forehead and smiled up into his face. 'That was beautiful,' she said and kissed his lips.

'I didn't think I could do it,' he said. His eyes indicated the two behind him who had now got up from their chairs and were already unzipping their flies. 'I've never had an audience before.'

'They're of no consequence now. We've done what we wanted to do,' she said softly and jerked her head towards the other two. 'But these guys are not going to be so lucky.' She winked.

James straightened. She got up. Richard reached to push her back down. She pushed him away.

McKenzie prepared himself to take the place of James. Liz kicked and caught him straight in the chest.

'Show's over. Get lost.'

He went sprawling.

'I don't understand!' cried McKenzie.

By the look on his face, she judged he really did not understand. It wasn't so much that he looked physically hurt. Wounded pride would be a better description.

'I choose the time and the place *and* the partner.' She almost spat the words. 'You two are like leeches. You sucked on us. You set us up and used us to get it up hard in your pants. Well, fine, Mr McKenzie; you too, Richard. But now you've got these hard-ons, you damn well go fuck yourself!'

'Liz! You can't say that!' cried a shocked Richard.

Liz slid her feet to the floor. 'I can damn well say what I like. I've had what I want. So has James. You two can take care of yourselves. How about getting off with each other?'

'Liz, you know I'm not that sort of person,' stuttered a reddening Richard.

'Don't knock it till you try it,' she snapped as she grabbed the clothes they had brought back down with them.

She turned to James. 'I'm getting out of here. Fancy a ride?'

He glanced at the winded McKenzie and the blushing Richard and, realising there was no future left with those two, he nodded.

'Then come on.'

'Liz! Please! We're soul-mates. I know we are! You like the things we do. I can see it in your eyes.

Don't deny it. Please, Liz. Don't leave. Come on; you're as decadent as we are!'

McKenzie sounded desperate. It surprised her.

But what he had said had hit a raw nerve. To some extent, he was right, but she certainly didn't want to feel so vulnerable and controlled as she had tonight. She'd been used. James had been used. And she did not approve.

Richard added his weight. 'Liz, there won't be a job for you when you get back if you walk out now.'

Trust Richard to use economic blackmail.

She spun round and glared at him. 'Go stuff your job. You're a boring man, Richard, and you run a boring company. We had some good sex, at times – but at others, we didn't. I'm out of here.'

She could see it was she who had now hit a raw nerve. No man liked to have his sexual prowess insulted.

She got into her clothes while James gathered his.

'Where are we going?' he asked, once they were outside and both dressed.

'The Highlands and lowlands – and possibly over the border,' she said with a laugh as her heels dug into the crunching gravel. Then she stopped dead in her tracks and looked at him very seriously. 'But only if you have the wheels.'

He raised a puzzled eyebrow. She was coming to the stage when she could almost time him doing it.

'A car,' she said. 'If you have a car, we can be up and away. I came here with the chauffeur.'

Instantly enlightened, he pointed towards a bright-yellow Citroen 2CV.

Liz shrugged. Not the most glamorous of vehicles, but better than walking.

He tucked his kilt around him.

'I'll get my things,' she said as he unlocked the car.

Strong fingers and palm landed on her arm. 'I'll get them.'

She sank into the front seat of the car. His skirt swayed gently from side to side as he strode towards the house. She watched him until he disappeared through the door. He was like a young stallion, she thought, well-hung and fired up with seemingly endless sexual energy. Just the thought of having him in bed beside her was enough to make her legs ease slightly apart and her nipples turn to iron. She could have him again and again and not tire of him – while he was around. It wasn't necessarily him that was in her mind. It was any young man. That virility and those firm young limbs were a constant aphrodisiac. Blow powerful men and all they had to offer. It was youth that gave her a buzz, that and an unquenchable sexual appetite.

'Where are you, James?' she said through gritted teeth, her eyes still fixed on the door.

Just as she'd feared, McKenzie came running out before James did. He was waving his arms. Richard stayed behind him in the doorway. He looked shell-shocked.

'Liz. Will I see you in London?' McKenzie called out.

As James pushed past him, she turned away. It amused her to think that McKenzie was somehow enthralled to her. That's how it was with some men. They appreciated a woman who thought of sex the same way they did, or at least appeared to. All the same, she still wanted revenge on him. Well, he'd submit to her will before she submitted to his. At some time in the future, the right moment would arrive. He would be in her power and she would make the most of it.

'Hit the gas, Jamie boy,' said Liz.

'I'll do my best.'

The little car lurched forward. When Liz last looked back, McKenzie was running some way behind them. Well, let him run. Let him lie in bed tonight and think about what he was missing. In the meantime, she had a firm knee beside her on which to rest her hand.

James smiled briefly before returning his eyes to the road. 'You can raise it higher, if you like,' he said a little sheepishly.

That, she realised, was what she liked about him. Sex was still fairly new, she guessed. He was little more than a boy, barely eighteen, and living in a place far removed from town centres, noisy discos and nubile young girls. In time, his bashfulness would fade away. But for now, it was sweetly stimulating. And during the next few days, he would cut loose completely from the innocence of his boyhood. She would take the boy and make him a man.

Chapter Ten

*T*he telephone rang constantly before she got to it.

'Hold it right there!' Rachel called out from the bathroom.

Once a towel was wrapped around her dripping hair, she ran quickly over the polished pine floor, scattering droplets of water behind her as she went.

The balcony door was open and the white muslin draped there billowed inwards. The breeze that came with it caressed her naked body.

'I wondered how you were getting on,' said a vaguely familiar voice.

'Mr McKenzie. Well, hello.'

'Mac,' he said. 'Call me Mac. Can you tell me yet how many skeletons are locked in the family closet?'

So far, her research had not strayed far from the book she had hijacked from the British Library. But she could hardly tell him that, could she? She bit her lip and thought hard before replying.

'Your aunt, Betty Jane, was certainly a mine of information. She led me to some really interesting stuff back in the eighteenth century.'

'Sounds interesting. Perhaps we could meet when I get back and you could tell me all about it.'

'Fine,' she said. 'I hear my mother's gone touring through the Highlands. I don't suppose you know exactly when I can expect her back?'

'Oh, a day or two. I suppose.'

She briefly wondered at his vagueness. Was the truth that he really didn't know – or did he have some secret he didn't want her to know about?

Her thoughts went back to the sexy underwear Ian had found in her mother's bedroom. Surely her mother didn't have affairs? Surely her father was the only sexual partner she had in her life? After all, she was of a more conservative generation. When you went to bed with someone, you did it for life – or a great many people did.

'I'm looking forward to seeing you again,' McKenzie added. 'I'm sure we can pass yet another entertaining evening together and, over dinner, you can tell me everything you've discovered about my family.'

'I will,' she said. 'Warts and all.'

He laughed. 'I hope it makes good reading.'

She eyed the book that now sat on the table. 'It does,' she said with a small smile. 'It certainly does.'

'You're looking bleary-eyed,' said Ian when Rachel met him for lunch. 'I know I'm not responsible. Can you tell me who is?'

I knew red was too strong a colour, she thought. She sat down and slid one satin-covered leg over the other. Perhaps satin pedal pushers were a bit OTT for midday, too. It had nothing to do with her skin or eyes looking tired. She threw him a disdainful glance then smirked. 'Caroline Standish.'

'Who?'

'What. It's a book,' she explained. 'I've been reading a book. It's all to do with this American guy who's looking for his roots. Mum asked if I could help him look into things.'

'Oh.' Ian looked away. It was as if the wine list seemed more interesting than she did.

'OK,' she said. 'So you don't like history.' She watched his fingers fiddling with the curling edge of the thick red piece of laminate.

He shrugged. 'It's not that I don't like it. I just don't see why anyone would want to know anything about long-dead people. What does it matter, anyway? They're all dead.'

'They like to know some of the finer details of their lives. You know: births, marriages, deaths, wives, husbands, lovers and bits and pieces about their daily habits.'

'Like going to the lavatory. That's a daily habit, isn't it?'

Rachel glared at him. 'Sometimes you come across as being really stupid, Ian.'

He hung his head. 'Sorry. I didn't mean to be vulgar. I know they didn't live like we do,' he said apologetically. 'They had different attitudes. I understand that.'

But it was too late. He'd niggled her and she wouldn't let it pass. Her eyes blazed. 'You're wrong. They weren't that different. For a start, some of them indulged in more sexual deviation

194

than you've ever come across in your suburban little life.'

Ian raised a finger to his lips as a few heads turned in their direction. Sex, Rachel thought with a smile, certainly commands attention. The lunch-time crowd lapsed into softer conversation, no doubt in a bid to hear more clearly what she was saying. And Ian, she could see, was beginning to feel uncomfortable.

'They had orgies,' she said a little more loudly. 'They'd pay whores to attend them then some of the guys would do three up. You know, one in one hole, one in another and so on . . .'

Ian's eyes darted nervously to either side of him. 'Rachel! Everyone can hear you. Keep it down!'

'Keep it down? Well, that's one thing they didn't do too much of in the eighteenth century. Keeping it up was their greatest concern. Anything that could make it stay harder for longer was treated like gold dust. Can you imagine that?' She frowned thoughtfully. 'Tell you what. The next time I go to Sainsbury's, I'll get you a can of spray starch. What do you think of that? Will that keep the stiffness longer? Certainly works for Dad's shirts, you know.'

Ian's neck began to turn pink. 'I've never had problems in that direction,' he said. 'You should know that.'

'Oh, and to what outstanding performance are you referring? The one the other night, perhaps? That wasn't really me fucking you, you know. It was objects. Purely objects.' She leant closer to him and laughed. 'Ever been fucked by a Pink Panther?'

His face turned puce. 'OK,' he said raising his hands, his face a picture of mortification. 'OK. You win. You want the world to know about this book and now they do.' He turned to each of the diners looking in their direction. 'Show's over, folks. But if you want to know anything more about the sexual perversions of the eighteenth century, just talk to my girlfriend here.'

His chair fell over as he got up from the table. He bent down, grabbed at it and slammed it upright on the floor.

'What about lunch?' asked Rachel.

'Enjoy your meal,' he snapped. 'I've got an errand to run. You can get yourself a taxi, can't you?'

He didn't give her chance to answer.

She watched him leave. How dare he! The bastard. She'd get even for this, and where the bloody hell was he going?

It was impossible to sit and order a meal for one. She got up and stormed out after him, threw a five-pound note at the cashier and slapped the door open. She was just in time to see him driving out of the underground car park. Just like she'd seen in the movies, she waved down a taxi. Not yellow of course. This was London and, in tune with the greyness of the city, the taxicabs were black.

'Follow that blue Vectra,' she ordered the driver. 'There's an extra fiver for you if you don't lose him.'

The traffic wasn't heavy. Miraculously, the lights stayed green for the Vectra and for the cab she was travelling in. The route was familiar. Eventually, they both spilt out on to the M25 heading for Heathrow.

Now why would he be going there? Fetching visitors from the airport wasn't part of his job in the city. Neither, as far as she knew, did he have any friends or relatives arriving back from abroad. And she had to ask herself why she was so concerned. I mean, it wasn't as if he were the love of her life or anything. It was just that his behaviour had altered slightly. He didn't dote on her and spring to her bidding as he had done.

Youthful pride made her curious. Pride could also cause her to be jealous. If it were one of her friends he was collecting or screwing or whatever, then there would be hell to pay. God, but she hated men getting the better of her. Was it perhaps something to do with reading the statements of those eighteenth century dandies who regarded women as having one use only? Maybe it went back even further than that. Convent education had a lot to answer for.

'Are we tailing a criminal?' asked the driver.

She disregarded the question. Explanations weren't something she wanted to go into at present.

The driver repeated his question. She heard him the second time, frowned, and opened her mouth, ready to snap at him not to be so stupid.

'That's right. He's a sex maniac.'

She saw his eyes open wide.

'You a cop?'

'What else?'

She could almost feel his excitement. His foot went down on the pedal. The cab sprang forward that little bit quicker.

'Don't get too close. Don't let him see us,' she said as they rounded the bend that took them to Arrivals – National. Ian had already pulled into a space immediately outside the doors. Whoever he was collecting must already be waiting there.

'Are we OK here?' asked the driver. 'We can't stop too long; you know what these security geeks are like.'

She ducked down behind the seat and peered over his shoulder. 'Wait a minute.'

'Is he picking up a victim?' asked the driver.

Rachel stared. Her throat was dry.

'What do you want me to do?' The driver looked over his shoulder and straight into her eyes.

Rachel stared at Ian – and at her mother. They shouldn't be kissing like that! Who did he think he was? This was her mother, for God's sake!

The exotic underwear! Surely it wasn't for Ian's benefit?

I don't want to see this, something said inside. Think of what Daddy will say. But will you tell him? No. You can't – can you?

She felt a sense of relief once they were both in the car. It gave her time to reflect on what she had seen. She might possibly be imagining things but it wasn't likely. Researchers have to be precise and observant.

With a pang in her heart, she watched Ian's car pull away.

'Follow them,' she gasped before slumping back in the seat. 'You don't need to drive too close. I know where they're going.'

Home, she thought. Obviously they would be heading for home, the place where she had grown up in the safety and security of an average family environment. One mother, one father and her.

But as the journey progressed it became obvious that they weren't going home. They were heading out of town towards Guildford. And they were no longer travelling on main roads. Despite house development and the proximity of two major airports, the area still had a maze of smaller roads and country lanes. The gap between the Vectra and the cab widened.

Fists clenched, Rachel leant forward.

'Put your foot down! Don't lose them but don't let them see us.'

If they'd both been acting out a part in an American thriller movie, the taxi driver could not have done a better job. When the Vectra came to a halt in a thickly wooded area off the road, so did they. Conveniently, there was a copse of virgin bushes between them.

Rachel grabbed the door handle, meaning to rush forward and confront Ian and her mother and ask them what the hell they were doing there. But she hesitated. Did she really want to know? And besides, perhaps they were just talking. Perhaps her worst fears were unfounded.

But men were capable of anything, according to the recent research she had carried out. So were women, if Caroline Standish was anything to go by.

She took a deep breath and opened the door.

'Wait here,' she ordered. The driver nodded vigorously.

She kept low. The bushes were sparse with green leaves and there were gaps where closed buds were waiting to spring open.

The car was no more then ten yards in front of her. Her mother was leaning against it, smiling. She was wearing a grey silk trouser suit and a peach-coloured scarf.

That's my mother, Rachel thought, and she looks incredibly sexy. The realisation took her by surprise. This was her mother, but first and foremost Liz was a woman. But it didn't stop Rachel from feeling angry.

Ian came round to join her mother. He had a look on his face she had never seen before. He rubbed his hands down his trousers. They're sweating, guessed Rachel. He's got the hots for my mother. Good God! What next?

'What do you want me to do?' she heard him say.

'Let me feel your body. Take off your sweater.' Her mother's voice trembled.

Rachel took a deep breath as Ian peeled off the green lambswool sweater he was wearing. She stared at his torso. Each contour seemed more pronounced. Each muscle seemed tenser. Why hadn't she noticed before?

Her heart thudded in her chest as her mother reached out and ran her hands over Ian's body. Slowly he began to fall away from her until he was lying over the front of the car, his feet still on the floor.

Rachel shoved her fist into her mouth as her mother undid the belt and zip on Ian's jeans. She heard him moan with delight as her mother pulled his cock out from within. It stood alone and untouched for a while. Her mother stood back, admiring it, smiling and looking at it through narrowed eyes as if remembering some dark, long-ago secret.

Then she enclosed it in both hands.

'Come here,' she said to him.

Rachel gasped as her mother pulled on his cock until he was upright. They stood close, face to face. Her mother took the scarf from her neck and threw

200

it to one side. Until that moment, Rachel had presumed she was wearing a shirt beneath her suit jacket. But there was nothing. Bare flesh shone warmly tanned against the grey silk.

She heard her mother say something as one of Ian's hands slid down the front of her trousers, while his other hand slipped inside her jacket. It had sounded like 'mutual satisfaction'.

This couldn't be happening. Yet here it was before her eyes. Her mother was pulling on Ian's cock and kissing him with the passion of a woman half her age. And there he was, the little schemer, rolling her nipple between his fingers while his other hand invaded her trousers.

Rachel covered her eyes. I can't let this happen! But she couldn't resist opening them again. It was only just possible to imagine her mother making love with her father. Never had she imagined Liz masturbating or engaging in reciprocal foreplay, as she was doing now, and certainly not with one of Rachel's boyfriends.

Part of her wanted to turn and run. But part of her was curious. Regardless of the fact that she had never considered her mother a sexual creature, she did now. It was like watching a professional, she thought, not a whore. Not someone who gets paid to have sex, but someone adept in the art of seduction.

But how had this happened – and, even more importantly, what would happen next? How would Ian come and what would her mother do with it?

They were both moaning in small, soft words between kisses. They were both tenser than they had been. Orgasm was approaching fast. Rachel found herself imagining how they were feeling. She imagined the thick vein running the length of Ian's prick pulsing with fresh semen, his balls bunching up into his body ready for the final thrust.

And her mother.

Her mother? The fact that this woman behaving so provocatively and obviously enjoying what she was doing was her mother somehow filled her with alarm. Earlier, it had been a sense of shock, almost of betrayal she had felt on seeing her mother on intimate terms with Ian. Now, as she imagined how her mother was physically reacting, she felt an affinity with her. Like her, her nipples would be hard beneath his fingers. A warm wetness would be seeping like honey over the hand that was doing such delicious things between her legs.

Gingerly, as if afraid what she might find there, her own hand slid between her legs. Her own lips parted and she felt the warm, wetness and the throbbing ache of aroused flesh.

Soon, she thought. Soon! And she breathed quickly.

She could see it. She could feel it. The man and the woman were lost in their pleasure. The woman convulsed and threw back her head. Her lips parted. Her cry was soft but impassioned. It rose to the treetops, like smoke lessening as it got higher.

She opened her eyes. Rachel looked to where Liz was looking. She was pulling on Ian's cock using both hands. She saw him stiffen, stand almost on tiptoe.

'Round here,' she heard her mother cry.

Obediently he turned and ejected a plume of foaming white over the car windscreen.

Rachel sank to the ground. Her face felt hot. Her hand felt wet. What should she do now? And why hadn't she run forward and told them to stop what they were doing?

She took deep breaths as the truth sank in. Any self-respecting voyeur would have enjoyed what she had just seen. Pleasure plus a sense of shame had taken over from outrage. At the end of it, they had merely been a man and a woman. But as her heartbeat slowed and her own pleasure died away, the outrage returned. She would confront her mother prior to telling her father. It had to be done. OK, Ian hadn't penetrated her mother. Not this time. But had he done so at some time in the past?

She was silent in the taxi, obsessed with her own thoughts about what to do. Even so she was aware that the driver was eyeing her in his rear view mirror.

'Did he rape that woman?' he asked in a tone that suggested he was aching to know the details of the incident, rather than if the man would be arrested.

'On this occasion, the victim consented to everything that happened to her.'

He nodded sagely. 'That does happen. I've read it all in the newspapers.'

The taxi dropped her at the end of the cobbled street rather than at the door of the building she lived in. No point in spoiling the illusion, she thought. The guy's had an exciting night supposedly assisting an undercover cop on a surveillance operation. Playing the part till the end seemed the fair thing to do.

A black limousine was parked half way down the street. They weren't that rare around the area, but no one she knew locally happened to have one. But she did know of one person who was using such a vehicle. She slowed her step. Leaning against a pillar outside her building she saw the broad-shouldered figure of Robert McKenzie.

He stepped forward to meet her.

'Thought I'd drop by to see how things are doing,' he said.

She side-stepped him and slid her security card into the anodised steel box in which the reader was situated.

'I told you that I would get back to you, once I had an overall picture to present of really interesting people.'

She turned quickly enough to shut him out, but changed her mind at the last minute. After all, he was fuelling her bank account with hard cash.

'There's something else,' he said. 'I thought I'd return these.'

He held up a fragile piece of mauve satin and lace. Rachel thought about snatching them out of his hand but changed her mind. He was the sort who would enjoy her embarrassment, just as his ancestors had enjoyed debauching young women purely for their own pleasure. In a small way, this was no different.

'You'd better come in,' she said, as she turned away and headed for the lift.

'Nice place,' he said as he followed her over the honey-coloured floor of her apartment. 'Lucky for you to have such great folks as parents. Generous to their daughter.'

He smiled. She did her best not to scowl. The scene between her mother and Ian was still in her head. Confusion over how she should react was making her blow hot and cold and there seemed precious little she could do to make it go away. All the same, she tingled in Robert's company.

Robert McKenzie walked over to the Mexican style dining table. The family papers and photographs he had given her almost obliterated a third of its dented surface.

'I don't see any research books.' He glanced at her then shuffled a few papers out of the order she had put them in. 'I thought you were getting some stuff from the British Library. How come I don't see any?'

'I have to borrow them on the spot,' she said adopting a slick, precise voice of the type that erects barriers between classes. 'I'm afraid one is only allowed to use them under the library roof so to speak. One is not allowed to take reference books off the premises.'

Thankfully he nodded, obviously satisfied with her explanation. His opinion of her might alter if he went into her bedroom and saw it sitting wide open on her bedside cabinet. There was more to read on Caroline Standish. Intrigue surrounded the woman. She had to know more about her. Once she had finished studying the woman, she would go back to studying Duncan McKenzie.

'Would you like a glass of wine?' she asked suddenly.

'Thanks.'

'Red or white?'

He'll have red, she thought.

'Red,' he said.

She smiled to herself. As she handed him the wine, he handed her the mauve panties she had seen him slipping into his pocket.

'Fair exchange,' he said.

With a sudden flush, she remembered the rest of the circumstances: the waiter watching as she had exposed her nakedness to the leather furniture and the lounge of the restaurant.

McKenzie made his way to the glass door that led out on to a small balcony. The lights of the city twinkled before him. The city breeze stirred his amazingly white silky hair.

'You obviously like a good view,' said Rachel.

He glanced over his shoulder at her. She saw his grin and the way his eyes raked her body. The meaning was clear.

'Tell me,' he said gesturing with the hand holding his glass at the panorama of London. 'Have you ever walked out here naked?'

She took a sip of her wine and looked at him over the rim of her glass. There, he had surprised her again! Her hair tickled the nape of her neck. The tingle continued all the way down her spine.

She swallowed. 'Only on warm nights.' It was true. On nights when she'd been feeling particularly sensuous, she had felt the chill night air against her flesh. Like ghostly hands, it had tantalised her breasts and her belly; like unseen breath, it had disturbed the crisp, dark curls that congregated between her legs.

He reached out an arm and drew her close. At first, she thought about refusing. Wasn't he a descendent of Duncan McKenzie? Was it possible that he abused women, just as his ancestor had done? But he had planted a picture, an experience in her mind. By doing so he had taken hold of a sensation. No matter who he was, she had to follow what she was feeling.

'Have you ever thought about leaning over that

balcony, your bare tits looking earthward while some rugged stud gives it you from behind?'

His hands roamed up and down her back, into the curve above her buttocks and up again.

'It's none of your business.'

'Tell me.' His voice was firm, demanding.

She tried not to let him see that her eyes were glancing at the surrounding windows. Of course she'd imagined such scenarios. But she'd never dared do such a thing. After all, she had to live here – and what sort of reputation would she have if someone saw her like that?

'I've never done that,' she said truthfully.

'Then you should,' he said and grinned.

She shivered and looked down into her wine. The seed he had planted was growing. Soon it might get too big for her to resist. A mix of measures designed to prohibit sexual experimentation popped unheralded into her mind. Those nuns of her youth had a lot to answer for. Celibacy had muffled their desires. To their logic, if they could live without sexual intimacy, so could every other woman on the planet. The nuns were sometimes cruel and quite usually perverse in exerting their beliefs and actions on others.

A pupil discovered indulging in masturbation at bedtime had her wrists tied to the sides of the bed. It never occurred to the sweet sisters that they might have left their charge open to sexual experiments by one or more of the other pupils. Some of the young charges ended up enjoying the wandering hands of their classmates. A number remained faithful to the ministrations of their own gender.

But the guilt they had implanted was still there. Every now and again it raised its ugly head. And every so often she battled against that guilt and the strength of her own desires.

'Let me put on some music,' she said suddenly.

He followed her back inside. She put down her wineglass. He followed suit. She put on a CD by Vangelis, vaguely aware she had borrowed it from her mother and not taken it back.

He stood close behind her. She marvelled at the fact that she could feel his warmth. It was as though his body was reaching out for hers.

Today, she had watched her mother seduce a young man. Now she was considering being seduced by a man old enough to be her father. Would she be giving in to him by way of revenge? After all, she would be encroaching on her mother's territory, her mother's age group. Was it fair? Would she feel better if she went ahead and did it?

She turned and was about to side-step him like she had before, when the mauve discarded knickers caught her eye. They were on the table next to the research papers and now the wineglasses. It was surprisingly hard to drag her gaze away from them.

He ran his hand down her arm, his wandering fingers leaving delicious trails of goosebumps over her skin.

'You liked performing, didn't you?'

She kept her eyes fixed on the scanty underwear. If she looked up into his eyes, she knew she'd be lost.

Keep this last vestige of control, she thought. Don't give in, yet – yet.

He stroked her hair. She liked that. It reminded her of being home for the holidays, of her mother stroking her hair and telling her how glad she was to see her. Even now, once someone stroked her hair, she was lost. All she wanted to do was give in, curl up and drift away.

Perhaps it was because she was feeling confused that she lay her head against his chest. She had still not decided what to do about her mother and Ian. But she didn't want to think about it any more tonight. Her head ached and McKenzie's hands were so soothing. She closed her eyes. Whatever he wanted, she would do. She wanted to forget what she had seen. She wanted to lose herself in her own sexuality.

As if in a dream, her clothes were removed, or did she remove them herself? She couldn't remember. It was like swimming with the tide: she just went with it.

His hands were warm upon her flesh. His words were like honey in her ears. She wanted to believe anything he said – only, more than that, she wanted him to possess her body. Just for once, she wanted to relinquish control.

She seemed to have drifted out on to the balcony. A thousand lights from a thousand windows winked throughout the city around her.

The night air was cool, just as she imagined it. His body was warm against hers. Hard between them, his cock rubbed against her stomach. His lips were hot upon her mouth, her cheeks and her neck. Delicious sensations curled around the nape of her neck, aroused by the stroking of his fingers.

He had such a way about him. He said the right words and made the right movements. She could not resist. She could only submit. She was his plaything and there seemed to be nothing she could do about it.

His hands slid down her spine. She arched her back and her belly met his. A mere smattering of body hair tickled her flesh. It was dark and contrasted strangely with the satin locks on his head.

Why are you doing this? she asked herself. You don't have to. You're just doing a job for him. Never mind about the night you went to dinner with him. Nothing happened. So you're not obliged.

No, of course she wasn't obliged. Of course she wasn't being seduced: not really.

And then the truth came to her, just as it had come to Caroline Standish. He's just a man, a vessel to give you pleasure. He may very well think that he is taking something from you. In truth, he isn't, because when you close your eyes, he isn't there. You only feel the sensations his touch and his smell are arousing in you. Forget about him. Let off the brakes and trust your body to respond for itself.

The night air did nothing to cool her ardour or make her change her mind. Lose yourself, a small voice said in her head. Lose yourself tonight. Find yourself tomorrow.

Shivers seemed to run just below the surface of her skin as his hands stroked her spine then grabbed her buttocks. He spread his fingers over them as if they were ripe fruit. The index fingers on both hands slid into the crack between, dipped into the well of juice between her legs, then smeared it between her buttocks as he brought his hand back up.

Only occasionally did she open her eyes. She hardly looked at him, although no doubt he would have liked her to. No, this was her event, her pleasure.

The scenery around her was reminiscent of the boxes and balconies of a giant theatre. She directed her gaze at the windows of her own apartment block and those around her. Some windows were lit. Some were in darkness. Were unseen eyes looking out and seeing her nudity? Would they be disgusted or would they ache with jealousy, their blood hot in their veins, their genitals alive with what could be experienced if one was a little more imaginative, a little more daring?

And there she was, performing – but not for them. Like Robert McKenzie, they were an important aid to her enjoyment.

I want them to watch me. I want them to see me writhe on his cock, rub my pubes against his pubes, and have him suck and nip at my breasts. Perhaps I also want to know what it feels like to have the fullness of an erect cock invade my anus. Never mind taboos. Never mind what he wants or what he thinks I want. Whatever I have is at my pleasure, even his orgasm.

She wrapped her arms around his neck and threw her head back as she slid upon his cock. Fetters that had held her in the past were discarded. No questions about why she was feeling as she did remained. Only the thought about how she wanted him to orgasm was fixed in her mind. The vision of her mother and Ian was still with her. This was the vision guiding her. Her mother had been totally in control. She had told him what she wanted but, when it came to his orgasm, she had grasped his cock and directed it to where she wanted his seed to land.

Suddenly she burst out laughing.

McKenzie smiled down at her. 'I hope it's not

my performance you're laughing at,' he said and kissed her forehead, then her eyelids.

'Not at all,' she said. 'You're doing everything I want you to do and exactly how I want you to do it.'

Her response to her orgasm was similar to that reserved for the chill breeze, so perhaps McKenzie didn't notice it. Once the spasms of sheer ecstasy had subsided in her body and his were about to climax, she jerked away from him.

She gave him no time to protest, no time to grasp her close and push it back into her. Quickly she gripped his cock with both hands, yanked on it again and again and again. As he cried out, she pulled him round to face the city lights, jerked his cock through the balcony railings and watched with delight as his semen took flight into the darkness of the street below.

She didn't let him stay the night, although he begged her and showered her with kisses and terms of endearment she didn't really want.

Once he'd gone, she got the book and opened it again at the proclamations of Caroline Standish.

Dear sister, if you are reading this, do remember that true sexual pleasure does not derive from a submissive demeanour – although some men seem to interpret it as such. Rather think of seduction in these terms:-
Ask yourself if he is handsome.
Does he have a good body?
Is he wealthy enough to keep you in style?
Is he busy enough not to notice that you

sometimes take pleasure elsewhere, if the mood takes you?

These are your first criteria and are derived purely by looking at your subject. Then, dear sister, ask yourself how his body would look naked. From then on, you will want to know how his naked body would feel against yours. If delicious shivers run up and down your spine and make your legs weak, then it is obvious you must take him.

Next, imagine his cock heavy, hard and entering your passage. Never mind about how it will feel in your hand or how his hands will feel on your breasts. Imagine only how the length and circumference of his weapon will feel as it pushes your pussy lips aside, like the plough does the furrow. My legs tremble and fall apart as I imagine his steed, his length, his iron rod filling the passage to my womb. If I concentrate very hard, I can feel it throbbing in time with my heart. And this, dear ladies everywhere, makes everything else worthwhile. What better delight to be generously plugged with a good-sized member? Never again feel you are being used. It is he doing all the work and all for your pleasure.

Rachel put the book to one side. An hour ago, she had orgasmed in full view of her neighbours. Thanks to Caroline Standish, she was aroused again.

Heart racing, she put the book to one side. She closed her eyes. Her fingers went to her breast. Her heaving hips beckoned. She writhed and the bed-clothes were kneaded into a clump between her legs. The cool cotton rasped against her moist flesh. Both hands covered her breasts, fingers pulled and played with her nipples.

She was lost in her own fantasy. Shadowy figures directed what was to happen to her. The hands on her breasts were no longer hers, yet they were just as cool and fine. The clump between her legs that rubbed and rasped against her clitoris started as a large hand then became something put there, some tool, some device designed to bring her to orgasm before the shadows fell on her and did everything for their pleasure alone.

Many eyes looked down at her, yet they only existed behind her closed eyelids. Many hands took it in turns to play with her breasts. Some had ten fingers on each hand. Some had red eyes that burnt into hers and left her feeling helpless, submissive to their will. Mouths leered and long tongues flicked out like small whips down over her belly.

'Give her more! Give her more!' they cried as her hips jerked and her fingers squeezed her nipples. 'That's it! Make her come until she can't come any more!'

The cries worked. The orgasm came. It racked her body, arched her back. Her thighs squeezed the appliance – which, after all, was only the bed-clothes – until the last spasm had come, shivered and died away.

Finally satisfied, she lay back on her pillows, one arm crooked up around her head.

She smiled. The shadows melted back into her mind. They had done everything she had wanted them to do.

Before dropping off to sleep, the thought of Ian and her mother came back to her mind. Ian had left a message on the answerphone for her to call him, but Robert McKenzie's visit had intervened.

Her mother had also left a message for her to ring, but she had hesitated in ringing back. What would she say? Could she come straight out and tell her she had seen Ian put his hand down her pants?

She wanted to sleep on it. It wasn't that she was angry. On the contrary, she was intrigued. But it was just that she needed to get things clear in her mind. Words might need some rehearsing before she voiced them.

When she fell asleep, she began to dream. Caroline Standish came to her, white breasts blossoming over the tight bodice of an empire line dress. 'Seduction should not be regarded as a submissive act. Is he busy enough not to notice that you sometimes have a need to seek pleasure elsewhere, if the mood takes you?'

In her dreams, Rachel looked up over the soft white bosom and came face to face with her mother.

Chapter Eleven

*I*t was Saturday the following day and, although she would happily have lain in bed an hour longer than usual, the sound of the security intercom buzzing brought her quickly to her senses.

Without dressing, she flew to the wall on which it sat and pressed the 'speak' button.

'It's me, darling.' She recognised the voice of her father. 'I've dropped your mother off at Harrods. What's the chance of coffee?'

'Good,' she replied and pressed the black button that would open the lobby door.

Still without dressing, she went to the kitchen and got out some decent filter coffee. Then she ran to open the door, just seconds after her father pressed the bell.

'Good Lord, Rachel! You could have got dressed.' He looked furtively to each side of him. The corridor outside was empty and low on lighting, so he was wasting his time.

She laughed a little nervously and kissed his

cheek. 'Come on in before the neighbours start talking.' Then she ran to the window and opened a fanlight. She felt light-headed and full of a need to dart around the place rather than sit down and look into her father's eyes. There was still the Ian/mother thing to deal with and she didn't want to mention anything to her father, just yet. In fact, she wasn't sure about mentioning it to him at all. But somehow she had to deal with it.

'Rachel,' said her father suddenly, a little louder and a little angrier, 'will you please put some clothes on?'

For some reason, his request stopped her in her tracks. She felt a little uncertain as she looked at him and knew she was standing awkwardly, as if she needed to apologise for childish sin.

'But you're my father,' she blurted.

He sighed impatiently and turned away. 'But I'm also a man.'

It seemed more than mere minutes before she turned away and walked slowly into the bedroom. His comment had meaning and triggered the memory of past conversations with her mother. If she remembered rightly, her mother had been peeved by her comment that she was too old to be watching Ian in the bathroom.

Suddenly, as she slid her slim thighs into grey slacks and pulled a black polo-necked sweater over her head, she felt guilty about what she had said. Her mother too was a person first and foremost. Why shouldn't the sight of a young male in a compromising position still arouse her?

Rachel ran a comb through her wispy haircut as the truth struck home. How arrogant youth could be. It was as if sex was theirs alone.

I need to make amends, she thought to herself. I need to say sorry. There's nothing to prevent me doing that, is there?

But there was one thing that stopped her. No penetration had taken place between her mother and Ian. But an intense intimacy on a par with full intercourse had occurred. So how did she cope with that? Did she tell her father that her mother was acting in an adulterous way? Or should she warn her mother that she knew about her and Ian and would spill the beans if she didn't stop doing it?

'You're taking your time,' her father shouted from the living room. 'How about us having breakfast down at the corner café?'

'Coming,' she shouted back. Silently, she made a promise to phone her mother when she got back.

The phone began to ring at the exact moment she reached for the door.

'Are you going to get that?' Her father nodded at the combined telephone/answerphone unit.

Rachel shook her head and snatched at the door handle.

In her absence, the voice of Robert McKenzie filtered out into the room. 'Rachel, I'm thinking about having sex with you again. Now what I'd like to do this time is this . . .'

'Did she mention it?' Liz asked Mark on his return as she put the last of the dishes into the machine.

He shook his head, took hold of his wife's hips and pulled her close to him. Her bathrobe opened slightly. Chanel No. 5 drifted from her flesh and into his nostrils. 'Does it bother you that much?'

218

Liz nodded. 'Darling, our daughter thinks people of our age shouldn't have sex.'

One corner of Mark's mouth turned upwards in a knowing grin. 'As long as you don't think that.'

She smiled. 'Any place, any time!'

He leant against her. Gradually, she inclined back against the central workstation.

'How about here – over the kitchen table, or whatever you call it?'

'No!' she jerked herself upright, her mouth a sudden grim line. 'Not the bloody kitchen.'

Mark looked sheepish but only in sympathy with her feelings, not on his own account. 'I forgot about that. It must have got you really riled.'

She'd already told Mark about what Mac had got her to do in the kitchen. The sex would have been fine, but treating her like a skivvy had not gone down well at all.

'I felt demeaned,' she said. 'It was as if I were a slave, not an equal. I won't have that, Mark; you know I won't have that.'

Mark nodded in understanding as his hands ran soothingly up and down her back. 'I understand. But I've got to do something with this, you know.'

He took her hand and placed it over the warm bulge in his trousers.

She reached up and kissed him and a fire ran through her. 'I'm sure I can take care of it,' she said. 'So how about making our way upstairs?'

His smile was enough of a reply for her to lead him to the stairs. When they got to the landing, he started to head towards their bedroom. Liz tugged him towards the bathroom.

'Let's play a game. You can be Ian and I'll be me.'

219

As she watched her husband make his way to the bathroom, she marvelled at how alike they both were. How many other couples could talk openly about their individual sexual experiences and still have a special place for each other? It was Mark who filled her with fire, Mark with whom she needed no fantasies, just the feel of his body against hers. A look was enough to set her off because, in that look, she saw everything she could possibly want. Like now, for instance. They were going to play games: adult games, in which they could share the individual experiences each had had with other partners.

Via the mirror on the landing, Liz watched Mark stand with legs slightly open before the pan. She heard the sound of his zip. A few seconds and his cock would be in his hand, its head aimed at the white china. Perhaps he might manage a few drops. Judging by the feel of his cock, she doubted it. He was too hard, too ready to fuck rather than pee.

The scene as viewed via the mirror was no longer enough. She turned from it. When she came up behind him, she leant her head on his shoulder and sniffed in his maleness then kissed his neck.

'Let me help you,' she said.

She wound her arms around his waist. Slowly, she slid her hands over his groin. He groaned as her fingers ran through the tough springiness of his pubic hair. She wound both hands around his cock.

'Heaven,' she whispered.

Backward and forward, backward and forward.

She pulled on him, her strokes as even as his breathing. They could make it last for hours, if they wanted. That was how they were together. In tune was a good description, but such harmony can only be learnt over a number of years.

He reached behind and opened up her robe. Then he hooked his thumbs into his waistband and jerked his trousers down so that his buttocks were exposed.

They were warm and firm against her belly. She hugged close, her hands tight on his cock, her pelvis tight against his arse.

They jerked slowly backward and forward, in time with the rhythm she was using on his cock.

Smoothly and slowly, she began to slide down his back. As she sank further, she nipped at his flesh through his sweater. It would have been better if his back had been bare. That was how Ian had been. He had only been wearing his jeans when she had first seen him peeing. The second time, he had been naked. But this was their game and they were playing it as they found it.

But his buttocks were bare. When she got there, she continued to pull on his prick. The fire within her body steadily burnt more brightly. When her lips came into contact with his behind, she nipped playfully at each firm orb and took pleasure from the taste on her tongue and the warm smell in her nostrils. Fired with enthusiasm and that ache for more, she went further. Her tongue flicked out at the cleft in between.

Lower again she sank. His trousers came with her. She brought her hands from around his hips. Both hands and lips sought the soft scrotum, the nuts within.

Her hands carried on through. Again she found his penis, which still throbbed and was still hard.

As she worked on his cock, her tongue flicked at his balls. With careful precision, she nipped the scrotal flesh. She sucked it into her mouth, rolled it around on her tongue. By tilting her head back, she could get more in. The thought of having this most delicate part of him in her mouth seemed to take possession of her. It tasted sweet and she felt that if she sucked really hard, she could have all of him in her mouth, her throat and, ultimately, her body.

Because of her closeness, every subtle movement of his muscles was clear to her. Tension and relaxation rippled through his body. One minute he sighed, the next he groaned with pleasure.

Soon, she thought, he will not allow this. Soon he will be all thrust and intrusion. And the thought thrilled her. Still being desired by many men, whether young or old, was eminently satisfying. Still to be desired by the same man after so many years was icing on the cake.

Just as she'd guessed, he was not long in slipping out of her mouth, turning and bringing her to her feet.

Their kisses were hot. His hands tore the robe from her body and her hands ripped his sweater off over his head.

They spun together out of the bathroom and on to the landing. Such was her enthusiasm, she slammed her back against the wall. His body slammed against hers, knocking what breath was left out of her.

'I'm going to fuck you,' he said. His voice was thick, as though his tongue as well as his cock was swollen with lust.

'Fuck me!' she murmured breathlessly. 'Fuck me!'

The moistness of his breath seemed to tangle in her hair. It felt warm and hot.

'I will,' he cried. 'I will!'

'Now,' she murmured. 'Now! Do it now!'

She raised her leg and grabbed his shaft.

He heaved his hips against her. She tilted hers. They pressed together, like two parts of one whole.

'Please!' she mewed. 'Put it in.'

At first, she felt only the soft warm head nudging her flesh. More followed. He fed it in slowly and she savoured the feel of it. Her body was slowly choking on it, but deliciously.

She mewed as inch after exquisite inch went in.

One hand grasped her neck and she groaned.

One hand clutched at her breast and she whispered the word 'More!'

His mouth sucked one nipple then the other and she sighed.

The tempo changed. She was impaled on him. His pelvis slammed against hers. The whole length was in. Ecstasy had been achieved yet again. Ecstasy with the same man after so long.

'Do I do it the best?' he asked, as if he had any need to ask.

'There's no comparison.'

'Do you want it fast?'

'Yes!' she shouted. 'Fast and hard! As fast and as hard as possible!'

He was like a machine. In, out, in, out, in, out, in, out, until she was breathless.

'Slower,' she cried out. 'Slow and easy, like you would do it to a virgin.'

The pace changed.

'Just take it easy,' he said softly against her ear. 'Don't get too tense, baby. Just take it as it comes.

Let your body hang loose. Enjoy the cock. Enjoy the fuck.'

They groped each other. They clung, they grasped, and they explored each other's bodies as if doing so for the first time.

They nibbled each other's ears; they sucked at each other's lips and the breath from their mouths mingled in the same way as the fluids from their bodies. They were one, just as they'd always been: just as they would always be.

Before making love, they had exchanged brief observations on their sexual experiences with other partners. Afterward, no mention was made of it. The more mundane matters of everyday living took over. But one particular scenario would not leave Liz's mind.

Mark was talking about making plans for two weeks away in their villa in Mijas. He'd been going on about one date then another. Eventually, he asked what Liz thought of the seventeenth of June.

'Yes,' she said absentmindedly.

They'd been married a long time, long enough for Mark to know when she wasn't listening.

'There's a murdered man in the back garden. I'd bury him in the cellar if we had one,' he said.

'Yes.'

Suddenly, she blinked as what he'd just said sank in. 'What did you say?'

She was sitting in a fat armchair by the window. He went over to her and rested his hand on her shoulder.

'What's on your mind?'

Liz sighed. 'Two things, really. I'm still damned annoyed at Robert McKenzie. I've never felt used like that before. And I'm still not sure whether to mention to Rachel that I saw her watching me with Ian.'

Mark shook his head. 'Hm, you should have avoided Ian. OK, have a young man if you want to, but not quite so near home. It was bound to come out.'

Liz frowned. Not because she was annoyed with Mark's observation but because she knew he was right. She shouldn't have been tempted. But she had been. On top of that, she'd been seen. Now what did she do?

'I think you've got to speak to her,' said Mark, as he stepped out on to the patio.

Liz got up from the chair and followed him. 'And say what?'

'Explain yourself.'

Liz looked up at her husband as though he were mad. 'Explain I fancy young men?'

'Why not? You said she didn't treat him as being anything special, so why should it upset her? It was just a fancy, right?'

Liz shook her head. 'Men find it so easy to explain away. It was just one of those things. OK, I can accept that. But Rachel isn't me. She's young and thinks that sex is love and fidelity is a more natural state than lust.'

'Heaven forbid!'

'Precisely. But that's you and me, not her.'

He held her shoulders and looked into her eyes. 'The alternative is to have it smouldering between you forever. Think of how horrendous that would be. Come on, get it out in the open. Come clean.'

Her jaw remained firm while she looked into his eyes. But eventually it had to give. She sighed.

There was no alternative. She had to speak to Rachel.

'I'll give her a ring and see if she'll meet me for lunch.'

'Or afternoon coffee in town,' he said. 'Remember, she had a big breakfast this morning.'

Liz patted his crotch and grinned. 'So have I,' she said and he smiled, too.

'If it's afternoon coffee, then perhaps I could also supply you with lunch.'

'That would be nice,' said Liz. 'Let me see what I can do. But, seeing as we've only just finished, I could do with some encouragement. What have you got to tell me?'

He put his arm round her and drew her out on to the lawn. 'I'll tell you about Meryl Lacock,' he said with a smile.

She looked at him with some surprise. 'Is that her real name?'

'Of course it is.'

'Go on.'

'Well,' he said as Liz kicked off her shoes, 'she's the MD of a company I've only just started visiting. It was passed to me only recently, after she'd met me at some business conference at the NEC. I didn't remember meeting her but, apparently, she remembered me. So there I was, sitting in her office at lunchtime. I should have realised things were going to be a little different, seeing that lunch and wine was already laid on. The outer offices were almost empty because people were out at lunch – celebrating someone's birthday, so she told me. Once I was seated, I heard her lock the door behind me. I knew what was coming. Someone back at the office had warned me she'd had one or two cases of sexual harassment brought against her by members of staff. He'd told me to look out but, if I wanted to do business, to grin and bear it – and he meant what he said. Theirs is a big account. I had to keep it.

'So there I was, waiting to be offered wine and food that sat on top of a long side table. But she was slow in offering.

'Now, before we go any further I have to describe her to you. She is over six and a half feet tall, has enormous breasts and heavy thighs. She has nice eyes and dark hair that also extends to her top lip. A couple of hairs have also strayed on to her chin.

'She moved round to the front of her desk in front of me, sat on it and crossed her arms. "I picked you because I think you can give me the service I require," she said. "I hope I'm right. If I'm not, then I want no more dealings with your company at all. You're not the only fish in the sea."

'I kept my cool.

' "Whatever you want," I said.

'She smiled and her mouth reminded me of a letter box, oblong and brightly edged in red.

'She continued smiling and began to nod.

' "Come here," she said.

'I stood up and stepped closer. She looked me up and down. Suddenly, I knew how a stud bull feels. Without me needing to remove a stitch, she stripped the clothes from my body.

'She took hold of my hands and put them on her breasts. They were huge breasts. I managed to cover a bit more than just her nipples, but not much more.

'She licked her lips and kept smiling. "Carry on," she said. "I want you to do it to me. I won't be doing anything to you. Oh, and don't bother to kiss me."

'Thank God, I thought. Imagine kissing that hairy mouth. Just then, it occurred to me that she might very well be pretty hairy all over. But I tried not to think of it.

'I did what she expected of me. I unbuttoned her blouse and heaved her breasts out of a satin bra that was big enough to use for paragliding. Her breasts were enormous. My hands ached as I kneaded them and squeezed the huge nipples.

'"Kiss them!" she demanded and, when I hesitated, she grabbed hold of my head and shoved it into her cleavage. At one stage, I thought I was going to suffocate. It was like fighting against an avalanche of flesh.

'When eventually I surfaced, I lost no time in sucking on her nipples. It was like suckling on a cow. It took both hands to steady her breast as I negotiated her nipple.

'But I must have been doing it right, because she started to groan.

'"Do it to me," she said. "Rip my knickers off."

'This time, I didn't hang around. I reached up under her skirt much quicker than I'd sucked on her breasts. There was no way I wanted my head to be pushed up under that skirt and between those huge thighs.

'Once her skirt was up and her knickers were off, I was treated to the full sight of her sex. Though full sight might be the wrong phrase. There it was, this mass of black silky hair spreading like a forest between her thighs and like a cobweb up over her belly. It even clustered around her navel and reminded me of a sparrow's nest.

'Obligingly, she lay back on the desk, her breasts sagging to one side, her thighs open and her springy black hair sat like a pillow in her groin. And among all that hair sat this pink object that jutted upwards like some raw penis. Of course, I knew what it was, but I had never seen one as big as that.

'Would it react like any other clitoris? I thought. Would it feel any different? Did it require more or less pressure than a normal-sized model?

'But I couldn't hang about asking myself questions. I had to get on with it or I might feel myself drowning in her juices and being smothered by her pubic hair. Take my word, she was big enough to overpower me.'

Liz, who had been chuckling throughout, now burst into loud laughter. 'I'm sorry, Mark. But I can't help laughing. This is harassment from the male point of view and it's the best thing I've ever heard.'

'You're not listening hard enough. Just lie down on the lawn here and listen properly.'

She did just that, but covered her mouth with her hands and continued to rock with laughter.

Mark shook his head in mock annoyance. 'You're not listening, Liz. I can't cope with that.'

So he didn't. He pulled two croquet hooks from out of the lawn, placed her arms above her head on the warm grass, and then fastened her wrists to the earth by hitting the hooks in really deeply.

'Now listen,' he said and she looked up into his eyes. As she did so, he began to slide her jogging pants down her legs. He also pushed her sweater up above her breasts. Her torso was free, open to the fresh air, the breeze and his open gaze. He stroked her breasts and restarted the story.

'It wasn't easy, but I was hard enough to enter her. I did the best I could, but that woman was huge. I was like a monkey pounding up and down on her. My cock was a mere pinprick in that cavernous sex. And all the time I poked it in her, an avalanche of fluid poured out over my cock and down my thighs.'

He didn't get any further but then, he didn't need to. Liz had the full picture. Besides, as he had described mounting the woman, he had mounted her – and what they were doing and what they achieved was far more important than telling a story.

Chapter Twelve

Rachel was angry after listening to her answer-phone. How dare Robert McKenzie presume he could order sex off some set menu created to his taste and his alone!

Angrily, she picked up the phone and tapped out the first few digits of his number. Then she stopped.

Don't tell him to get lost, said a small voice inside. And the voice was right. Hot words weren't enough to rebuke him or to satisfy her fury. There had to be something better. Slowly, a plan began to form. Let him think she was putty in his hands. Beguile him with sweet words and the promise of her body on any terms and in any way.

Ask him over. Say you're willing to discuss his requirements with him. Then, once you get him here . . .

'So you think you've got me in the palm of your hand.'

Her voice echoed around the green metal rafters

and bare brick walls. It sounded menacing but it also sounded oddly enticing – just like her. Oh, yes: she could be very enticing, if she wanted to.

She smiled to herself. Yes! That was the way it would be. She planned carefully. Get him over here. Talk about the research, first. Play at being serious. Get him panting for it. Have him drooling with anticipation until you could almost imagine the pain of keeping a cock restrained behind a closed zip.

Once it was obvious that his sexual intentions were overriding his interest in family history, she'd lead him in the direction she wanted him to go. But, of course, he wouldn't know that. He would be begging her and he would follow.

She tousled her short-cropped hair and chuckled at the thought of it. Never mind leading him by the nose. She would be leading him by a larger, stiffer organ of his body.

The giggles had to stop. She cleared her throat and tapped at her ribcage in an effort to control herself before dialling his number. She curled up on the sofa, her legs folded beneath her. She hugged them with her free arm.

He answered. As usual, he sounded full of confidence, so bloody arrogant, thought Rachel. It would have been great to tell him so. But that would spoil things.

Briefly, she placed her hand over the mouthpiece. Like an actress about to take the stage, she took a deep breath and talked courage. 'Come on, Rachel, baby, let your words drip with honey.'

She removed her hand from the mouthpiece.

'Robert. I got your message. I must admit, I found it very interesting.'

'Good,' he replied. 'I guessed you would. I'm looking forward to coming over. Let's see . . .'

She could imagine him looking at his watch or perhaps even his diary. Most probably, he had fitted her in between a dental appointment and a trip to the hairdresser. Like them, she was one more convenience.

'I should be over in about an hour,' was all he said.

Bastard! What a nerve! No asking for her opinion or agreement on what he wanted to do. No enquiring whether she would be around in one hour. He presumed she would be there. *Presumed*! And that was what annoyed her about him.

But she controlled her feelings.

'Sure. Whatever you want.' Her voice was pure sugar.

'Then get yourself ready, baby.'

'Sure,' she replied with as much saccharine as before. 'I'll be ready for you.'

After she'd put the phone down, she fetched the book from the bedroom. There was one particular piece of prose she wanted to read again before he arrived. Once again, she turned to the chapter regarding the ebullient Caroline Standish, and what she read made her smile.

I never allowed men to use me. They might have thought they were, but the truth always hurts, does it not?

One man in particular caught my eye among all those who were given access to my body. He was a well-endowed man, his rod thick and long, his thighs well muscled and his upper torso rippling with vigour.

I had always given the impression of being of a good family who required that I marry as best as I could, most particularly above my station; I set out to bend him to my will. His name was Duncan McKenzie and he had a house in London and a castle in Scotland. Castle Cael, I believe it is called.

He was handsome – although his family, he told me, were prone to go white headed very early in life. I did not mind that, I told him. In fact, I regard a man having any hair at all as preferable to having none! And besides, he is a young man. The white mane is a family trait and very well it looks, too.

So I planned to trap the man. I wanted him to know that I was as much in control of his body as he might be of mine. One day, I got him to call at my home and hinted that I would be willing to do anything he wanted. He came, of course, but when he did it was I who took advantage of him. Using a suitable ruse, I tied him up. I beat his posterior with a riding whip. As I had him hanging from a hook in the ceiling, I also did things to his manhood that he would never have dreamed of having a woman do to him. I told him I wanted him to marry me and he laughed. So I told him there was no getting away from it and he would be mine regardless. No longer would he wish to frequent the Hellfire Club and show off his rude length to all his male friends. He laughed at this, but when I showed him the special ink I had got and explained I would prick it into the surface of his cock, his jaw dropped and he cried out for mercy.

But I did what I said I would do and, to add to my hold on him, I also branded his buttocks with the motif 'Pty of Caroline'. Property of Caroline.

As the hot iron marked his flesh, I thrust my finger up his hole and jerked it backwards and forwards. Once the branding iron had left his flesh, I continued to fuck his arse with my finger. The action obviously helped soothe his scorched posterior. Now that my other hand was free, I also rubbed at his scrotum and his rod until they were hotter than his buttocks. I milked him of his seed and, all the while, his buttocks clenched my finger and his hips moved gently up and down with the rhythm of my other hand.

The feeling in his behind must have come back, once he had spent his come. He fainted but, with a little wine and the sight of my mossy mound before his eyes, he saw the error of his ways.

'How could I do without you, he said?

They were the words I wanted to hear. I promised I would be a good wife and would give him many children to carry on his name.

Of course, I still maintained I was a lady of good breeding. I never told him the truth, that I was in fact a woman of the gutter. I was one who had sold her body to dozens of men, until hearing of men's treatment of chaste women at the Hellfire Club and hatching my plan to use my experience to trap one into marriage. And, as he was substantially older than I was, my needs might outweigh his after a decent length of time. Servants are plentiful; so are those young men who wish to further their status in society by pleasing a lady of wealth and social standing. Many young bulls would come to my byre before I breathed my last breath – so too might some hot young heifers.

Rachel sighed as she put the book down. Her hands felt cool against her face. What a woman! Although separated by the centuries, Caroline Standish had made her want to do all the things she had read of in the book. Not all were unfamiliar to her. Sexual fantasies, she now realised, had a basis in reality. She couldn't help breaking into a smile. What would Robert McKenzie do when he found out he was descended from a debauched pervert and a well-used whore?

What price now that North Atlantic arrogance?

Her thoughts turned to planning how she would trap him and what she would do to him. How easy it would be to treat Robert McKenzie in the same way Caroline had treated him. And didn't he just deserve it? She bubbled with energy as the scenes of his downfall appeared in her mind.

'Yes!' she said springing to her feet. 'And that is what I shall do too. If it was OK for Caroline Standish, a few centuries ago, it's OK for me now!'

First, she would dress appropriately. She went into her bedroom, her bare feet padding on the polished pine floor.

Creamy muslin draped from the bedroom ceiling, like the sails of a sailing ship. At one end, two steps led to a raised area on which was her bed. It was as wide as it was long and covered with the same muslin that hung in great drifts from the ceiling and was caught by green metal rods running just above the windows.

In vivid contrast to the puritanical plainness of the décor, something red, boned and trimmed in black lay there.

Rachel reached out and touched it. The feel of soft satin and rough lace made her shiver. It was a recent acquisition, bought on impulse after reading the exploits of Caroline Standish. Now she would re-enact something similar to what that woman had done. To some extent, she would even become her and McKenzie, unknowing, would in effect become his ancestor Duncan McKenzie.

She peeled off her everyday wear and stood naked in front of the huge mirror that was fitted between two windows.

She ran her hands down over her belly and tweaked at the clutch of dark hair beneath it. Holding her head to one side, she lifted her breasts so that they were high and held tight against her body. The tightly boned corset she had bought would hold them there like that. Just thinking how she would look made her tingle with excitement. She was still tingling when she was actually wearing it. The red satin made her skin seem creamier. The rigid bones trapped her breasts so that they half spilt over the lace edged cups. Black silk stockings accentuated the naked whiteness of her thighs. High-heeled suede boots completed the picture.

There was no point in wearing panties. Besides, she thought as she surveyed herself at the same time as spraying on her favourite perfume, my quim matches the black lace trim.

'Quim!' she exclaimed and laughed at her use of the old-fashioned word. It wasn't just that it seemed quaint. It was almost as though the woman she had modelled herself on was resurrected. If she'd believed in ghosts, perhaps she might have thought the woman was in the room with her.

After covering her profane appearance with a black silk cheongsam her mother had brought back from a holiday in China, she gathered the items she would need.

There was rope, there were belts, plus a pot of moisturiser and an indelible marker, such as used in marking valuable items.

'There,' she said at last. 'I'm all ready.'

The music was soft, the blinds were drawn and the lighting was low, by the time the intercom announced his presence.

There was just time to light some heavily scented joss sticks before he actually rang the doorbell.

She pinched her cheeks and showed a little more décolletage before opening the door.

'Mac,' she said in a hushed, breathless way. 'How nice of you to come.'

He looked good. She had to give him that. He was wearing a navy blue ribbed sweater and lighter blue slacks. They were good quality and definitely not chainstore.

He took her in his arms. His kisses were hot and demanding, his tongue parting her lips and laying on top of her own.

Gently but firmly she eased him away from her and all the time her lips and her eyes smiled with promise.

'There's no rush, is there?' she said.

'Not particularly.'

'That's good. The door's locked, the answerphone is on and you've got me all to yourself.'

He smiled back at her.

You pompous ass, she thought. And although she had plans to humiliate him and abuse his body as one of his ancestors had abused –

She had to stop thinking like that. She wasn't some woman from an old book. She was a modern woman and she was going to enjoy this because, basically, he was a very good-looking man.

She asked him if he wanted wine.

'Yes. An aperitif would be a good way to start.'

Even as she poured she could feel his eyes boring into her back. In his mind she was already undressed, laid out and tied hand and foot, while he did all that he wanted to.

She turned and offered him a glass of dark red liquid.

His fingers brushed hers. His eyes sparkled. I'm down on you, she thought. In your mind, I'm kneeling naked in front of you, my lips and tongue tasting your flesh.

Like a cat waiting to be stroked, she stretched out on one of the two white sofas set at an angle to each other.

'You really do like to play things slow,' he said. His eyes never left her face.

'If a thing's worth doing . . .' she replied and licked the wine from her lips.

He shrugged his shoulders and a thrill ran through her. McKenzie knew that heads turned when he passed by. He was different but was also as dramatically appealing as the dominant male in every woman's fantasy.

'I'm glad to hear it,' he said. 'I'm a man of fastidious tastes and I know what I want.'

Rachel regarded him over the rim of her glass.

Then she laughed. 'Inherited tastes,' she said blithely.

At the mention of inheritance he looked at her with renewed interest. 'What have you found out about my family?'

Don't tell him everything. Tease him. Make him want to know more. Once you've got him where you want him, then you can tell him.

'They used to own property in London and a castle in Scotland,' she said, glancing to add meaning at the notebook sitting on the coffee table in front of her. 'The London house was destroyed in the blitz. The castle in Scotland still exists. Castle Cael, I believe it is named.'

McKenzie almost leapt off the sofa. Elbows resting on knees he leant towards her his face beaming. 'Are you sure about that?'

She threw the sort of look that dared him to doubt her. 'Of course I'm sure. I'm very thorough in my research; besides, your aunt's papers pointed me in the right direction.'

'Phew!' He slumped back against the soft upholstery. 'How about that! I knew I had a certain affinity with that place.' He leant towards her again. 'Did you know that's the place I've been renting in Scotland?'

Rachel shook her head. 'No, I didn't. My mother never told me that.'

He looked at her a little strangely. 'Your mother?'

It suddenly occurred to her that Liz had not divulged their relationship. She had only told him that Rachel carried out freelance research. She decided not to tell him, either.

'Yes. She knows a little about the place.'

He smirked wickedly. 'She wouldn't know about

240

the dungeon.' He reached out and ran his hand over her hip. 'We could have fun there, you and I; we could play games you've never even dreamed of. We could be really dirty with each other, play a little rough and play a little smooth, if you know what I mean.'

She smiled. She knew what he meant, all right. But she had never been too sure about bondage. Tying him up was one thing. Her being tied up was another matter entirely. But she'd think about it.

He knelt before her and rested his hand on her hip. His gaze went to her cleavage, which held his full attention. At no time did he notice the fact that she was wearing suede boots with a lightweight wrap.

'I think I can fit in taking you up to the castle before I go back to the States. Then we could play. Really play.'

She noticed he didn't ask if she could fit him in. But it didn't really matter. She could tell her temporary aloofness was affecting him. For her own part, she was looking forward to fulfilling her plan. She would enjoy it. He might enjoy it, too, but that wasn't really the point. She also wanted him to feel used – just as sometimes he made other women feel used.

'Do we have to wait till then?' she asked sweetly.

He bent his head and kissed her cleavage. 'No, of course not. I haven't come all this way for nothing.'

She tousled his hair and smiled triumphantly. Her plan was working.

Gently, she pushed him away. 'Then we'd better

get started. I wouldn't want to waste any of your precious time.'

She stood up. He remained kneeling. She let her robe slip to the floor. She saw the wonder on his face as he looked up at her. He ran his hands over the black silk stockings. But of course he couldn't stop there. He breathed in the musk of her sex, then pressed his face into her pubic hair. His hands clutched her bare behind as he buried himself in her.

This was bliss. His tongue probed between her pubic lips. So delicate was its touch, yet so firm. His hands kneaded her buttocks. She murmured her approval. This was the best way to enjoy a man. Providing he had the right tongue, the right touch. And he was on his knees before her. This was good, really good. If she closed her eyes he disappeared. He became merely a thing designed to give her pleasure.

But this was only a preliminary. It excited her, but there was more excitement to come. Soon, she would be dizzy with sensuality, as long as this man submitted to her will.

It wasn't easy, but the present pleasure had to stop. Shame, she thought, but there it is.

'Enough,' she murmured, her voice husky with a mix of pleasure and lust. She side-stepped away from him. His fingers trailed across her belly then cupped her moistened sex.

'You can't stop now.'

She smiled down at him. 'I don't intend to.' She reached out and tousled his hair like she had before. It was silky to the touch. 'But this is my castle, Mac and so we play the games on my terms. OK?'

For a moment, she wasn't sure he was going to agree. His face was expressionless. She sensed some turmoil going on behind his eyes. Then he grinned; then he smiled.

'I think that sounds real fair. Whatever you want, honey. It's your place and your game.'

Sex in itself was pleasure. Sex mingled with power, well that was something else.

'Then follow me into my bedroom,' she said in a voice husky with lust.

He started to get up. She lay a heavy hand on his shoulder.

'Naked,' she said, 'and on your hands and knees.'

Again he hesitated. But desire was in his eyes. She could imagine it racing through his body, quickening his heart, hardening his cock.

She watched as he undressed. Each time he tried to stand up and take something off, she pushed him back down again. He was on his hands and knees before her and that was how she wanted him to stay. My, but how easy it was to dictate terms when the subject was fired up with the need to fuck.

Just as she had guessed, his cock was hard as rock. She licked her lips. Somewhere in her mind, the vestige of a fantasy came to her. In the fantasy, she had been lying on the floor, a brute of a man sucking her sex while his huge cock fucked her mouth. For a moment, she wanted to get down under Mac and have him do the same. But her own willpower stopped her. After all, a fantasy was one thing. Reality was something else. She might not like physically carrying out such a scenario. In time, she might gain more experience of such things. But, for now, she was content to use her fantasy for what it really was – a means to an end, a spur to a better orgasm.

Finally, he knelt naked, his eyes shining as they looked up into hers. Quickly, without warning, she grasped his head with both hands and pressed his face to her pubic hair.

'Smell me,' she said. 'Breathe me in so that your body is ready to be my slave and do everything I want it to do.'

He grasped her buttocks like he had before. Obligingly, he rubbed his face against her crotch.

'That's the spot,' she gasped and pressed him hard to her, before pushing him away again.

'Now you know the smell of me, you can follow me into my bedroom by scent alone.'

She took the silk scarf she had secreted away earlier from behind a cushion.

He looked incredulous for a moment. 'You're going to blindfold me?'

Rachel smiled reassuringly. 'That's the whole point of knowing the smell of me. You should be able to follow by smell alone. And anyway, you can't fall over and hurt yourself if you're down on all fours can you?'

He let her apply the blindfold.

'Just a minute,' he said as she turned her back on him. 'If I'm to follow your rear, I need to smell you from behind, too.'

She should have expected it.

'All right,' she said.

The feel of his nose nudging between her buttocks was not unpleasant. On the contrary, it felt good to have something other than a cock or a finger exploring a crevice that was almost as sensitive as her sex.

She could not help half closing her eyes as the pleasure of what he was doing spread through her senses. She did not protest when he reached round to tease her tingling clit and dip his fingers into the wet flesh surrounding it.

Before leaving the room, she picked up the leather belt that had held up his trousers.

Obviously, the smell of her had taken his senses. He had no trouble following her into her bedroom. He neither bumped into anything, nor did he lose his way.

She saw him shiver.

'Have you got a window open?' he asked.

'I like fresh air,' she countered.

She bent down to him and stroked his head, held his chin and kissed his lips. He reached for her breasts that pouted so provocatively above the tightly boned corset.

He cried out and turned a little tense when she hit his hands away.

'Now my pet, let me put your leash on and then you can fondle my breasts.'

Once he'd visibly relaxed, Rachel bent down, looped the belt around his neck and slid the leather through until it was tight but not obtrusive.

'Come this way,' she said and tugged at the strap.

He crawled after her, not knowing she was leading him into the bondage he had thought to lead her.

The drapes that hung tent-style from the ceiling were caught with iron rods at both the top and bottom of the windows. This was where she led him.

'Stand up,' she said in a soothing voice. 'It's time for you to really get involved with the game.'

He did as he was told and did not protest as she spread his arms wide above his head and fixed them with strips of copper wire to the iron rod running above the window.

'What are you doing now?' he asked.

'Be patient and you will find out. I guarantee it will be an exciting and unusual experience.'

An exciting and unusual experience for her; she wasn't sure how he would view it, but she couldn't imagine him not liking the experience.

His body tensed slightly as she wound the cold, thin copper wire around all three components of his genitals. Swollen, erect and hot with lust, his genitals bunched forward as she fastened the wire to the bottom iron pole. His back arched. His hips jerked forward so as to ease the pressure.

She rested his chin on her table. If he hadn't been blindfolded, he would have seen her saucy smile.

'How does it feel?' she asked.

He hesitated. She wondered for a moment if he was going to beg her to let him go. If he were that afraid, she would indeed release him. But if he were a truly curious and sexual man, then he would stay. She was sure of it.

She ran her hand down his naked back and slowly tickled his spine with soft strokes.

'Do you like the way I look?' she asked. She teased her nipples from the tight restriction of her bodice, then rubbed both her breasts and her pubic mound against his behind.

'Oh, yes!' he said. 'Red's my favourite colour.'

She picked up a long, slim riding crop, a leftover from her childhood hobby. With slow attention to his responses, she ran it down his spine. The fine strip eventually slid between his buttocks.

'Do I look like a whore or a mistress?'

Lines of concentration appeared on his brow. He was obviously wondering what he was supposed to answer, because she was directing this scene. He plumped for the right answer.

'A mistress. You're my mistress, aren't you?'

She feigned anger. 'You question my position?'

'No! I just thought that was what you wanted me to say. It's all part of the game, isn't it?'

She maintained the anger. 'You're questioning my position. I can tell you are and, just for that . . .'

The crop rose, hissed as it travelled through the air and made a loud slapping sound as it hit his buttocks.

McKenzie cried out. His hips thrust forward. His cock pulsated.

'There!' she exclaimed. 'That's what you get if you doubt my status. And, if you're not very careful . . .'

She ran the fragile end of the crop over his genitals. He shivered with apprehension.

'You wouldn't!' he exclaimed. His erection never faltered.

I must be doing it right, thought Rachel and that fact alone made her feel sexy.

Again she raised her arm. McKenzie tensed. The intercom buzzed in the hallway.

'Damn! Who the hell is that?'

'You don't have to answer it,' said McKenzie.

She smiled at the broad back. You want more,

she thought. You really want me to thoroughly enjoy your body, perhaps in the hope that your compliance will be reciprocated.

'I don't,' she said, 'but I will.'

Out in the hallway the intercom buzzed again. She sighed impatiently before picking it up. There was an ache between her legs. She was enjoying what she was doing. Exploring a man's body and reactions was a very appealing weekend occupation.

She lifted the receiver.

'It's me,' said a voice she recognised.

'Ian. What do you want?'

'You,' he wailed. 'I just want you.'

He sounded drunk.

'Well, you can't have me: not just like that, anyway.'

'Rachel, please listen to me. I've got a confession to make.'

She had been just about to put the receiver down. But his talk of confession made her pause. He'd been having sex with her mother: that's what he wanted to confess. Well, he didn't need to. She already knew. And besides, she had McKenzie all ready to play with in the other room. Still, she paused. Something about Ian confessing his sins appealed to her. The thrill of having two men to play with instead of one was too good to resist.

'OK,' she said slowly as a new thrill ran through her. 'Come on up.'

She was waiting for him behind the door when he rang. Because she was standing behind it, he did not at first see that she was wearing little except a tightly fitting corset, black silk stockings and thigh-high suede boots.

248

He gasped with shock. His eyes and mouth opened wide. 'What are you dressed like that for?' He sounded incredulous

Smiling, she undulated her half-naked flesh against him. 'Didn't you know? It's required uniform for those who have to listen to confessions. It doesn't have to be a black-frocked priest, you know.'

He stared with a mix of amazement and adulation. Although his eyes roamed her body, his features seemed to crumple as if he'd suddenly remembered something. He hung his head.

'I'm sorry, Rachel, but I just have to tell you this. It's the worst thing I could do.'

'Telling me?'

He shook his head somewhat forlornly. 'That's bad enough. But having to tell you that I've had sex with . . .' He took a deep breath and hung his head more deeply – if that were possible.

'A young boy!' Rachel exclaimed

'What?' He stared at her.

'Is that what you wanted to confess? That's something really naughty, isn't it?'

'Yes,' he started. 'No! No!' He hung his head and shook it. Then his gaze ranged her body again. 'How I can I talk seriously, with you dressed like that. Am I missing something around here?'

Rachel took hold of her breasts and pulled them completely out of their cups so they sat proud and pointing forward.

'These, perhaps?'

Her hand dropped to her genitals. She ran her fingers through her pubic hair. 'And this?' she added. Seductively, she opened her legs, so he was in no doubt of what she was offering.

'Oh, Rachel!' he groaned. His head dropped to her bosom. Gently he kissed one breast then the other. Then his lips closed over her nipples and he sucked hard and long on each in turn.

'That's enough,' said Rachel at last. Of course, it wasn't, really. She would have liked him to do more. But she was sure things could be even better. Her decadent thoughts of having two men were still with her. Now for the right implements, the right words.

'Let me see you naked, Ian.'

He did not hesitate. Soon, his clothes were in a neat pile next to the pink velvet hall chair. It wasn't the only thing that was soft to touch and shaded pink. His cock rose proud from his loins and his balls seemed to heave up with each lustful throb.

'I see you're ready for me,' she said. She kissed him. At the same time, she tapped the head of his rod with the tips of her fingers. He groaned.

'Please,' he said and his voice seemed to fade as all his power flowed to his loins.

She cupped his face in both hands and kissed him deep and long, her tongue sliding through his lips and rolling around his mouth.

'Bend down, get your belt out of your trousers and pull them down.'

Silently he stared, but only momentarily. He did what she asked quickly and without question. But that was Ian. He aimed to please. All that rankled was that he aimed to please mother as well as daughter.

'And I want you down on your knees. Do it now.'

He did exactly as she said. From below her belly his awe-struck eyes looked up at her like some submissive spaniel. Yes, she thought, that's exactly what he was: a spaniel. A docile, submissive spaniel.

There was another scarf tossed carelessly over the back of the pink velvet chair. She took it and began to blindfold him.

'Now,' she began. 'I want you to smell me.' She held his head with both hands and pressed his face to her mons. 'Breathe me in. Swallow my scent.'

She sighed as she felt his nose and mouth against her most sensuous parts. She rubbed herself against him and sighed again as his tongue flicked delicately through the covering of pubic hair.

'Now,' she said, breathless as she let him go. 'I want you to follow me on all fours. But don't worry. I will use another scarf as a leash. You won't get lost.'

He submitted immediately. Like the spaniel she had judged him to be, he moved on all fours alongside her high suede boots.

When she got him into the bedroom, she lost no time in tying him up in exactly the same position as McKenzie.

'Have you got someone with you?' asked McKenzie.

'Who's that?' Ian sounded nervous. 'Rachel!' he cried as he began struggling against the bonds that tied his wrists. 'Let me go.'

She came close to him. 'I won't let you go. And don't struggle too much. That's copper wire tied around the family jewels. You don't want to lose them, do you?'

'Rachel!' It was Mac this time.

'The same applies to you, Mac. Remember the copper wire.'

'You can't do this!' Mac's voice was angry but high-pitched from fear.

'Oh, come on, Mac. It's my game, remember? My rules. Who said I've got to work out with just one guy? Isn't two supposed to be better than one? And anyway, neither of you can see the other. You can just feel what I'm going to do to you. You'll be able to hear the other moan and groan at will. Nice, huh?'

She strode like a gladiator around the arena, stroking their cocks with the riding crop and giving each of them a swift cut across the buttocks just when she felt like it. To see red stripes appear on their white, firm flesh gave her a big thrill. At times, she just had to rub at her sex. It was as if she were putting the fairy back into the box – just temporarily, of course.

Now, what was she going to do next? She could whip them a few more times across their behinds. Or she could fondle their cocks, perhaps even bring them off each in turn. But she felt there had to be something more, though she wasn't sure quite what.

Perplexed into inaction, she stood in the middle of the room, arms crossed and brows furrowed. Then the intercom buzzed again.

'I'll ignore it,' she said, but it sounded again and again.

Without bothering to ask who it was, she pressed the door release. Doubtless one of her neighbour's visitors had pressed the wrong button. Well, they'd find their own way to where they were going, once she had let them in.

Presuming she was right, she made her way back

into the living room and was only partly through the door when the doorbell rang.

Panic suddenly enveloped her. What if it was one of her parents? What if it was a friend? She couldn't possibly let them see what she was up to. She slammed the bedroom door behind her.

Quickly, she grabbed her dressing gown, went to the door, peered through the spyhole and saw – her mother!

What was worse, her mother had seen her. There was no going back. She had to let her in.

They exchanged the usual kisses. Her mother entered the flat slowly, cautiously, as if the floor were scattered with eggshells and would break if she stood on them.

'I wondered if you were still talking to me,' said Liz.

Rachel noticed her eyes take in the fact that she was wearing something stiff beneath the bathrobe. Not only that but she was also wearing high suede boots.

'Have I interrupted something?' she asked.

'Just Saturday afternoon relaxation,' returned Rachel.

Liz nodded slowly but her eyes never left her daughter's face, except to take in the details of how she looked.

Liz automatically made her way into the living room. Rachel kept herself between her mother and the door.

So far, no comment had been made about the way she was dressed, yet she was sure her mother had noticed.

'I wanted to say . . .' Liz paused and glanced at

253

Rachel's boots. 'I don't think you would make a very good secret agent, Rachel.'

Mother's eyes met daughter's.

Rachel raised her eyebrows disdainfully. 'I wasn't intending to be one.'

'Really? Then perhaps a private detective. They're the ones to follow adulterous wives, aren't they?'

Rachel lowered her eyes and sat on the arm of one of the sofas. Suddenly, her cream and peach décor was just too bright, too sophisticated to live in. She had a strong urge to curl up and tell her mother she had a headache. At least, she thought, it will get me back in next door.

But she knew this confrontation had to be faced. She raised her eyes and looked into her mother's face. What good bone structure she had: what youthful skin and sparkling blue eyes. Yes, she could see why Ian had fallen for her. In fact, she could easily see why her father had.

'Are you going to confess to me about Ian?'

Her mother looked at her oddly. 'Confess? I think that's the wrong word. We had a liaison. I wanted to feel a youthful body against mine. An older woman besotted him. There's nothing wrong in that, is there?'

Rachel stared at her mother, as if for the first time. There she was, dressed in a coffee-coloured suit with an oyster-coloured blouse. Three pearls were clustered in a group on each ear lobe. Her hair was beige-blonde and cut in a classic bob to chin length. She looked every inch the successful woman, both in marriage and career. But what was she really?

'But you're married!' Rachel blurted at last.

Liz smiled and shook her head a little sadly. 'What you mean, Rachel, is that I shouldn't be lusting after younger men. But I do lust after young men and sex on the side does me good.'

Rachel sprang to her feet. 'I can't believe I'm hearing this! It's crazy. What will Dad say?'

'He knows.'

At first, Rachel did not hear her. But as the word sank in, she turned round and frowned. 'What did you say?'

With a casual elegance born of confidence, her mother sank on to the opposite sofa. Then she smiled and shook her head.

'You have a lot to learn, Rachel. You're young and endowed with the arrogance of all youth. You look at your parents and think, yes, these are what they are. They are my parents. They are a bit like a cat and a dog, very domesticated and settled in their ways.'

She leant forward, her eyes gleaming. 'We still have passions, your father and I. We are committed to each other but we also enjoy a varied sex life. There are no secrets between us. I am a passionate woman. He is a passionate man. You have to understand that, if you are to understand why the fact that you saw me with Ian does not matter.'

Rachel felt her face flushing. 'But it might matter to me! Ian and I have been seeing each other for a while.'

'I know you well, Rachel. You are blood of my blood.' Liz stood up, walked over to her daughter and caressed her cheek. 'If I had thought you and Ian were a real going concern, I would not have let it happen. But that isn't so, is it? You dally with him, just as I did: just as you would dally with

255

anyone else who took your fancy. And besides, he liked me doing things that you would never do with him. I like variety, you see. In my youth, I depended on fantasies to fuel my libido. But with experience it became obvious that these were not enough.'

Rachel looked at her in disbelief. 'What are you saying?'

Liz laughed. 'That you don't fool me, Rachel.' She flicked her hand at the loosely draped robe. 'What sort of scenario are you playing at? Are you playing alone, relying on plastic toys to pleasure yourself? Or do you have some willing man to play your games with?'

Her mother was putting into words everything Rachel was doing. Somehow, any guilt she might have felt about her fantasies no longer mattered. They couldn't be bad if even her own mother had experienced them. But what else was it she was saying?

As if reading her thoughts, Liz put the facts into words. 'It's not shameful to act out your fantasies. It's only shameful when someone tries to make you do something you don't want to do.' She glanced swiftly aside for the moment, as if a certain name had come to mind.

Suddenly, it was all clear. 'Mum!' Rachel flung her arms around her mother's neck. 'I know what you mean. That's why I'm dressed like this.'

She flung off her robe. Her mother looked her up and down. 'Very nice, dear. Tell me, who's the lucky man?'

'I don't know if either of them are lucky.'

Liz raised her eyebrows. 'Two?'

Rachel nodded. 'It was only Mac, to start with. I

wanted him to know that I had to be in control now and again. Then Ian arrived, wanting to confess about you. I haven't let him do that, yet.'

'So where are they?' asked Liz.

Rachel smiled. 'I just left them hanging around. Do you want to have a peep?'

Smiling and looking excited, Liz nodded.

Rachel opened the door quietly. Liz held her breath. Her eyes widened when she saw what her daughter had done. Her jaw dropped with amazement. She nodded at her daughter to close the door. 'Marvellous,' she hissed once it was closed. 'But you have to let me have some part in this. I'd really like to make Robert McKenzie more than a little uncomfortable. Do you mind your old mother participating in this?'

Rachel did not hesitate. 'I'd love you to.'

Liz immediately began to disrobe. 'I think I'm dressed for the part.' As she did this, Rachel told her about the book she had found and how she intended to copy what Caroline Standish had done.

'What fun!' said her mother. 'In Ian's case, it will be like declaring our mutual ownership on his cock or his backside. In Mac's case, it will be like stamping a passport. He'll be reminded of the print on his backside each time he travels abroad.'

'In which case,' said Rachel, 'we're not very likely to see him again. His pride will be too dented.'

'Will I do?' said Liz at last, once her clothes were folded and placed neatly on the arm of the sofa.

Rachel gasped. Her mother's underwear was of white satin with silver strands running through it. There was nothing remotely high street about it. It gleamed with value, just as much as the pearls in her ears and round her throat.

'Shall we?' said an excited Liz.

Rachel nodded.

The phone rang just as they were about to enter the bedroom and deal with the two men tied up within. Rachel answered it. 'It's Dad,' she said. Her hand shook slightly as she passed it to her mother.

'Is everything all right?' asked Mark.

'Very,' said Liz. 'We're just about to impose the rights of women on the bodies of men. As soon as we're finished – and they're finished – I'll be home for dinner. I'll tell you all about it then.'

A stunned Rachel stared as her mother put the phone down.

'You're just like her,' she said.

'Like who?' said Liz.

'Caroline Standish.'

'Obviously an admirable woman,' said Liz. 'Would she have approved of what we're about to do?'

Rachel laughed as she pushed the bedroom door open. 'Most certainly she would!'

BLACK LACE NEW BOOKS

Published in July

ASKING FOR TROUBLE
Kristina Lloyd
£5.99

When Beth Bradshaw starts flirting with handsome Ilya, she becomes a player in a game based purely on sexual brinkmanship. The boundaries between fantasy and reality start to blur as their games take on an increasingly reckless element. When Ilya's murky past catches up with him, he's determined to involve Beth, who finds herself being drawn deeper into the seedy underbelly of Brighton where things, including Ilya, are far more dangerous than they seem. This is a hard-hitting story of sex and crime.

ISBN 0 352 33362 6

WICKED WORDS
A Black Lace Short Story Collection
Edited by Kerri Sharp
£5.99

Black Lace anthologies have proved to be extremely popular. Following on from the success of the *Pandora's Box* and *Sugar and Spice* compilations, *Wicked Words* takes the series in a dynamic new direction. This time the accent is on contemporary settings with a transgressive feel. The writing is fresh and upbeat in style and all the stories have strong characters and a sting in the tale. This is an ideal introduction to the Black Lace series.

ISBN 0 352 33363 4

Published in August

LIKE MOTHER, LIKE DAUGHTER

Georgina Brown
£5.99

Mother Liz and daughter Rachel are very alike, even down to sharing the same appetite for men. But while Rachel is keen on gaining sexual experience with older guys, her mother is busy seducing men half her age, including Rachel's boyfriend.

ISBN 0 352 33422 3

CONFESSIONAL

Judith Roycroft
£5.99

Faren Lonsdale is an ambitious young reporter. Her fascination with celibacy in the priesthood leads her to infiltrate St Peter's, a seminary for young men who are about to sacrifice earthly pleasures for a life of devotion and abstinence.

What she finds, however, is that the nocturnal shenanigans that take place in their cloistered world are anything but chaste. And the high proportion of good-looking young men makes her research all the more pleasurable.

ISBN 0 352 33421 5

To be published in September

OUT OF BOUNDS

Mandy Dickinson
£5.99

When Katie decides to start a new life in a French farmhouse left to her by her grandfather, she is horrified to find men are squatting in her property. But her horror quickly becomes curiosity as she realises how attracted she is to them, and how much illicit pleasure she can have. When her ex-boyfriend shows up, it isn't long before everyone is questioning their sexuality.

ISBN 0 352 33431 2

A DANGEROUS GAME
Lucinda Carrington
£5.99

Doctor Jacey Muldaire knows what she wants from the men in her life: good sex and plenty of it. And it looks like she's going to get plenty of it while working in an elite private hospital in South America. But Jacey isn't all she pretends to be. A woman of many guises, she is in fact working for British Intelligence. Her femme fatale persona gives her access that other spies can't get to. Every day is full of risk and sexual adventure, and everyone around her is playing a dangerous game.

ISBN 0 352 33432 0

If you would like a complete list of plot summaries of Black Lace titles, or would like to receive information on other publications available, please send a stamped addressed envelope to:

Black Lace, Thames Wharf Studios,
Rainville Road, London W6 9HT

BLACK LACE BOOKLIST

All books are priced £4.99 unless another price is given.

Black Lace books with a contemporary setting

PALAZZO	Jan Smith ISBN 0 352 33156 9	☐
THE GALLERY	Fredrica Alleyn ISBN 0 352 33148 8	☐
AVENGING ANGELS	Roxanne Carr ISBN 0 352 33147 X	☐
COUNTRY MATTERS	Tesni Morgan ISBN 0 352 33174 7	☐
GINGER ROOT	Robyn Russell ISBN 0 352 33152 6	☐
DANGEROUS CONSEQUENCES	Pamela Rochford ISBN 0 352 33185 2	☐
THE NAME OF AN ANGEL £6.99	Laura Thornton ISBN 0 352 33205 0	☐
SILENT SEDUCTION	Tanya Bishop ISBN 0 352 33193 3	☐
BONDED	Fleur Reynolds ISBN 0 352 33192 5	☐
THE STRANGER	Portia Da Costa ISBN 0 352 33211 5	☐
CONTEST OF WILLS £5.99	Louisa Francis ISBN 0 352 33223 9	☐
MÉNAGE £5.99	Emma Holly ISBN 0 352 33231 X	☐
THE SUCCUBUS £5.99	Zoe le Verdier ISBN 0 352 33230 1	☐
FEMININE WILES £7.99	Karina Moore ISBN 0 352 33235 2	☐
AN ACT OF LOVE £5.99	Ella Broussard ISBN 0 352 33240 9	☐
DRAWN TOGETHER £5.99	Robyn Russell ISBN 0 352 33269 7	☐
DRAMATIC AFFAIRS £5.99	Fredrica Alleyn ISBN 0 352 33289 1	☐

Black Lace anthologies

------------✂-------------------

Please send me the books I have ticked above.

Name ....

Address ....

....

....

.... Post Code ....

Send to: **Cash Sales, Black Lace Books, Thames Wharf Studios, Rainville Road, London W6 9HT.**

US customers: for prices and details of how to order books for delivery by mail, call 1-800-805-1083.

Please enclose a cheque or postal order, made payable to **Virgin Publishing Ltd**, to the value of the books you have ordered plus postage and packing costs as follows:

UK and BFPO – £1.00 for the first book, 50p for each subsequent book.

Overseas (including Republic of Ireland) – £2.00 for the first book, £1.00 for each subsequent book.

If you would prefer to pay by VISA, ACCESS/MASTER-CARD, DINERS CLUB, AMEX or SWITCH, please write your card number and expiry date here:

....

Please allow up to 28 days for delivery.

Signature ....

------------✂-------------------